THE
HUNTED
SERIES
Seduction

IVY SMOAK

To my Hunted series family.

Writing about these characters always feels like coming home.

CHAPTER 1

Tuesday

James would be home any minute. I'd spent all day cooking a homemade meal for my husband. Yes, I could have just asked our housekeeper, Ellen, to prepare something. Her cooking was better than mine. But it was the thought that counted. I even set the dining room table, which we rarely ever used. We tended to eat at the kitchen island together most nights. But tonight was a special occasion. I lit the last candle and stepped back. It was perfect.

The last few weeks James had been busy getting ready for his first day back teaching. He'd gotten a job at a university in the city. Today was his first day and I just wanted to show him how happy I was for him. For taking this big step. For doing what he loved again.

"He's going to be excited, isn't he?" I said and put my hand on my stomach. I had a very tiny baby bump. And ever since I'd started showing I'd been talking to him. No, I didn't know if it was a boy. But James' brother, Rob, talked about it being a boy so much that I believed him. Rob could be very persuasive. Besides, I loved the idea of having a little James running around.

My phone buzzed and I hurried back into the kitchen. I picked it up off the kitchen counter to see Ian's text: "We just parked. He's on his way up. Have a fun night!"

I texted our driver back: "Thank you so much, Ian." I put my phone back down on the counter. Oh, I hoped James would like this surprise. I'd somehow managed to squeeze myself into the outfit I'd worn the first day I'd met him. A pair of leggings and a tank top. I'm pretty sure the leggings were about to rip though and I was suddenly overthinking all of it. I wasn't a 19-year-old college student anymore. My pregnant belly made the outfit look anything but sexy. Yes, it was a super small bump right now. I only just started showing. But every time I looked down I felt like I looked bigger. And now that I was thinking about it…this outfit had never looked sexy. I looked down at my red rain boots. What had Melissa constantly called them back in school? I was pretty sure the word *hideous* had been tossed around quite a few times.

But before I could kick them off, I heard the front door opening. I couldn't help but smile. James was home. I ran into the foyer.

My smile grew when I saw that he'd pulled on a sweater over his button-up shirt. One of the sweaters he used to wear when he'd been my professor. I didn't even know he still had those. It felt like we were completely in sync. Me wearing my leggings and rain boots and him wearing that sweater.

I wasn't sure if he'd worn it all day or if this was just a treat for me. But I didn't care either way. God, he was so freaking handsome. It was like I was transported back in time to the coffee shop when we first met. And for just a second I stared at him. Losing my words again like I had when we first met.

"Hey, baby," he said, his eyes trailing down my body. "You look amazing."

His words snapped me out of my trance. I wasn't just some random student he'd just bumped into on the first day of classes. I was *his*. Forever and always. "Happy first day…" my stomach churned and I put my hand over my mouth. *Shit.* I ran to the downstairs bathroom, dropped to my knees in front of the toilet, and threw up everything in my stomach. Which fortunately wasn't very much.

I closed my eyes tight. *Damn it.* That was not the way I'd wanted to start tonight. I heard James walk into the bathroom. I hated when he saw me like this. I always told him to just leave me alone when I had morning sickness, but he swore he didn't mind. How could he not mind? I unceremoniously spit once more into the toilet bowl. It was disgusting.

"They shouldn't call it morning sickness if it's not just in the morning," I said and leaned my back against the vanity.

He sat down next to me on the bathroom floor, pulling me close so I could rest my head on his shoulder.

"I was trying to plan the perfect night and now I smell like vomit."

"No. You don't." He kissed the side of my forehead.

It was a lie. But I didn't even care. I was just glad he was here beside me. I was happy he was teaching again, but I'd missed him today. "It's supposed to be over by now. Why won't it stop?"

James kissed the side of my forehead again, rubbing his hand up and down my arm. "I'm sure it'll be over soon."

"I hate being pregnant."

He laughed. "Yesterday you were just saying how much you loved being pregnant. You said you wanted a million babies."

"I thought my morning sickness was over yesterday."

He grabbed my hand, running his thumb along my palm. He always knew just how to calm me down. But now when he did this, it also somehow made my stomach settle. Like his hands were magical.

I looked up at him. "What I was trying to say earlier was happy first day of classes. How did it go?" I kept going when he didn't respond immediately. "I really hope it went well. I missed you so much today. And I really like your sweater."

He smiled. "You have a lot of pent-up energy, don't you?"

"I'm used to hanging out with you all day." We'd been home together for months. He'd been recovering from his surgeries and we'd agreed to stay home together, enjoying the start of my pregnancy. The time had flown by way too fast. "And even though Ellen was here for most of the day, she doesn't want me to help with anything. She swatted my hand when I tried to fold laundry." Not that it mattered. I was supposed to be writing, not hanging out with Ellen. But it was easier to write when my laptop was in the family room and my feet were propped up on James' lap. His face was always good motivation.

"It's only two classes this semester. And only two days a week. I'll be home with you all day tomorrow."

"No office hours the other days?"

He smiled. "I scheduled them for Thursdays while I'm already on campus. Why, are you worried about my office hours?" There was a teasing glint in his eyes.

"I know girls are going to come in and flirt with you because of course they will. Look at you. But no, I'm not worried. If I recall correctly, it was never *students* plural that you were interested in. Just one student."

"Just you." His eyes wandered down to my boots. "Those boots have always done something to me."

I smiled. They weren't hideous at all. They were sexy. *I knew it!* All I wanted to do was straddle him and kiss him. But…I'd just thrown up a minute ago. I wasn't about to subject him to that awfulness.

Instead, I leaned forward, resting my chin on my knee. "I'm sorry. I just wanted tonight to be perfect."

"Every night with you is perfect."

"Not when your son is being terrible and making me sick."

James stopped rubbing my palm and put his hand on my stomach. "You mean when our *daughter* is being terrible and making you sick. I don't know why you believe Rob is right about this. He's rarely right about anything."

"That's not true. And I really think he's right this time." I had no idea why, but it was like I just knew it was going to be a boy. Rob and I were both adamant about it. There was no changing our minds. I knew no matter how much I believed it, it didn't necessarily make it true though. It could be a girl…*not*.

A small part of me wanted to know for sure what we were having. But a much larger part of me liked not knowing. I wanted to believe we were going to have a little James running around soon. I put my hand on my stomach. "Despite what you think, Rob is rarely wrong about anything."

James shook his head. "Rarely wrong about anything? Do you not remember when he thought you were a prostitute?"

I laughed and lightly pushed James' shoulder. "Well he never would have thought that if you didn't keep me a secret from him."

"Touché." He pulled me back into his arms. "We did not stay a secret for very long though." He kissed the side of my neck. "I couldn't keep my hands off you."

I tilted my head back as his trail of kisses fell to my clavicle.

"I still can't."

God, just a few kisses and I was melting.

His lips wandered back up my neck to my lips.

"James!" I pushed on his chest. "It's one thing for you to sit here when I puke, it's another to kiss me. I need to brush my teeth a thousand times first." I slowly stood up, everything moving a little slower these days. "Give me a minute and then meet me at the front door. I want a do-over. Tonight is still going to be perfect."

"You got it."

I ran upstairs to our bathroom and brushed my teeth twice and used way too much mouthwash. I hurried back down into the foyer.

James was standing at the front door, leaning casually against the doorjamb.

My heart started racing when I saw him. That sweater on him really did something to me.

"Happy first day back at teaching," I said as I walked up to him. "If I recall correctly, you were not wearing this sweater when you left today." I placed my hands on his abs, easily feeling them through the fabric.

"No, this was all for you."

"Is that so, professor?"

He nodded, placing a hand on the side of my face. "And if I recall correctly, you were not wearing this outfit when I left for work today."

I shook my head.

His hand wandered down the side of my neck, down the front of my chest, pausing between my breasts. "You can still see the stain."

"What?" I looked down. And sure enough there was a very faint brown stain on my tank top where the coffee had spilled. How had I not seen that? "Well that's not very sexy."

"Everything you do is sexy. If your goal was to seduce the new professor, you're doing a very good job. I give you an A+."

I laughed, but the sound died in my throat when he pressed my back against the wall. "Dinner's going to get cold," I said, not that I cared.

"I'm only hungry for one thing." There was that hunger in his eyes. I loved when he looked at me like that.

Again it felt like I was transported back in time. But this time it was like we were back in his old office at the University of New Castle.

"Remember the last time we negotiated grades?" he asked.

I swallowed hard. "Yes."

"I thought I'd fuck you that day and get you out of my system." He knelt down in front of me and slowly pulled off one of my boots and then the other. "That I could literally fuck away the craving." He reached up and grabbed the waistband of my leggings, pulling them and my thong slowly down my thighs. He leaned forward, leaving a trail of kisses down the path of my leggings. He pulled them the rest of the way off and then his hot breath paused between my thighs.

He looked up at me. "But one taste was never going to be enough." He thrust his tongue inside of me.

"James," I moaned, burying my fingers in his hair.

His tongue swirled slowly at first, teasing me. He knew just how to get me to the edge of oblivion.

But then his lips moved to my clit, his finger replacing his tongue.

My head leaned back against the wall. I needed more. I needed everything.

It was like he could hear my silent pleas as he slid another finger into my wetness.

"Oh God, James."

His lips fell from my clit a second too soon. "Penny." He kissed my hipbone. "We're not in public. Don't you remember what I told you all those years ago?"

I swallowed hard. I remembered. We both had very fond memories of sneaking around. He'd always be Professor Hunter to me. "Then you should probably punish me, *Professor Hunter.*"

He groaned and placed another kiss on my hipbone before standing back up. "Say it again, baby." He slowly unzipped his pants, pulling out his erection. "You have no idea how many times I jerked off to you saying my name just like that. How many times I imagined your soft lips around my cock." He ran his hand up and down his shaft.

Each word out of his mouth turned me on even more. I watched him run his hand down his length again. I couldn't wait another second. "Fuck me, Professor Hunter."

He lifted one of my thighs and slammed into me.

Jesus.

His thrusts fast and hard.

"Professor Hunter!"

His fingers gripped my ass, somehow pulling me even closer.

"Just this once my ass," I said.

His laugh was hot against my throat. "We were never going to be a one-time thing. Not when you were everything to me." He thrust into me faster.

I moaned.

He bit down on my earlobe, harder than I think he meant to, the pain somehow swirling with pleasure.

"I feel you, baby. Let go. I want to feel you come."

I started pulsing around him.

He groaned as he emptied himself inside of me. Again and again.

We melted to the floor together as we caught our breaths.

I nuzzled my face into the side of his neck, breathing him in. "How is it that we can have sex and I somehow wind up completely naked and you're fully clothed?"

He pulled off his sweater and handed it to me.

I smiled and pulled it on.

"I love you just like this." He leaned over, brushing a strand of hair out of my face. "Flushed and happy."

"You mean freshly fucked?"

He smiled. "Exactly. I think we really turned tonight around, don't you?"

"Yes." I leaned closer, pressing my lips against his. "Oh my God, the dinner!" I stood up and ran into the kitchen. I was probably seconds away from burning the entire building down.

CHAPTER 2

Friday

I should have been writing. Instead I kept stealing glances at James. We were sitting on the couch, my feet propped up on his lap. He was working on his lesson plans for next week. And he assumed I was working too. But...I wasn't. I'd been distracted all day. By him. No one should be allowed to look that sexy in sweatpants. I looked down at my own sweatpants. I looked anything but sexy. But somehow James looked like a million bucks.

Instead of working, I'd been taking turns staring at James and staring at a scene I'd already written. It was the third sex scene I'd put into the novel I was working on and I was only halfway done. I never meant for my book to be so explicit. But sex was an important part of my relationship with James. And I really liked reliving those scenes. A lot. That was part of the reason I kept staring at James. I was so turned on it was hard to think straight.

And then there was a nagging thought in the back of my head. That things wouldn't always be this way.

I looked down at my stomach. A baby was going to change things. I knew that. In five months it wouldn't be just the two of us anymore. It would be the three of us. I was so excited to meet our baby boy. It was easy to daydream about the three of us being a family. But I was a little worried about how different everything would be. I hated change. And I could already see my body changing.

James seemed excited about having a baby. He kissed my stomach goodnight every night before he kissed me. It was the sweetest thing ever. He was embracing change so easily. He even seemed to be looking forward to it. But what about after the baby is born? When I'll have stretch marks everywhere? And the baby will cry all night and we won't be getting enough sleep? We had no idea what we were walking into. Would James still look at me with stars in his eyes then? When we'll be sleep deprived and grumpy and I'll be covered in stretch marks?

I bit my lip. *Maybe he'll still look at me the same.* Or maybe the next five months of just us were going to be our last semblance of normalcy. I needed to take advantage of that while I still could. And it needed to start right now. I'd dressed up to surprise him after his first day of classes. I never expected him to be wearing that sweater I loved so much. He wanted to take advantage of these moments too. I could tell. And I wanted to step up my game even more while I could still fit in normal clothes.

"James, it's past 6." I lightly nudged his thigh with my foot.

He looked up from his notepad. "We should probably get ready for dinner. I still need to shower." He tossed his notepad down on the coffee table and stretched.

We were going out with our friends tonight. One night a week we always went out with our friends. Which was always fun, but a little less so now when I was the only one not drinking. I'd been looking forward to turning 21 in the city two years ago. To finally be able to enjoy the city nightlife like all my friends. James had snuck me into the bars they went to before I was legal. But it was different when I could flash my ID and walk in without a bribe. Plus I enjoyed a good tipsy night.

And it had been fun. So much fun. I remembered tons of weekends where I'd be celebrating time off from classes and they'd be celebrating the end of a work week. I'd dance until my feet were sore and sweat was dripping down the back of my neck, my body pressed against James on the dance floor. His hands possessive on my hips, the small of my back, my ass. Like he was claiming me even with our clothes on.

God, I'd lived for those nights. It made all the late night studying and cramming for tests worth it. I hadn't expected that time of my life to be so short lived. I put my hand on my stomach. A wonderful albeit unexpected surprise. Now we usually just went to a restaurant and caught up. Which was fun too. I loved seeing our friends. But I missed the dancing sometimes.

"Let's not get ready quite yet," I said. I closed my laptop, placed it on the coffee table, and then moved so I was straddling James. "First we should celebrate you finishing your first week teaching again, Professor Hunter."

He smiled as his eyes locked with mine.

Yup, there were stars in his eyes. Well, not really stars. More like a hunger. I loved when he looked at me like that. Like he was starving and I was the only thing that would satiate him.

"You know...whenever you call me that, I want to call you Miss Taylor." He placed his hand on the side of my face. "But I much prefer calling you Mrs. Hunter."

"It's much sexier to be a forbidden student than a boring housewife. Call me Miss Taylor again and see what happens." I was going to devour every inch of him.

"Boring? Hardly. I'm happier now that you're my wife. And you get sexier every day."

I laughed. "About that. I was thinking…things are going to be very different once the baby gets here."

"Yeah. We'll have a little you running around."

I shook my head. "It's going to be a boy, James."

"I don't think so."

I smiled. "Either way…everything will be different. I'll look different."

"Right. Sexier." His hand slid down the side of my neck. "Since you look sexier every day."

"You're incorrigible. You know what I mean, James. Stretch marks."

"You don't have any yet."

I shook my head. "He's barely a bump. I'm sure I'll get them."

"And I'm sure I'll love them." His hand wandered down, past my breasts, to rest on my stomach. "They'll remind me about the gift you're about to give me."

It was the perfect thing to say. But I didn't really believe him. "They'll be ugly."

"No. They won't."

I exhaled slowly. "Some women's feet grow."

"That's okay. Your feet are too small if anything."

I laughed. He just wasn't getting it. "I'll have leaky boobs."

"Leaky boobs?" He put his hands on my breasts. "I don't think that sounds right. Because I've been doing some research and I've read they get even bigger."

I laughed.

"And that the milk is rather sweet. I'm kind of excited to try that."

I laughed harder. "No, that's so weird."

"Is it?" He pulled down the front of my tank top. I refused to wear a bra while I was writing. I needed to be comfortable in order to work. So when he pulled down my tank top, there was nothing to hide my exposed breasts. "You don't seem to mind when I suck on them now." His lips fell to my nipple. But instead of being gentle, he bit down and tugged.

Jesus. It was like the action had a direct line to my clit.

He slowly swirled his tongue around my nipple.

"James." I was trying to get his attention, but his name was more of a moan. I couldn't help it. His mouth was magical.

He shifted forward, letting us fall to the couch. He was careful to catch himself so that he wouldn't smush me. Although, I was pretty sure he was more worried about smushing our unborn child. I loved when he was rough with me, and I could already see him being more tentative. Things were already changing.

He tilted his hips, pressing his erection against me.

I desperately wanted to just rip his clothes off. But I had something important to say. I put my hand on his chest before he went any further. "Wait, this is important. What I was trying to say was that we should really make every moment special before the baby is born. Especially the holidays. All the holidays should be extra sexy. Really, all our days should just be riddled with sex. Five months of crazy seduction. Before my body is ruined."

He smiled down at me.

God I loved that smile. I'm pretty sure my heart still skipped a beat whenever he flashed his smile at me. I hoped it never stopped. "Does that sound good?"

"Are you seriously asking me if I want all holidays and all days to be extra sexy? Because that's a ridiculous question. Of course my answer is yes. I'll take your five months of seduction. But I raise you a lifetime of it." He leaned forward, placing a gentle kiss against my lips. "Because your body is not going to be ruined."

"What if it is?" I knew James loved me with all his heart. I knew that. And yet…I was a lot younger than him. He fell in love with me in part because of the way I looked. Yes, we were perfect for each other. But our sexual tension is what started everything. Hence the three sex scenes in my book so far.

"I will love you always and forever. Even when we're both old and gray."

"You'll be old and gray a lot sooner than me."

"Very funny." His fingers found the waistband of my sweatpants. "I should punish you for that comment."

I was already wet. I was always ready for him. Just being in the same room as him had me practically soaked.

His hand dipped lower, sliding underneath my thong. He groaned when his fingers lightly touched me. "You're so fucking wet, baby."

I lifted my hips slightly. God, I needed him. Just one light touch and it was like I was dying for more.

"Too bad it'll have to wait." He removed his hand from my skin and stood up.

"What?" I stared at the tent that was forming in his sweatpants. It wasn't like I was the only one that wanted this right now. "Come on, we can make it quick." I sat up and reached out for him, but he caught my hands in his.

"I'm not doing quick with you tonight." He dropped my hands. "Besides, you'll be even sexier in…" he looked at his watch "…three or four hours."

I gaped at him.

He ran his thumb along my bottom lip. "Don't worry, baby. I'll be dying for it too. Tonight I'll show you that I won't be old and gray for a long time." He slid his thumb into my mouth and groaned when I sucked on it. "Tonight is going to be fun."

"Mhm," I said around his thumb.

He exhaled slowly. "You should probably get dressed."

I swirled my tongue around his thumb.

"Penny."

If he was going to torture me all night, the least I could do was torture him back.

He pulled his thumb out of my mouth, trailing it down the side of my chin. "In a few hours it'll be my cum dripping down your chin."

I swallowed hard. "Is that a promise?"

He nodded and then grabbed the back of his shirt, pulling it off. He tossed it at me.

I laughed and caught his shirt. *Such a tease.* My eyes traveled down his six-pack to the sexy V in his waist. "Where are we going for dinner tonight?" I asked, keeping my eyes trained right above his sweatpants. I was going to lick every one of those muscles tonight.

"Some new place Rob found. It looks…tropical."

"Tropical?" I laughed. "What does that mean?"

"Like a laid-back beachy vibe. Apparently there's parrots. Fake ones," he added before my mind ran wild with that tidbit of information.

Tropical vibes in the city? *Interesting*. But I already had an idea forming in my head on how to make tonight even more fun. I could do tropical.

"What are you thinking? You have a devious look in your eyes," James said.

"Me? Never."

James smiled. "I'll be down in a bit."

I watched him walk away. He looked just as good coming as he did going in those sweatpants.

I stood up and stretched.

I wondered why Rob chose a new place for dinner. When it was his turn to choose he always picked the same place – a bar nearby that had exceptionally busty waitresses. And darts. He was weirdly good at darts. But it made sense that he'd chosen someplace new, since we all refused to play with him now. He liked to bet on darts, and no matter how much money I technically had now, I still didn't feel comfortable betting thousands of dollars on a game. Especially one I was terrible at. One time I almost hit one of the busty waitresses.

Either way, a new place sounded fun. Tropical. A theme night sounded like the perfect way to start five months of seduction. I was going to tease James so much tonight that we were going to start this whole thing off with a big bang. Literally.

CHAPTER 3

Friday

I wasn't a crazy person, so I wasn't wearing like an overly tropical dress or anything. A theme restaurant didn't mean cosplay. But I still fit into a sundress that I liked to wear on trips to the beach with James. It was what was underneath that was going to surprise him. I'd slipped into his favorite bikini, one he'd bought me during our first few weeks of dating. Because I'd lost my other one. And by lost I mean we went skinny dipping and had sex in the ocean. And while we were doing that, a bunch of horny little boys stole my bikini. James had replaced it with this one…which was much nicer.

I was lucky that it still felt more like summer than fall, because even though my dress would have looked cute with boots, my bikini would not have. I pulled on my high heeled sandals and strapped them up tight. And then I contorted my arm into an awkward angle so I could zip the back of my dress without assistance. My reveal was supposed to be a surprise. So if James zipped me and saw the bikini, the whole thing would be ruined. I turned to look in the mirror. The dress was flowy over my stomach, so it masked my growing baby bump. *Perfect*.

James emerged from the bathroom, a cloud of steam billowing around him. The towel around his waist was just begging to be pulled off.

"You're licking your lips," James said.

Really? Oops. "I was not," I said with a laugh.

"Mhm." He walked into the closet and grabbed a pair of khakis he usually saved for teaching.

Was he trying to torture me? He knew what him dressing like a professor did to me. I didn't even pretend not to gawk at him as he dropped his towel to the floor. I don't know if I'd actually been licking my lips earlier, but I definitely was now as he slid his tight ass into his boxers. I shamelessly watched him finish getting dressed.

He walked out of the closet, rolling up the sleeves of his dress shirt.

Fuck me now.

Instead, he grabbed me around the waist, pulling me close. "You look breathtaking."

I smiled. *Just wait until you see the bikini.* "You too."

He laughed. "I look breathtaking? That sounds so weird when you say it to me."

I placed my hand against his strong chest. "You'll be horrified to know that I describe you as gorgeous in my book then."

"Gorgeous? That is a very unmasculine term."

"Don't worry. All the things you do to me in it are very masculine."

He raised his left eyebrow.

"And as much as I'd love to recreate one of those moments right now...we're going to be late." I slapped his butt and then stepped away from him. *Two could play the teasing game.*

He ran his fingers through his hair as his eyes drank me in. "So tonight's the first night of our five months of seduction?"

Oh yes. I was going to seduce the crap out of him. "Just you wait and see." I grabbed his hand and led him out of the bedroom. I could feel the sexual tension in the air when we stepped onto the elevator. James gripped my hand a little tighter.

I smiled up at him.

And he winked at me.

"What was that wink for?"

"You'll see," he said.

"What are you planning?"

"You'll see," he said again.

He wasn't supposed to be planning anything. I'd already planned something. I was the one seducing him for a change.

He guided me out of the elevator and out the front doors of our building.

Ian was leaning against the car, talking on his cell phone.

"I gotta go," he said as we approached. "I love you too." He quickly hung up, looking a little embarrassed.

"How is Jen?" I asked.

Ian glanced at James and then back at me. Jen was James's sister. Ian had been dating her since our wedding. But it was long distance and I was really hoping she'd move back to New York soon.

"Good," he said and cleared his throat.

I could tell he felt awkward about this whole situation. But it didn't have to be weird. I looked at James and he was scowling. Okay, fine…it was a little weird. But love was love.

Ian quickly opened the door for me.

I thanked him and ducked my head to climb into the back seat.

James joined me on the other side.

"Why are you being weird?" I asked. "They make such a cute couple."

"That's fine. But I don't want to hear about it."

"It's not like he was going into intimate details about their sex life."

James made a funny face.

"Ian wouldn't do that. And I'm sure he's very nice to your sister."

"Can we please stop talking about this? I just don't like when my friends date my sister. It's awkward."

I laughed. "Are you talking about when Matt dated your sister? Because from what I heard they weren't really dating. It was just sex. Kinky, primal sex."

He glared at me.

"I'm just kidding you." I nestled into his side as Ian climbed into the driver's seat. As great as our sex life was, James was a little bit of a hypocrite for not wanting to hear about anyone else's. But I got it. I'm pretty sure if I had a brother I wouldn't want to hear about my friend banging him. I guess that was a plus side to not having any siblings.

I put my hand on my stomach. I wanted my son to have lots of siblings. A whole house full of love and laughter. James and Rob practically grew up with their friends Mason and Matt. It would be fun to have four kids that were as close as them.

Ian pulled the car away from the curb and we started zooming through the city.

James looped his arm around my shoulders. "What are you thinking?"

"About having all the babies," I whispered. I always whispered when we were in the car. As awkward as James thought hearing about his sister's sex life was, I didn't really like anyone to overhear our private conversations. I guess I was the hypocrite.

"All the babies?"

"Yeah, a whole bunch. That can grow up the way you, Rob, Mason, and Matt did. Well, not exactly that way. Your mom is terrible."

James laughed. "Yeah, I wouldn't wish my childhood on anyone. Speaking of childhood…" James cleared his throat. "Mason and Matt's parents are starting up their annual Halloween party again. If you want to go."

"Um…of course I want to go. Is that even a question? You know how much I love Halloween. That sounds amazing. And their house is perfect for a spooky party. With those gargoyles and everything."

James laughed. "It really is."

"You said starting it up again? They used to have one every year?"

"Mhm."

"What made them stop?"

James looked out the window. "Just…they got busy I guess. Mr. Caldwell is retired now though."

"It's cute that you still call him Mr. Caldwell."

"You do too."

"Only because that's what you call him. And the fact that Maxwell Caldwell is kind of a ridiculous name."

James laughed.

"When was the last Caldwell Halloween party you went to? In college or something?" It was a silly question. But I kind of wanted to know if he'd taken Isabella. I hated picturing them together. Even though she was gone, it still turned my stomach. Thinking about James with anyone else made me feel sick. But the image of Isabella and him together was a special kind of torture.

"No. They stopped doing it after my senior year of high school."

"Wow, it's been a long time then."

"I'm not that old. What's with all the digs at my age tonight?"

I laughed. He wasn't old. He was only 30. But it was fun to mess with him. "I know. I just meant...it's been a while since they stopped hosting their annual party then. It's weird that they just stopped all of a sudden. You'd think they'd keep doing it until at least Matt graduated. Since he'd still be home for Halloween even though you and Mason went off to college."

"Yeah, Matt doesn't really do Halloween."

"What do you mean he doesn't really do Halloween?"

"Have you really not noticed that Matt never comes out with us on Halloween weekends?"

"No...I..." *Huh.* The first year I moved here was after Halloween. The next year I'm pretty sure Matt said he had another party to go to. And the year after that he'd been sick. "Wow, yeah. I've never even seen him in a Halloween costume. That's blasphemy."

James laughed.

"Is he scared of clowns or something? I've heard that lots of people don't do Halloween because they're terrified of clowns and so many people dress up as them. It's a thing."

"Yeah, I don't think he's scared of clowns."

"Then why doesn't he do Halloween?"

- 24 -

James shrugged. "You should ask him."

"Okay…" I stared at him. He was hiding something. I could tell. "Or you could just tell me."

"You should really ask him."

I pressed my lips together. "Okay. I will." I already had an idea in my head. Matt was young at heart. I bet he did something really embarrassing one Halloween and swore everyone to secrecy or something. That was probably it. I'd get the truth out of him. And even if I couldn't…he had to come to the party. His parents were throwing it. I could be very persuasive when I needed to be.

Ian pulled to a stop in front of a…ridiculous looking restaurant. There were parrots painted all over the sides of the exposed bricks. Really big parrots in tons of bright colors. And the Parrot Palace was scrawled above the turquoise front door. The Parrot Palace. I smiled. What a funny name.

"It looks very tropical," I said.

James laughed. "Just wait until you see the inside. They really went crazy with the theme."

"I can't wait."

Ian opened my door. I grabbed his hand and stepped out.

"Tell Jen I say hi," I said.

He smiled. "Of course."

"Thanks for the ride, Ian," James said. "See you in a few hours." He gave him a curt nod.

I waited until Ian climbed back into the car to turn to James. "You have to get over it. Ian and you are close. Stop being so terse with him."

"I'm not being terse."

"Every time you talk it looks like you're gonna rip his head off."

"I would never do that."

I laughed. "I know that. But he's probably worried you're going to fire him or something. Which you can't do. Because we need him."

"I'm not going to fire him."

"Good." I stared at him.

"Good."

He hadn't agreed to be nice. But I'd pester him about that later. Right now I needed to see what the hell was inside this tropical restaurant. I'd painted a picture in my head of very over the top tropical décor.

We walked inside and it was like we were transported to…well…some tropical place. If anything, it was more extra than I'd even pictured ahead of time. The walls were all painted with waves. The tables were made of worn-down beach wood. There were stuffed parrots perched on fake palm trees. I wasn't even sure that was accurate. Weren't parrots in rainforests or something? But it didn't really matter. It all somehow worked, even though it was way too many decorations for a restaurant. I wondered if Matt and Mason's parents went all out like this for Halloween. Probably. Mrs. Caldwell always threw a good party.

I swore one of the parrots' heads moved as we walked to the hostess stand. "Did you see that parrot move?" I asked.

"What?" James looked over at the parrot. "No."

I swore it was looking at me. Maybe I was already at a Halloween party. But then I heard music. Ah! My eyes abandoned the creepy parrot. There was a DJ and a dance floor. I hadn't been expecting that. Right now the DJ was just playing some Beach Boys music pretty quietly. The restaurant had a romantic, intimate feel despite the creepy birds. But fingers crossed it was going to get crazy in a couple of hours.

CHAPTER 4

Friday

Rob waved at us as the hostess led us toward their table.

"This place is insane," I said when we got to the huge half-circle booth.

"Isn't it perfect?" Rob said. He was at one end of the booth, his arm was wrapped around Daphne's shoulders. Mason and Bee were already there too…smushed together in the middle of the booth. It was actually kind of funny seeing Mason sitting in a booth. He was still wearing his expensive suit from work and he stuck out like a sore thumb here. All the employees were dressed in bright, floral Hawaiian shirts. The vibe was chill and laid back and not at all what Mason was wearing.

James slid in beside them because he knew I'd want to be close to the end so I could go to the bathroom. I was barely showing and I already felt like I needed to pee every few minutes. I didn't want to think about what it would be like in a couple of months.

Bee leaned forward. "So is the food really good here or something, Rob? Why'd you choose the weirdest place in the city?"

He laughed. "It's not weird. It's perfect," he said again and looked over at Daphne.

She grabbed her glass of water and downed half of it without making eye contact with anyone.

I looked over at James. He was already staring down at me. And we shared the "what the hell is going on right now?" look with each other.

"They don't even have darts," Mason said. "How are you expecting to con me out of all my money tonight?"

"No kicking your ass tonight," Rob said. "Just a memorable night with my favorite people. Speaking of which...where is Matt?" Rob rolled up his sleeve to check his watch. "He's five minutes late."

James and I both looked at each other again. Rob never wore a watch. And now that I thought about it...he was always late for our weekly dinners, usually the last to arrive. What the actual hell was going on right now?

"He said he'd be a few minutes late," Mason said. "Speaking of being late...nice watch. Please tell me you're not dying or something."

Rob laughed. "Nope, I'm very healthy. Virile, actually. But I'm a grownup now and grownups wear watches." He pushed his sleeve back down. "I'm a freaking adult."

Oh God, is he dying? "Are you sure you're feeling alright?" I asked. I couldn't help but worry. He was acting very strange.

"He's fine," Daphne said and elbowed him in his side.

He smiled down at Daphne.

They'd only been dating a few months so they still had that thing where everyone else faded into the distance when they were together.

James placed his hand on my thigh. I looked up at him and he was staring at me the same way Rob was staring at Daphne. I guess we still had it too. I felt my cheeks flush.

This was the look I was worried would fade though. Once I was the size of a blimp.

His hand slid farther up my thigh, his fingers absent-mindedly playing with the hem of my dress that had risen *very* high. His fingers gently dipped below it.

Oh my God, what is he doing?

But his fingers froze a little farther up.

I breathed a sigh of relief. If this man was thinking about touching me in a booth surrounded by our friends, he was out of his damn mind. It wasn't like I could scooch in my chair to hide it better. Because we were in a booth, and it was nailed to the ground.

"Sorry I'm late," Matt said and slid into the booth next to me. "Hey, Penny."

"Hey. Long day at the office?"

"Yeah." He adjusted his collar.

I was pretty sure he was hiding a hickey or something. Okay...not a late day at the office then. Well, maybe. And I couldn't exactly fault him for mixing business with pleasure. It sure worked for Mason and Bee.

I was just about to ask Matt about Halloween when James' thumb slid closer to where I needed him most. God, was this how he was going to torture me? Just tease me all night, inching closer but never touching me? And why the hell did I want him to touch me right now? We were in the middle of a crowded restaurant.

"I'm so glad we're all here tonight," Rob said. "To-gether. All my favorite people. I want to make a toast." He drummed his hands against the table. "We need more than water though. Where is our waiter? I swore I just saw him over by that palm tree a second ago."

Okay, something was definitely up with him.

"He's probably dry humping a parrot," Matt said under his breath.

I laughed and Matt smiled at me.

But my laughter died in my throat when James' hand rose higher up my skirt. I looked over at my husband and hoped he could tell what I was thinking – that Matt had a clear view of my lap…and his hand under my skirt, only an inch away from touching me now.

James' eyes dropped to my lips, sending a chill down my spine.

Oh God, he is going to touch me, isn't he?

He lowered his eyebrows.

Yeah, he was definitely going to. That was what the wink in the elevator was about. He was going to torture me slowly beneath the table all night.

Rob waved his hand in the air to get our waiter's attention.

The waiter hurried over. "I see that your whole party has arrived. Welcome to the Parrot Palace. I'm Randy, and I'll be your Parrot Palace party person this evening. What can I get y'all to drink?"

Parrot Palace party what now? I pressed my lips together so I wouldn't laugh. His southern accent didn't really fit the vibe of the restaurant. And for some reason that was the final straw for making this place crazy. Seriously…where were we?

"We're going to need champagne," Rob said. "And…" he turned toward the table like he was counting us even though there were always seven of us "…six glasses. Yeah six. And what do you want to drink, Penny?"

"Iced tea, please."

- 31 -

"Champagne and iced tea," Rob said. "And make it snappy."

Daphne touched his shoulder.

"Make it two iced teas," Rob said. He looked over at me. "My sister-in-law looks thirsty."

Excuse me? What the fuck does that mean?

Matt laughed.

I looked over at James. "Did your brother just call me a thirsty bitch?" I whispered.

Mason started laughing now too. "He definitely did."

The waiter hurried off.

James shrugged. "Do you think he's high or something?"

"I don't know." I turned to Rob. "Seriously, Rob, is everything okay?" I was just wearing a sundress. I didn't look *that* thirsty. I wasn't even taking any selfies! He was usually very nice to me. And a little inappropriate.

"What? Yeah. We're good. I'm just excited." He looked at his watch again.

"When did you buy a watch?" Matt asked. "I thought you didn't believe in the concept of time?"

"I'm an adult, Matt. Of course I believe in the concept of time. And I need to make sure I'm not late to anything important. Like important life events. It's an adult thing. You wouldn't understand."

"He's definitely high," Matt whispered to me.

James' hand rose higher on my thigh when Matt leaned in to whisper to me.

Jesus. "Do they have dinner rolls or something here?" I opened up my menu. "I'm starving." I needed a reason to unroll my napkin and place it on my lap before the whole table saw what James was up to. He was inches away from touching me. And if I was a woman with less restraint, I would have shifted on the booth so his fingers would finally reach me. As it was…I was used to him torturing me.

Instead, I crossed my legs. But that somehow just moved his hand closer. I swallowed hard. *I will not moan in front of our friends. I will not moan in a crowded parrot restaurant. I will not.*

A waiter was walking by with exactly what I was looking for. "Excuse me," I said. "Could we have some rolls too?"

"No problem. I'll be right back with those."

Thank God. Now I had an excuse. I'd just asked for food, so getting my napkin right now was normal, right? I didn't even care. Un-normal was better than being kicked out of the restaurant for indecent exposure. I unwound the fabric from the utensils and draped the napkin over my lap.

Apparently James had been expecting me to do that, because his fingers finally slid up, brushing his fingers against my bathing suit bottom.

Fuck.

"Eating for two," Rob said and smiled at me. "The miracle of life. It's been really fun the last few months watching my nephew grow inside of you."

James' fingers stopped.

Yeah, this was super weird. I didn't want Rob saying weird things about the miracle of life when James was touching me. "Rob…"

"Where is our champagne?" Rob said.

"Maybe he snorted cocaine," Matt whispered and tilted his head to the side to study Rob.

Rob fidgeted with his watch again.

Matt nodded. "Yeah…it's probably cocaine."

I stared at Rob too. I wasn't sure if Rob was on drugs. He just seemed…nervous or something. Which was weird. Because I'd never seen Rob nervous. Maybe none of us had, which is why we thought he was high out of his mind. Rob was confident in everything he did. Including his decision to not wear a watch. What the hell was going on?

"Huzzah!" Rob yelled a little too loudly when the waiter came back with our drinks and the basket of bread I'd awkwardly asked another waiter for.

Oops. It was fine if two baskets were coming though. I really was hungry.

Rob grabbed the champagne bottle and opened it with a satisfying pop. He barely spilled a drop before catching it in one of the flutes.

"Did you want me to pour those, sir?" Randy our Parrot Palace party person asked.

"No, I got it." Rob grabbed another glass and hurriedly poured the champagne.

He handed a glass filled to the brim with champagne to Daphne. And she looked just as confused as the rest of it. She quickly set the glass down.

"Are you ready to order?" Randy asked.

We all said yes, except for Rob, who said no. When we all stared hungry daggers at him, he shook his head. "Fine. But make it quick."

But we all knew it couldn't be quick…because Daphne was here. And Daphne was very slow at ordering food. She passed after Rob ordered and lifted her menu a little higher.

The Parrot Palace party person took all of our orders, collected our menus, and then went back to Daphne.

I grabbed a roll and slathered it with butter. This was going to take a few minutes. I bit into my roll. *So good.*

But I almost choked on it when James' index finger slid beneath my bathing suit bottom, sliding against my wetness.

His breath was hot in my ear. "Are you wearing a bathing suit?"

Damn it, he was ruining his surprise! "No." It came out airy and weird.

"Are you sure about that?" He gently circled my clit.

Fuck. I almost squashed the bread in my hand.

"Because it certainly feels like a bathing suit."

I shoved a piece of bread in my mouth to stop the moan that wanted to leave my lips.

He traced my wetness again and now I was worried I'd moan and bread would fly out of my mouth. What was he doing? I'd be lucky if we made it through the night without getting arrested.

Rob was high or something and James had clearly lost his mind.

"I can't wait to get you back home alone," James whispered. "Because I'm only hungry for one thing." His eyes landed suggestively on my lap.

"Maybe we should go to the bathroom," I whispered back. It wasn't like it would be the first time we'd fucked in a bathroom stall. At least we'd have a little privacy there.

"I think I'd rather take my time with you right here." His finger slid inside of me.

A small moan escaped my lips but I covered it with a cough.

Yeah…we were definitely going to get arrested.

CHAPTER 5
Friday

"James, please," I whispered.

He slid another finger inside of me.

That was not what I was saying please for. Or...was it? I had no idea anymore.

He moved his fingers faster.

Yeah, I probably was begging him to keep going at this point. God I was so close. I bit the inside of my lip so I wouldn't scream.

"You okay?" Matt asked. "You look a little pale."

Okay, no. That's enough. I was not going to come when Matt was staring directly at me. This was too weird. I coughed and slapped James' hand. And then slapped it again when he didn't move it.

He laughed and slid his hand out from underneath my skirt. He picked up my half-eaten bread and took a bite, licking his fingers like he'd gotten butter on them. But I knew what was on his fingers. His eyes locked with mine as he licked off the last drop. I felt myself clench and shifted awkwardly in my seat. I was supposed to be the one seducing him. He had no business torturing me like this. But I'd be lying if I said I didn't love every second of it.

"Hmm," Daphne set the menu down. "Well, what kind of cheese do you put on your cheeseburgers?"

Was she seriously not done ordering yet? I'd almost come and she was still going over burger options.

"American," Randy said.

"Is it like a thin slice or a thick slice?"

"Pretty thin I think."

"Could I get two slices then?"

"Sure." Randy wrote it down and was about to walk away.

"Wait," Daphne said. "I still have more questions."

"Okay…"

"What kind of bun is it?"

"Like…a normal cheeseburger bun."

"With sesame seeds?"

"Yeah."

"Okay, that'll be fine I guess. But if you had one without sesame seeds, I'd really appreciate it. Also, if it wasn't a sesame bun at all and was a wheat bun that would be even better. And could I have all the toppings on the side? But please, no pickles at all. I don't like when they touch the rest of my food."

She was going to be horrified in a few minutes then. Because I'd ordered double pickles and I was going to devour those things. I craved them constantly.

"Sure thing," the waiter said and was about to walk away again.

"Wait," Daphne said. "It comes with fries, right?"

"Fries and coleslaw."

Daphne made a face and then shook her head. "Could I get two vegetable sides instead?"

"Yeah. The side substitutions are on page three."

She flipped to the page. "Is your broccoli steamed or roasted?"

"Roasted I think."

"Hm. What about your green beans?"

Good God. I loved Daphne to death. But eating out with her was a nightmare.

"I think those are steamed," Randy said.

"Oh, good. I'll take green beans and…is your applesauce homemade?"

"No."

"You know what? I'm feeling crazy. Let's get the fries after all. So fries and steamed green beans."

She did realize that she basically just ordered the normal menu item right? All she had to do instead of all that was ask for all the toppings on the side and green beans instead of coleslaw. It would have saved our Parrot Palace party person a whole lot of time. But I knew Rob always tipped well to make up for Daphne's weird ordering habits.

"And actually could I get a turkey burger?"

Rob groaned. "Babe, the reviews here are great. I'm sure the normal burger is fine. Let's get a move on."

She glared at him.

Rob cleared his throat. "A turkey burger for my girl, please," he said to the waiter.

"Very well." Randy took one step back and paused, like he thought Daphne would demand something else. When she didn't he practically ran away.

Rob kissed Daphne's cheek and whispered something in her ear that made her smile.

I swear, if James ordered food that way I'd probably murder him in his sleep.

"I swear," James whispered to me. "If you suddenly started ordering food that way I'd murder you in your sleep."

I laughed. "I was just thinking the same thing about you. What happened to loving me forever and always?"

"It's the one thing I wouldn't be able to keep my vows for. I'd have no choice but to murder you."

I laughed. Speaking of murdering people...I needed to ask Matt about Halloween. But before I turned to him, I saw that Daphne hadn't given her menu back to the waiter. *Good God, someone take that away from her.*

She flipped another page. "Maybe I should have ordered..."

"Nope," Rob said and slammed her menu down on the table. "It's time."

Her face grew pale.

"Seriously," Mason said. "What is going on? You're freaking us out."

Daphne took a deep breath and exhaled slowly. "We um..." she looked at Rob and then back at us. "We have some news." She started to smile, but it looked like she was holding it back. "Really crazy news, actually. We..."

"I'll take it from here," Rob said, cutting her off. He stood up and lifted his glass of champagne in the air. "I want to make a toast to Daphne. For being the best girlfriend in the whole world."

Okay. That was kind of a slap in the face to Bee and me, but I got the idea. I lifted my glass of iced tea in the air. "Hear, hear," I said. Wait, was that the news they wanted to share?

Rob smiled at me. "Come on everyone. Glasses up."

Everyone else at the table lifted their glasses.

"Daphne and I met under very weird circumstances. A weekend that would change our lives forever. Luckily Mason and I forced James to have a bachelor party. Or else Daphne and I never would have met at the Blue Parrot Resort. I never would have fallen in love with my other half." He smiled down at her.

And Daphne smiled up at him.

Oh. The Blue Parrot Resort. Is that why we were at this parrot themed restaurant? I'd never been able to find pictures of that resort. It was super exclusive and fancy. Kind of the opposite of this place. I looked behind me at the parrot with the strange eyes and immediately snapped my attention back to Rob. That winged beast had been staring right at me, I swear.

"You and I all started with a bracelet," Rob said. He reached into his pocket and then shook his head and reached into his other pocket. He pulled out a small box.

"What started with a bracelet?" I whispered to James.

"It was that weird sex game at the resort."

Right, I remembered hearing about it. All the girls wore bracelets and the guys had cards with chips in them that could unlock the bracelets. Most of the cards were crazy. Like…Get topless. It helped people at the resort flirt or whatever. Probably more than flirt. And the girls had to do whatever the crazy cards said if a man unlocked their bracelet. But James swore he didn't play the game. He'd given his cards to Rob and Matt.

Rob handed Daphne the box. And I finally registered how small it was.

James put his hand down on my thigh, dangerously high again.

But I wasn't even thinking about how much I wanted him. I wasn't sure he was thinking about that either. I put my hand down on top of his. And then I held my breath. I was pretty sure we were all thinking the same thing. That Rob was about to propose in this weird parrot restaurant.

Daphne gave him a funny look and then opened up the box. I shifted a little closer, moving James' hand higher, his pinky brushing against me again.

I gasped.

Daphne laughed. "It's not a ring, you guys, it's just a bracelet."

I was really glad they thought I was gasping because of that. I tried to ignore James' hand as I watched Daphne lift the bracelet.

"Um…thanks, Rob," she said. "This is beautiful. But it has nothing to do with our news."

"Right. I just wanted you to have this."

She smiled sweetly at him as he reached out and clasped the bracelet on her wrist.

"It looks just like the ones from the resort," James whispered at me.

"Huh?" I was having a hard time paying attention because his fingers were too close to me again.

"The bracelet. It looks like the ones from the Blue Parrot Resort."

Oh, that was a sweet gift. To remind them where they met. I wasn't sure why we were all watching this though. Was the bracelet their news after all? I feel like we didn't need to be here for this…

"Cool," Matt said. "I hope the food comes soon. I'm starving."

"That wasn't the news," Rob said. "This is our news." He pulled a card out of his pocket.

Daphne was smiling at all of us and was about to open her mouth to finally share the news, but she stopped when Rob handed her the card.

She took a sip of her water before looking down at the card. Before she could see it, Rob pressed the card against her bracelet and the bracelet fell to the table. And then she immediately spit the water all over the table.

I jumped back, trying not to get sprayed.

And Rob dropped to one knee.

Oh my God!

He pulled out a smaller box from his other pocket.

"What is happening right now?" Daphne said and put her hand over her mouth.

"Didn't you read the card?" Rob said. "Read it out loud for everyone."

"It says…marry me." She started blinking away tears.

"Will you make me the happiest man alive and marry me, Daphne? Not that you have a choice. You have to do whatever it says on the card. It's in the rules."

She was full on crying now. She couldn't even respond.

"But please say yes. I can't wait to start the rest of our lives together."

She just nodded her head because she was crying so hard.

Rob slid the ring onto her finger and then she jumped off the booth and into his arms. Their kiss was sinful and not at all suitable for a public restaurant.

But I'd been reading sex scenes all day and James' hand was up my skirt. So I didn't find it unusual at all. "Congratulations!" I screamed at the top of my lungs.

Our whole table started cheering.

Then everyone in the restaurant was cheering too.

And then the weirdest thing happened. All the parrots in the restaurant started singing in harmony *Wouldn't It be Nice* by the Beach Boys. Apparently they were all robotic. They started flapping their wings and swaying to the beat of the music. It was perfect timing. Hence the watch that Rob was wearing for the first time in his life.

It was so freaking cute.

"You're crying," James whispered.

Am I? I touched my cheek and sure enough, it was wet. Anything could set me off recently. But I wasn't surprised I was crying now. This was amazing. I loved Rob and Daphne together. And I'd just gained the world's best sister-in-law.

Rob stopped kissing Daphne long enough to say, "You didn't read the whole card."

"What?" asked Daphne.

He reached behind her and grabbed it off the table.

She looked at the card and then back at him. "You're crazy, you do know that?"

"I do," he said. "Is that still a yes?"

"A thousand times yes."

He kissed her again.

"What else is on the card?" Matt asked.

Rob held it up in the air as he started making out with his fiancée again.

Matt stood up and grabbed it. "It says marry me…in two weeks."

"No, sir," Rob said. "I will not."

Matt hit him in the back of the head.

I laughed and then stopped. "Wait, two weeks?!"

Rob smiled at Daphne. "I don't want to wait another minute for you to be my wife."

She nodded. "I love you so much."

"We have a wedding to plan!" Rob said.

Two weeks was not a lot of time. But if there was anyone who could do it… "I know exactly who to call." My wedding planner, Justin, was the only person I'd trust for the job. He was going to freak about the two weeks' notice. But he'd also see it as a challenge. He'd make it magical for them.

"Good, because I don't know the first thing about planning a wedding," Daphne said. "Oh my God, I need a dress." She shook her head. "And a venue. Can we really do this in two weeks?"

"We can do it," I said. Well…I couldn't. Justin could. And I'd definitely be there to help with anything they needed. We needed to make a list of everything we had to do. My mind was going a mile a minute, but it came to a halt when Matt screamed at the top of his lungs.

One of the parrots was attacking him.

He screamed again and slapped the parrot.

I screamed too and ducked under the table. But I could still see the action. Some of the parrots were flying around the restaurant now, flapping to the music. The creepy parrot with the wandering eyes only had one target, though…Matt. Its mechanical wings flapped violently as it belted out the lyrics to *Wouldn't It Be Nice*, trying its best to hit Matt in the face. Matt was trying to swat it away, but it kept coming back for more.

I started laughing because I didn't know what else to do. And Matt's screams were so high-pitched.

Matt dodged another attack and then swatted once more at the bird before ducking under our table too. "What the fuck?" he said.

I started laughing even harder.

"It's not funny. That bird tried to fucking kill me." But he started laughing because I was laughing so hard.

"Did you see its eyes?" I said through my laughter.

"Yes, they were staring right at me."

James ducked his head under the table as the song came to an end. "It's safe to come out now, you two."

I lifted my head back up. The whole table was laughing.

"Part of this place's charm," Rob said. "Singing birds on the hour every hour." He unhooked his watch and then threw it on the table. "I don't need that thing anymore. Watches suck."

Of course. Rob was timing this out perfectly. And murderous tropical parrots were the perfect way to celebrate a proposal. The night made a whole lot more sense now.

The food came out a minute later. "Sorry about that," our waiter said, nodding at Matt. "Patty the parrot has a certain route around the restaurant and you were in the way. We've never had that happen before."

"Was I in the way?" Matt said. "Because I was just standing by our table."

"We always suggest that our guests stay seated during the show. For their own safety."

"I didn't know there was a show," Matt said.

"Oh. That's why everyone comes here. For the parrot show and the delicious food." He turned to the newly engaged couple. "Congratulations, you two," Randy said. "Dessert is on the house tonight. And you know...we do weddings. You could have it here."

Good God no. Accidentally being attacked by parrots on your wedding day did not sound like a good plan.

Rob nodded at Randy, but he didn't say yes. I was hoping it was more of a polite nod. Not a...yeah we'll have our wedding at the Parrot Palace kind of nod.

Daphne and Rob climbed back into the booth. They both looked so happy.

Which reminded me of how nervous Daphne had been to tell us the news. "Wait," I said. This night made no sense at all. "Daphne said you guys had news. But she was totally surprised about the proposal. Was there other news?"

Daphne opened her mouth but Rob cut her off.

"Yeah, we probably should have warned you," Rob said. "There were terrible reviews for the burgers here. Their beef is super rancid."

What? I'd ordered a burger... I looked around at the rest of our meals. We'd all ordered burgers.

"I can assure y'all that our beef is not rancid," Randy said.

Rob looked down at Daphne's plate. "Oh, then maybe it was the turkey then. Well, either way, she can't eat this. The pickles can't be anywhere near her plate. And there are pickles there. We talked about this."

I'd never seen Rob complain about any food. Or care about any reviews. It was sweet that he was taking care of Daphne though. And I didn't want to get sick from rancid beef. Or turkey. Or whatever.

"Sorry. I'll take it back right away." Randy grabbed the plate.

"Wait. I'll take them." I leaned across the booth and grabbed the pickles off her plate.

Daphne looked horrified when I shoved one in my mouth.

So freaking good.

James laughed. "So the turkey is rancid?"

"I promise you nothing is rancid," Randy said again. "Will you guys please stop saying that," he said, dropping his voice so the other patrons would stop staring at us.

"Just the turkey," Rob said with a nod and then whispered something in Daphne's ear.

She nodded.

Screw it. I didn't know what those two were up to. But that pickle was amazing. And I was starving. "I guess we'll find out," I said and took a big bite of my burger. It didn't taste rancid. It tasted like heaven.

James shrugged and started eating too. The rest of our table followed. Minus Daphne because she'd ordered the rancid turkey meat. But I didn't think she was that hungry. She seemed perfectly fine making out with Rob.

I took another bite and then all the lights in the restaurant turned off.

What the hell is happening now?

CHAPTER 6

Friday

I grabbed James' hand. If a parrot restaurant was this scary to me, maybe I should skip the Caldwell Halloween party. Apparently I couldn't handle scary stuff anymore.

"What is going on?" I said.

"I don't know," Rob said. "I only knew about the parrots."

It was seriously pitch black. I couldn't see a thing. I held James' hand tighter.

And then the beat dropped. The dance floor in the back lit up. It was like we'd been transported to a disco. Minus the parrots flapping to the music.

"Ah there's dancing!" I said. I suddenly wasn't hungry anymore. I put my burger down. "Who wants to dance?"

James had a mouthful of burger.

"I'm in," Bee said. She hadn't touched her food. She was probably worried it was rancid. "Daphne get your butt on the dance floor, us girls need to celebrate!"

Daphne threw her hands in the air. And the three of us maneuvered out of the booth and ran over to the dance floor.

Before I started dancing, I threw my arms around Daphne. "Congratulations!"

Bee put her arms around us too. "You and Rob are perfect together."

"Stop it, you're going to make me cry again," Daphne said and stepped back. "And I want to celebrate." She started jumping up and down to the beat.

Bee and I joined in. Although I was jumping significantly less than they were. As much as I'd been dying to dance, I wondered if jumping around was good for the baby. I started swaying my hips instead.

It felt so good to be dancing again. Bee and I sandwiched Daphne on the dance floor. I was in front of her and I leaned over. Daphne smacked my butt. I laughed and looked over at our table. James was staring at me. That familiar heat in his eyes. God, he was going to fuck me so hard tonight.

I was still bent over when I pointed to him and crooked my finger. As fun as it was dancing with my girls, I was really wound up. And very much in the mood to grind against him.

I closed my eyes and let the beat guide my hips.

It only took a few seconds before I felt James' hands around my waist. He pulled me against him, his erection already pressing into my lower back.

I opened my eyes and tilted my head to the side so I could see him behind me.

"You're driving me crazy." His voice was barely audible over the music. He grabbed my hips more firmly.

He'd been the one in control at the table. But I had him just where I wanted him now. I dropped low and slowly rose up, sliding my ass against him.

He groaned.

God, I needed him. I'd been desperate for him all night. I looked around for the restroom signs.

But before I could find one, Daphne joined us. "I'm going to be your sister!" she said and threw her arms around James.

James caught her at an awkward angle so she wouldn't accidentally hit the tent in his pants.

Rob had joined us on the dance floor too. "I'm getting married, big bro!" He threw his arms around James and hugged him too.

I laughed as Rob leaned back, lifting James slightly off the floor. If he wasn't careful he was going to throw out his back.

I looked over at Bee who was dry humping Mason in the middle of the dance floor. I laughed and searched the rest of the dance floor for Matt, but he wasn't there. I turned back to our table. He was sitting there staring at his food. It looked like he was lost in thought. I pressed my lips together. *Oh, Matt.* I couldn't imagine what he was thinking. He was the last of his friends to find his person. But I was sure she was out there somewhere. I knew it had been hard on him ever since Rob started dating Daphne. He was the last single member of our friend group. Dancing would cheer him up though. Matt was a great dancer. I left the dance floor to go grab him.

"Dance with us," I said.

He looked up at me. "I'm actually gonna get going."

"No you're not. Come dance with us."

"But I um…I got another thing."

"Another thing? Your best friend just got engaged. Nothing is as important as this." I put my hand out for him.

He looked at my hand and then back up at my face. "I really gotta get going."

Seriously? "Scoot." I pushed on his arm for him to move over in the booth. I sat down beside him. "What other thing?"

"A work thing."

Bullshit. It was Friday night. I knew what this was about. "You're going to find your person, Matt."

He drew his eyebrows together. "No. I'm not."

"Of course you will. Did you ever in a million years think I would have found love with James? He was my professor for goodness sakes."

Matt shrugged.

"And I'm pretty sure that Mason was up to very sinful things when he met Bee. Did you ever think he would settle down?"

Matt pressed his lips together.

"And Rob and Daphne? That is a very unlikely pair. Carefree Rob with a woman who orders food like it's the biggest decision in the world."

Matt finally smiled. "She really shouldn't be allowed into restaurants."

I laughed. "Come on. Celebrate with us. You'll find your soulmate soon."

His smile faltered.

What was going on with him? I slid out of the booth and put my hand out again. "Don't leave me hanging here, Matt. I don't have a partner on the dance floor and I need you." I looked over to where Rob was trying to lift James again. *What on earth are they doing?*

Matt slid his hand into mine.

I pulled him out of the booth and dragged him to the dance floor. I took a few steps backward and pretended to cast a fishing rod. "You," I mouthed, like I'd just caught him.

Matt wiggled toward me like he was the fish I caught, and then grabbed me and dipped me.

I laughed as he pulled me back to his chest.

"Feeling better already, aren't you?"

He shimmied in response.

I smiled. I had no doubt in my mind that Matt would find someone soon. The guy was a total catch. Speaking of catches...I glanced over at James. All our friends were dancing in the middle of the dance floor. I grabbed Matt's hand and pulled him over to the rest of our friends.

We all surrounded Rob and Daphne in the middle of the dance floor and cheered for them again. They started pausing in their dance in funny poses like they were posing for paparazzi.

"Work it, girl!" Bee yelled and pretended to take a photo.

Which somehow ended in us all taking turns in the middle, posing for fake photos.

I was smiling so hard my cheeks hurt.

James grabbed my hips again, pulling me against him. I reached behind me, grabbing the back of his neck. And I moved my body slow to the music. Torturously slow. I never knew a restaurant filled with creepy parrots could be so erotic, but I swear I was soaked.

"The things I'm going to do to you," he whispered in my ear.

I moaned and it didn't even matter because the music was so loud.

I wasn't sure how long we danced for. But I felt the sweat dripping down the back of my neck. It was just like it was before I was pregnant. Dancing until my whole body was sore. Until I was drenched in sweat. My ass pressed against James' length.

"I need you," James said. "Right now."

"But I never got to congratulate Rob…"

"You can congratulate him later." He grabbed my hand and pulled me off the dance floor. I thought he would be taking me out of the restaurant and back to our place. Instead, he turned left.

Ah, so that's where the restrooms have been hiding.

He looked both ways before opening the door to the woman's restroom. There was no one inside. He locked the door and then pressed me against it.

God, yes please.

I buried my fingers in his hair and pulled his face down to mine. The kiss was dizzying. It was like I was starving and I needed him. He bit my bottom lip and I moaned. His mouth truly was a miracle. His hand slid up my thigh, lifting my leg around his waist.

I don't know why I opened my eyes. I was caught up in the moment and I wasn't a weirdo who opened my eyes during a kiss. But it was like I suddenly knew we weren't alone.

I stared in horror at the mechanical bird perched on the corner of the sink. Staring directly at us with his beady little eyes. It slowly lifted its robotic wings and flapped. I put my hand on James' chest. "Oh my God, it followed us in here."

"What?" James turned around to see what I was looking at. "It's just one of the dumb birds, ignore it."

"It's not just one of them. It's *the* one. The creepy one with the eyes that follow you." I moved, peering over

James' other shoulder. The little demon bird was still staring at me.

"It's fine," James said as he kissed the side of my neck.

I closed my eyes and tried to ignore the bird. But then it squawked.

"Nope." I stepped back from James, letting my thigh fall from around his waist. "I can't. It's too freaking weird."

James laughed and looked back at the bird. "Okay, it is a little weird. Wasn't that the one at the front of the restaurant? How did it get in here?"

"I don't know. Let's get the hell out of here." I unlocked the door and pulled James back out into the disco Parrot Palace party. Just as we stepped out, another bird started flapping toward us. We ducked to avoid its party path, or whatever the heck our waiter had called it. "Yeah, this was all too freaking weird. "Let's just go home," I said. "You're right. I can congratulate Rob later."

James smiled. "I'm so glad you said that. Ian should be here any second. I already texted him."

"But…" I glanced back at the bathroom door. "We were just going to bang in there. Why'd you already text him?"

He pulled me in close. "Did you think I was only going to have you once tonight?" His fingers slid down and squeezed my ass. "You know that once is never enough."

"Come on, before we get arrested." I reluctantly pulled his hands from my butt and we made a run for it. We dodged one more beady-eyed beast and pushed out the front doors of the restaurant. We couldn't tell from inside, but it was pouring out. It only took a few seconds before we were both completely drenched.

I laughed and turned to James.

He stepped forward, cradling my face in his hands. "Does this remind you of anything?"

I swallowed hard. "Our first kiss." I remembered it perfectly. He'd driven me home. And instead of walking me to my door like a gentleman, he'd pressed me against the side of his car and kissed me. Just thinking about it made my heart race.

"It took every ounce of my restraint not to fuck you right there against the hood of my car."

Jesus. I blinked fast as I stared up at him, trying not to let the rain fall in my eyes. But honestly, I didn't even care about the rain. I was wearing a bathing suit after all. And I loved the rain. I'd fallen in love with James in a storm.

I stood up on my tiptoes and closed the distance between us.

His hand found my waist, pulling me closer.

I buried my fingers into his wet hair. I'd dreamed of running my fingers through his unruly hair all the time when I was his student. And now I took full advantage of the fact that I could do it whenever I wanted.

The rain started falling even harder. I could feel it dripping from my eyelashes. I could taste it in our kiss.

"Our car is here," James said.

I didn't care. I deepened our kiss. And I practically whimpered when his hands fell from my waist. I stared up at him. He was so soaked that water was dripping from the scruff on his chin. God he was so fucking sexy. If Ian wasn't sitting in the car waiting for us, I would have licked the water off of him.

James pulled me over to the car and opened the door.

"Crazy storm," Ian said.

"Mhm." *Crazy perfect.* I'd been planning on seducing James in the bathroom of a tropical restaurant. That hadn't exactly panned out. But my bathing suit worked for the new plan forming in my head too.

James climbed into the other side and slammed the door.

I slid to the middle seat. He'd teased me in the restaurant, so I was going to tease him all the way home. I looked into the rearview mirror to make sure Ian wasn't looking, and then reached out for James' belt. I managed to unbuckle it before James caught my hand.

"It's five months of seduction both ways, James," I whispered into his ear. "Which means I get to seduce you too." I lightly bit down on his earlobe as I unbuttoned and unzipped his khakis. "You know how turned on I get when we might get caught. You're the one that told me that. You've taught me a lot of things about myself." I slid my hand under the waistband of his boxers, lightly dancing my fingers down his length.

His breath was labored, like he was trying to control himself. I knew what he wanted to do. Flip me over and fuck me right here in the car. I hoped that would happen. Desperately so. I needed him so deep inside of me that I'd have no choice but to scream his name. Just not quite yet. After all, Ian could easily see us in the rearview mirror. And I liked the fear of getting caught, not *actually* getting caught.

"Penny…"

I wrapped my hand around his thick erection and he stifled a groan. "Yes, James?" I didn't wait for a response. I leaned forward and did what I wanted to do outside. I licked the side of his jawline, tracing the path of the rainwater. I kissed the side of his neck. Every inch of his skin was wet from the rain. But he'd also been sweating from dancing, and it tasted salty on my tongue. It was the most delicious taste in the world.

He grabbed my hand, stopping me from giving him an amazing hand job. "I'm not going to cum in my pants," he whispered. "Get over to your side of the car. Now."

I loved when he used that demanding voice with me. I tried to raise my eyebrow at him, but I wasn't nearly as good at the stern look as he was.

He reached out, wiping some of the water off my collarbone. Stopping his hand before it dipped between my breasts. "I promise it'll be worth the wait."

I bit my lip and slid to my side of the car, re-buckling my seatbelt. But just because I was on the opposite side of the car, it didn't mean I had to behave. I pushed the skirt of my dress up.

James' eyes landed on my exposed thighs.

I grabbed the waistband of my bikini bottoms and slowly slid them down my legs. I pulled them off the heel of my sandal and tossed them at him.

He shook his head at me, but he was smiling. He pocketed my bikini bottoms and his eyes landed back on my thighs. The hem of my dress was dangerously close to revealing everything. And the steamy glances he gave me all the way home were almost as satisfying as his touch.

I swear I was panting by the time Ian parked the car in the parking garage under our building. And I hoped James was ready...because I was about to give him the time of his life. It had been a while since the last time we'd fucked in a car.

CHAPTER 7

Friday

James cleared his throat. "Thanks, Ian. We're going to need another minute. You can head on up without us."

"No problem," Ian said.

He obviously knew what was going on, but I didn't even care. All I cared about was the fact that in a few minutes James would be deep inside of me. I'd be screaming his name so loud I'd probably wake up the whole building.

Ian tossed the keys into the back seat without turning around. Probably because he was scared we were already going at it.

James caught the keys in one hand and raised his eyebrow at me.

Yeah, he definitely did that stern look better than me. I swear whenever he did that I was putty in his hands.

Ian closed the door behind him and it was only a matter of seconds before I was straddling James in the back of the car.

"I knew you were wearing a bikini," he said as he pulled down the straps of my dress to reveal my bikini top. The soaked fabric of my dress clung to me and he pulled it lower, almost ripping it. He buried his face between my breasts as I grinded against him.

God, I couldn't take it anymore. "I swear if you don't fuck me right now, James, I'm going to die."

He laughed. "I love when you're pregnant. You're insatiable."

"If I recall correctly, you called me that before I was pregnant too."

"You're right. I just fucking love you."

"And I love fucking you."

"Is that really what you want right now?" He tugged on my hair, exposing my neck to him. His tongue traced my throat. "Because it's been a while since I was rough with you." He lightly nipped the side of my neck.

I moaned, grinding against him again. I knew he'd been more gentle with me recently. It was part of the whole reason why these last five months were important. It might be our last chance to go crazy. Hopefully not. But it was better to live it up while we still could. "Fuck me. Now."

He grabbed my ass, lifting me closer as he roughly tore my bikini top down, giving him access to my breasts. He swirled his tongue around my hard nipple. My skin pebbled under his tongue.

What the hell was he trying to do to me? I didn't need to be teased. I needed to be thoroughly fucked. So hard that it was hard to walk. Just thinking about it had me dripping.

He lightly bit down on my nipple.

Jesus. I grabbed the front of his shirt and yanked. The buttons flew off in every direction. *Oops. Not.* I leaned forward, tracing his wet skin with my tongue again. I would seriously never get enough of the taste of his salty skin. I tried to push his shirt off his shoulders, but it was wet and sticking to his skin. I groaned in protest to the stupid shirt. I wanted to see all of him. I loved the way his tanned skin glistened when it was wet. I tore at the fabric like a wild animal, so distracted that I didn't even realize that he'd lifted me up so that he could shove his pants down.

He pulled down on my hips, slamming his erection deep inside of me.

James. My nails dug in to his shoulders as we both moaned. God I felt so full. There was nothing better than being full of him.

He lifted my hips and slammed me down on him again.

Fuck. I take what I said back. There was nothing better than this feeling. Him guiding my hips for his pleasure. Like he was using me for his own release. I loved what my body could do to him. And even though he was in complete control, it made me feel like I was in control too. Each groan that escaped from his lips? That was because of me.

He started moving my hips faster, our wet skin sticking slightly. Adding this tiny slice of pain between the pleasure.

I didn't even care that my knee was against a seat buckle or that I was dangerously close to bonking my head on the roof of the car. I just needed more. More of his mouth. More of the taste of his skin. More of him.

I finally managed to push his shirt off his shoulders. The friction of our wet skin pressed together and I moaned again. I ran my hand down his abs, tracing the muscles with my fingers.

He grabbed my jaw, probably harder than he meant to, and brought my lips back to his.

God, I loved when he was rough with me like that. I was panting. Moaning. Seconds away from screaming his name.

"Ride me, baby," he groaned, his fingers easing their pressure on my hips.

He let me set the pace. But I didn't slow down. If anything I was going faster than before. I spread my legs farther as I shamelessly rode him.

His fingers tangled in my wet hair, tugging hard, as he kissed my neck again. I could tell he was bruising my skin as he sucked on my neck, but I didn't even care. He sucked even harder and it was like it had a direct line to my clit.

Yes, God, just like that. "I love seducing you," I moaned.

"Oh, baby. You're not seducing me." He gently kissed the skin he'd just bruised. "*I'm* seducing *you.*" He grabbed my hips again, his fingers almost painful as they dug in to my skin.

I pressed my hand against the roof of the car to make sure I didn't slam my head against it. And it was the perfect leverage to match each of his thrusts.

One of his hands lightly grabbed my breast and his groans drove me mad.

"James, I'm so close."

He flipped us over, my back slamming against the back seat of the car. He leaned over me and thrust into me hard.

"Yes, James. James!" I reached behind me to the door to try to get leverage again. And somehow in my ecstasy I grabbed the handle of the car and opened it. The cool air hit my skin.

I tried to reach behind me to close it, but James slammed into me harder. I didn't know if he didn't notice that the door was open or if he didn't care, but his pace made me forget about it too.

I pushed his pants further down so I could grab his tight ass.

He groaned. "Come for me, baby." He tilted his hips, hitting that place that always made me come. Every time. I felt myself clench around him.

"James!"

He ran his thumb gently across my clit, making me shiver as he thrust into me faster. And then I felt him pulse inside of me. Again and again.

I'm pretty sure my chants of his name echoed around the parking garage. And as soon as I came back to my senses, I remembered the car door was opened and laughed. My laughter caused me to tighten around him.

James groaned. "That was..."

"Epic?"

"Epic." He leaned forward, making me moan again, as he grabbed the door handle and closed it.

"We're going to get arrested," I said. "I just know it."

"Five months of seduction and this is how we wind up on the first night? Yeah, you're probably right." He smiled down at me, sweat dripping from his forehead.

"Just for the record...I totally seduced you. With the bikini and everything."

"What bikini?"

I looked down. I'd thrown my bikini bottoms at him earlier and my top had been abandoned somewhere in the last several minutes. "Very funny. I seduced you."

"Baby, at the end of these five months, you're going to finally admit that I'm the one seducing you." He gently kissed the side of my neck.

"Never." I wrapped my arms behind his neck. "I'll be seducing you way more over the next few months, Professor Hunter."

His eyes grew dark again.

"See…I'm doing it right now."

He leaned down, running his nose down the length of mine. "Remember when we fucked in my car back on campus?"

"How could I forget?"

"Then you shouldn't forget this…" he leaned forward farther, shifting in me again.

How was he still that hard? He was touching that place again and I knew my lip was quivering.

"Your pleasure is mine," he said. "To give or take." He reached down.

My dress was bunched around my waist. For a second I thought he was reaching down to adjust it. Instead, his thumb found my clit again.

"James…"

"Remember what I told you that night back on campus?"

I remembered all of it. We couldn't keep our hands off each other. And we didn't want to wait to drive back to his apartment. We'd fogged up the whole car, just like we did tonight. I still remembered my handprint on his window.

"I told you that you were mine." He moved his thumb in slow circles and I started to squirm.

"Yes!" *God.* "I'm yours."

He leaned forward, opening up the car door again.

"James…"

"Say it again, baby. I want everyone to know that you're mine."

Wasn't the ring on my finger and his baby growing inside of me proof enough of that? Every inch of me belonged to this man. My heart, my soul, everything.

He pressed down on my clit.

"Yes! I'm yours!"

He pressed down harder and I came again. Harder than the first time. With his cock still hard inside of me and my name on his lips.

My chest rose and fell as I stared up at him. I remembered that time in his car back on campus perfectly in my head. This was better. A thousand times better. Because unlike back then, I was certain every inch of him belonged to me too. His heart, his soul, everything.

"See," he said. "I'm the one seducing you." He slowly pulled out of me.

I was going to protest, but I felt his cum leak out of me. Right onto the back seat of the car. "Shit." I looked around for something to wipe it up with.

James leaned over the front seat and opened the glove compartment. He pulled out a few tissues and then tried to clean up the spot.

But it wasn't coming out. I grabbed the tissues from him and started scrubbing. It was useless. "Ian's going to know what we just did." I put my hand over my eyes.

"Baby, everyone in the building knows what we just did."

I laughed, because it was all I could think of to do. Had he really just made me orgasm with the door of our car wide open? Holy shit, the door was still open! I grabbed my dress and pulled it back into place before a passerby could see my boobs.

"It's late," James said. "I doubt anyone else is even in the parking garage." Somehow in the past few minutes while I worried about the stain, he'd managed to get dressed. Well, as best as he could with all those missing buttons. But I knew I still looked like a hot mess, while he was quite composed.

We both heard the quiet beep of someone locking their car.

I could feel my face turning bright red.

James leaned forward. "Okay, so maybe one person heard us."

"Shhh." I put my hand over his mouth. "Maybe they won't know which car the noises came from."

He slowly slid his hand up my thigh.

I kept my hand over his mouth.

He inched a little higher.

"James I swear…"

He lightly licked my hand.

I laughed and removed it from his mouth just as he thrust two fingers inside of me.

"What are you doing?" I moaned.

"I'm going for a hat trick."

"I swear to God…" my voice trailed off with another moan. *Fuck it.* Who cared if someone heard or saw us? This was going to be the best five months of my life.

CHAPTER 8

Saturday

I was pretty sure my favorite thing in the world was waking up with my limbs tangled up with his. I smiled and opened my eyes, staring at my husband. I was still getting used to thinking of him as my husband. He'd barely ever been my boyfriend, but he'd been my fiancé for a long time. And now? My husband. I loved him more than ever.

The morning light coming through the blinds made his skin almost glow. And there were shadows from his eyelashes, dusting across his cheeks. I didn't care how unmasculine he thought my adjectives were. James Hunter was gorgeous. I ran my fingers along his tattoo, tracing the heartbeats. And then my hand wandered to his ribcage. I felt the scar beneath my index finger. I moved my hand lower, brushing my fingertips against the scar on his stomach. His perfect abs marred by the raised skin.

But I didn't see it as a flaw. Just like the tattoo he'd gotten as his wedding gift to me, these scars were proof that he'd fought his way back to me. Fought his way back to the life he'd promised me. A life filled with love and laughter and us. I ran my finger along the scar on his bicep too.

Three scars. Three chances for him to stop breathing. But he'd kept breathing for me. I'd almost lost him. I'd almost never known what it was like to be his wife. And ever since then...I hadn't taken a day for granted. Not one. I was going to take advantage of these next few months where we were still just the two of us. *Us against the world.*

James slowly opened his eyes and smiled at me. "Good morning, beautiful."

I let my hand fall from his bicep. I knew he wanted to pretend it never happened. He didn't want me to notice that every now and then he got out of breath. Or had to pause in doing something. James wasn't weak. And I had no problem ignoring those moments, knowing that doing so was giving him more strength to keep going. He was a fighter. And I loved him for coming back to me. "Good morning, handsome."

He reached out, pushing a strand of hair out of my face. "What do you want to do today?" he asked with a yawn.

He was doing so much better. But I still thought he should sleep in more. Give his body more time to heal. "You should sleep in."

"I'm not tired anymore." He grabbed my ass, pulling me into his side.

I laughed. "But I have a million things to do today."

He pressed his lips together. "What happened to taking weekends off?"

We'd gotten into a good rhythm over the past couple of months. And that involved leaving work for the weekdays. It was the one rule we had in our house. No work on the weekends. The weekends were lazy days walking around Central Park or spent in bed. But not sleeping. No, we never got much sleeping done when we stayed in bed all day. I bit the inside of my lip, thinking about all the sinful things we'd already done last night. He'd successfully gotten his hat trick. And as much as I wanted to repeat that...

"I have to call Justin," I said. "Rob and Daphne are getting married in two weeks. It's practically an emergency situation."

James yawned again. "Isn't that kind of their job to do all the planning?"

"You're going to be his best man." I lightly shoved his shoulder. "Which means you have to help. This planning is going to take an army to pull off. They'll need all the help they can get."

"Rob hasn't asked me to be his best man," James said.

"He will."

"He might ask Matt."

Was that a twinge of jealousy in his voice? "Nope. I don't think so."

"Technically they're best friends," James said.

"Brother trumps best friend. Trust me."

James laughed. "How would you know? You don't have any siblings."

"You wound me, good sir."

James smiled.

"I think of Rob as a brother. And I'm sure I won't be Daphne's maid of honor. But I can probably squeeze in as a bridesmaid since it's so last minute. So I have bridesmaid duties."

"She hasn't asked you."

"Pessimist." I stuck my tongue out at him.

"The things I want that tongue to do this morning. Come back to bed."

"Just let me give Justin a quick call. To at least set things in motion. Rob and Daphne need us. Even if they don't realize it yet." I climbed out of bed and grabbed my phone off the nightstand.

I clicked on Justin's name and lifted the phone to my ear. He answered in two rings.

"Penny, my favorite redheaded goddess, please tell me you're renewing your vows and need my help. The bigger the celebration the better. Let's make it a night to remember."

"I can do you one better. But don't freak out."

"Don't say that. Now I am freaking out. Stop freaking me out right this instant!"

This was already escalating quickly. I shouldn't have started with 'don't freak out'. "Remember James' brother?"

"Yes, just as handsome as James. How could I forget?"

I laughed. "Well…he's getting married. And we need your help."

Justin squealed. "Of course! Tell me everything. Let me grab my planner. Are we talking next year or a later date? Hit me with it, and I'll make it happen."

Next year or later? God, he was definitely going to freak. I started pacing around the bedroom. "Um…the fall."

"Are we thinking next October? October is a great time. Not too hot and not too cold yet."

"September actually." I heard him flip a page in his planner.

"Oh I can do the second weekend of September. The leaves won't have started changing yet. Unless there's a drought in the summer. Fingers crossed for no water next year! Drought, drought, drought!"

"Yeah, the second weekend of September is perfect." I stopped pacing. "But we need to make it…this year. Not next year."

Silence.

"Justin?"

"What the actual fuck are you saying right now?"

I'd never heard Justin curse before. "This September."

"This September?!" His voice was so shrill I had to pull the phone away from my ear for a second.

James started laughing. Apparently he could hear the whole conversation from bed.

"Yes," I said and started pacing again. "Two weeks. I know it's short notice…"

"Short notice is a year in this town, honey. What do you expect me to do in two weeks?"

"Magic."

He sighed.

"It would mean the world to me, Justin."

He groaned.

"Justin, come on. We can figure it out together. I'll help."

"Who is this woman who wants to get married in two weeks? She must be barbaric!"

"Justin, come on. Don't be rude."

He huffed.

"She's super sweet. You're going to love her."

He huffed again.

"Justin, please."

"I can't," he said. "It's literally impossible." There was a long pause. "Which means I'm the only one that can do it. Fine! Damn you and your beautiful husband. I hate you."

James laughed again.

I lifted up a pillow and tossed it at him. "You don't mean that, Justin."

"Of course I don't. I love you both, you know that. But you're testing me. God, there's no time for dillydallying. I'm coming over right now. Make sure the barbarian woman is there so we can hash out the details."

"Her name is Daphne."

"I don't care what her name is!" he screamed. "Ah! Sweet baby Jesus! I have to go!" He hung up the phone.

"He seemed calm, cool, and collected," James said.

"It's fine. Everything's fine." But...was it? Because Justin was the best wedding planner in the city. And if he couldn't handle this, no one could. "I better call Daphne," I said.

Her phone went straight to voicemail.

"Shit, they're probably super hungover from last night."

"How about you just come back to bed," James said, pushing the covers down so I could climb back in.

That invitation was super tempting. How was I supposed to walk away from a shirtless James? I turned away from him so I wouldn't launch myself back in bed and molest his abs. "Nope. Bridesmaid duties." I walked into the closet and pulled off James' shirt that I'd worn to bed. If Justin said he was coming over right away, he was serious. I quickly changed into a stretchy dress. I had a feeling I was going to need to be comfortable today.

"You're not a bridesmaid until she asks!" James called after me as I ran out of the bedroom.

Where were we going to find Daphne a dress that could be altered so quickly? And bridesmaid dresses. God what if they wanted the whole thing to be parrot themed? Justin was going to freak. He hated corny themes more than anything else in the world. Well, not more than children ringbearers. He seemed to really hate those with a passion. He said they always stole the show.

I pulled open the freezer door. We were going to need something quick for breakfast. I grabbed the box of frozen waffles, pulled out a few, and put them in the toaster. I also started the coffee maker to make James a cup. My fingers drummed along the kitchen counter while I thought about how long it had taken James and me to plan our wedding. How each decision had seemed momentous. Could we have done it in two weeks?

No. definitely not. But...I would have eloped with him if he'd wanted to. I didn't need a big fancy wedding. Maybe Daphne and Rob would want something simple. Did Justin do simple? I wasn't sure.

The waffles popped out of the toaster just as the doorbell rang.

"James!" I called up the stairs. "Breakfast is ready and Justin is here!"

"I'll be down in a second!" James called from our room.

I put the waffles on plates and then hurried to the door. I threw it open and Justin was standing there, his arms full of magazines, three-ringed binders, and clear storage boxes. Or at least, I assumed it was Justin. Because the stack was so high it was covering his face.

"Hi, Justin. Let me help you with those."

He sighed when I lifted half of the stuff out of his arms, then he kicked the door closed with his foot. "Where. Is. She?" He sounded furious.

"Don't freak out. But Daphne hasn't answered my calls yet."

"Stop telling me not to freak out! It's too late! This is chaos!" He shook his head and took a deep breath. "Sorry. Two weeks isn't enough time. But enough about the barbarian for a moment. Penny, you're glowing. Pregnancy looks good on you." He kissed each of my cheeks.

"Thanks, Justin." I walked through the foyer, balancing the binders in my arms before depositing them on the dining room table.

"Is it a boy or a girl?" Justin asked.

"We want it to be a surprise."

"You're just full of surprises, recently, aren't you? Speaking of which….call the barbarian woman again."

"Justin, stop calling her that," I hissed.

He pressed his lips together in a thin line.

"Be nice."

"I'm stressed! I need a mimosa!"

"Um…how about some coffee? There's a fresh pot in the kitchen." I regretted the offer as soon as it came out of my mouth. Justin was already acting insane. He definitely did not need any caffeine.

I pulled out my phone to call the barbarian again. I shook my head. Daphne, not the barbarian. Justin was getting to me. I was just about to click on Daphne's name when she started calling me.

"Hey, Daphne," I said. "Remember last night when I said I'd ask Justin to help with the planning? Well…he's here. Can you come over? I really think we should start tackling the planning right away."

"Yes! You're a lifesaver. Rob and I can be there in...twenty minutes."

"Okay, great."

"Really, Penny. This means the world to me."

"It's not a problem at all. He's the best."

"I know, your wedding was beautiful. Okay, gotta go get ready. See you soon!"

I hung up and smiled at Justin as he walked into the room with a coffee cup filled to the brim. "Rob and Daphne will be here in twenty minutes."

"They better be. I have a wedding I need to get to in..." he looked down at his watch and his eyes grew round. "We have two hours. To plan this whole thing. Because if I don't start booking things right this second you can call the whole thing off. As it is the only venues left are probably prison yards and whore houses. Or worse...city hall." Justin gasped. "There isn't time! We can't..."

"We can do it in two hours. Don't panic."

"You don't panic!"

I just stared at him. I wasn't panicking. He was.

He huffed and sat down at the dining room table. "I take it back. This woman isn't a barbarian. She's a sadist. The devil herself!"

"Would you quit it." I lightly shoved his shoulder.

"Fine. I'll behave. But..." his voice trailed off as he steepled his fingers together on the table. He cocked his eyebrows up. "But I need a few things in return."

"Whatever you want," I said, sitting across from him.

He smiled for the first time since arriving. And then leaned in like he was about to launch into a ton of negotiations. "I want three things."

"Okay."

"First, I want double my normal rate."

"Done." That was a low ball ask. Even if Rob didn't want to foot the bill, James would take care of it.

"Second, I get to plan your baby shower."

"I thought you wanted to focus on weddings?"

He took a sip of his coffee. "I do. But I make exceptions for the people I actually like. And you and James are lovely. I'll probably like the little one too, I guess."

I smiled. When I said Justin hated children ringbearers, I meant he just hated all children. "I'd love it if you planned my baby shower, Justin."

"Good. Besides, your maid of honor was flaky and I don't trust her to throw you a good one. You need me."

He just had to add the sass to his previous compliment. "Melissa and I were going through some stuff. She'll be there for me now. But of course I need you."

"You really do. Regardless of Miss Flaky, it's now my duty. And that's all you need to know about that. Because obviously it's going to be a surprise. And it's going to be beyond fabulous."

That sounded fun. I smiled to myself. So far these negotiations had been easy. I was just nodding along. "And what's the third thing?"

"My favorite of the three. I get to come to the bachelorette party."

"Why would you want to come to the bachelorette party? You don't even like Daphne."

"Because I need a break!"

"Okay…"

"And who said I didn't like her?" he asked.

"Um…*you*. A bunch of times. You keep calling her a barbarian. And the devil."

He waved his hand through the air. "I'm just frazzled. I'm sure she's lovely. So I can come to the bachelorette party?"

Honestly that was kind of up to Daphne. Or one of her bridesmaids that was throwing it for her. And as James had so kindly pointed out…Daphne hadn't actually asked me to be a bridesmaid. But I wasn't really good at negotiating anything. I had no practice. So instead I just nodded. "Of course. We have a deal." I stuck out my hand.

Instead of shaking it, he grabbed it and lifted it up to his lips, placing a kiss on the back of my hand. "Good." He dropped my hand with a flourish and stood up a little straighter. "Now let's plan this thing. Just because it's a shotgun wedding doesn't mean it can't be beautiful. How far along is she?"

"It's not a shotgun wedding."

"Don't even with me, honey. If this Daphne woman isn't a barbarian, then she must be pregnant. It's the only thing holding me together. Because that means I get to plan two baby showers. Just added a fourth thing. You'll have to let her know the contingencies at your earliest convenience."

I just shrugged. Daphne wasn't pregnant. But at this rate, she was probably going to have to promise her firstborn to Justin in order for him to pull all this off. "Sounds good, Justin."

He spread out an array of color palettes, bridal magazines, pictures of designer gowns, pulled out miniature tables to depict seating arrangements, and somehow managed to get sparkles all over the dining room table.

"Shouldn't we wait for Daphne?" I asked.

"No. I don't like her."

I gave him a pointed stare. "We just talked about this."

"I'm joking. Ha. Ha. Oh, James, you're here too! Yay!" Justin stood up just as James walked into the room. "And yay for gray sweatpants season," he added. "I'm a lucky man."

I looked down at the sweatpants James had pulled on. He should have known better when Justin was around. I commented on them enough. Seriously…you could see every outline. Everything. I bit the inside of my lip.

Justin gave James a big hug and kissed both his cheeks. And then he giggled. "Your scruff tickles my lips. Best shave that for the wedding, yes?" He patted James' cheek. And then the patting turned into more of a gentle stroking.

James just laughed. "For the pictures or for you?"

"Both."

"It's good to see you, Justin. Where are Daphne and Rob?"

"Who cares," Justin said. "This is a great threesome right here. Come, sit next to me." He sat down and patted the seat next to him. And when James didn't move, Justin crossed his legs as he waited, drumming his fingers on his knee.

"Did you say something about breakfast, Penny?" James asked, ignoring the offer to cozy up next to Justin.

"Yeah, I almost forgot. The plates are in the kitchen. Could you grab mine for me?" I turned back to Justin. "Did you want a waffle too?"

He gasped and put his hand to his chest. "Do I look like I eat carbs? How do you think I fit into this number?"

His suit was indeed very fitted. I wasn't sure anything was worth giving up carbs for though. What was life without hot bread?

"Coffee is fine for me. Another cup?" He handed James his empty cup.

Wow, he seriously downed that coffee. He was going to be very hyper during this wedding consultation. I hoped Daphne and Rob were prepared because they were in for... a lot.

Justin blew some of the sparkles off his binders and right into my face.

I coughed and waved my hand through the air.

"Sorry about that," Justin said. "But everything in life is better with sparkles."

CHAPTER 9

Saturday

Daphne bit her lip while she flipped through the pages of one of the binders. "I don't know," she finally said.

"We don't have time for indecision," Justin said. "We need a color scheme pronto." He was holding a pen in his hand so tightly that his knuckles were turning white.

Daphne looked over at Rob.

"How about we go classic," Rob said and grabbed her hand on the table. "Black and white."

Daphne nodded.

"Oh, I love it," Justin said. "You have amazing taste, Rob, you sexy man beast. It's perfect. Classic elegance. And we don't have to worry about things coordinating. Unless one of your groomsmen is colorblind and shows up in a navy tux." Justin shook his head. "Speaking of which…let's talk wedding party. How many people?"

"Let me think," Rob said. He didn't seem at all phased by Justin calling him a sexy man beast. They'd always gotten along well. I think Rob just took Justin's flirtations as a joke. Since Rob always flirted with me as a joke. But I was pretty sure Justin was not joking.

"It's going to be three groomsmen for me," Rob said. "Yup. Three."

I waited a beat for Rob to ask James to be his best man…but Rob didn't offer any more information.

"Three is a nice, good number. I love doing things in threes. Especially when it involves two big, strong men." He winked at James.

James coughed on a sip of coffee.

"And how about you?" Justin asked and turned to Daphne.

"Oh. Um…everything is so last minute. I don't know if Alina or Kristen will be able to make it. Especially since they both just took vacation time for Alina's wedding."

"We don't really have time for indecision," Justin said. "I'm just going to put down three and we'll figure it out, okay? Because you need to make sure the parties are even. You don't want an uneven party. It looks ridiculous in pictures. And I don't do ridiculous. I do perfection."

"Okay," Daphne said.

"Now most importantly…we need to pick a caterer, the DJ or band, find a dress, and book the venue."

That was a lot more than one 'most importantly'.

Daphne looked so overwhelmed.

"I was thinking…" I said. "Did you guys want a really big wedding, or maybe something simpler would be easier with such short notice?"

Daphne smiled at me. For the first time since she'd walked into the apartment, she looked a little relieved.

"Nonsense," Rob said. "I've thrown a lot of parties in my lifetime and this one has to trump all the rest. It has to be epic. Huge."

"Sensational!" Justin added. "It's a wedding, Penny, not a backyard barbeque. Get on our level."

James laughed.

I shot him a look, but he didn't seem to be bothered, the humor still dancing in his eyes.

I pressed my lips together. I said *simple*. Not *backyard barbeque*. That was quite a leap. But what was so wrong with a backyard wedding? It sounded magical to me.

"Enough talk about lame simplicity," Justin said. "Do you guys have a venue in mind that will fit our vision?"

"Hm." Rob rested his chin in his hand as he thought.

"Well…the restaurant where Rob proposed said we could have it there," Daphne said.

"Splendid. Which restaurant?"

"The Parrot Palace."

Justin blinked. "The place with the singing birds?" He laughed, but when he saw that Rob wasn't smiling, he coughed. "Good God, please no. I can't. You can't make me."

"Do you know of any places that have openings?" I offered. "A nice backyard perhaps?"

"Penny I love you, but stop it with that nonsense. This is a classy affair. Not a clown rodeo."

A clown rodeo? Where was he coming up with this stuff?

Justin started flipping through a binder, his face growing paler by the second. "Two weeks isn't a lot of time. Are you guys certain it has to be so quickly?"

"Yes," Rob said.

Justin flipped more pages. "All the best venues in the city are booked months if not years in advance. I don't know…"

James cleared his throat. "Are you two dead set on getting married in the city?"

Daphne glanced over at Rob. "No, not necessarily."

"That opens things up a bit. I bet we could find a venue in Jersey." Justin made a face. "No, not Jersey. I can't do Jersey. It's just as bad as a backyard. I'll look desperate."

"How about Penny and my country club?" James said.

Oh my gosh. Of course! It was perfect! "The Hunter Creek Country Club is so beautiful," I said. "You guys could get married on the golf course somewhere. It's very scenic."

"Where is it located?" Justin asked.

"In Newark, Delaware."

"Delaware?! How am I supposed to plan a wedding in Delaware?!" He slammed a binder shut. "Wait, do they have catering?"

"Yes," James said.

"Getting a caterer tied into a venue at this point is a must. And I'm guessing you can call in a favor. And a country club is always an elegant choice. We can make the distance work. Call them immediately."

James looked over at Rob and Daphne. "Would that work for you guys?"

"It doesn't matter what they think! It's our only option!" Justin shrieked.

Daphne looked relieved. "Actually, that sounds perfect. Rob and I went to dinner there about a month ago after walking around the University of New Castle campus. It really is beautiful. I can picture it there." She smiled at Rob.

Justin clapped his hands. "James, call them now. Do it. Do it!" he screamed when James didn't immediately pull out his phone.

"Give me a minute," James said. He stood up, pulled his phone out of his pocket, and left the room.

"Back to business," Justin said. "Where were we...crap, flowers. What kind of flowers do you like?" An alarm on his phone started going off. "Gah!" He ended the alarm. "I have to go. This is insanity. But I'm going to leave all this here. Look through every inch of material and make decisions. We can meet up again tomorrow morning, okay? Oh, and you have an appointment at the same place Penny got her wedding dress today at 4 pm okay? And right after that you have an appointment for bridesmaid dresses, so figure out your bridal party ASAP. This is dire."

Daphne nodded. "Thank you so much, Justin. Seriously, I can't thank you enough."

"Going to your bachelorette party and getting double my normal fee is thanks enough. Gotta run!" He actually ran - sprinted right out of the dining room and I heard the door slam closed a second later.

"Double the normal fee? Bachelorette party? What?" Daphne asked.

"He had a few contingencies. Don't worry, I negotiated him down." *Not. Whatever.* It was fine. Justin wasn't asking too much. This *was* insanity. In two weeks they'd be walking down the aisle. I smiled. Sometimes insanity was really fun.

Rob laughed. "I love that guy. He's hilarious. Do I get to come wedding dress shopping with you?"

"No," Daphne and I said at the same time. She smiled at me. "Do you think you could come with me, Penny? And we could call Bee too. It would be fun to do it with you two."

"Of course. I'll call her right now."

"Thank you so much."

I excused myself from the table and walked into the kitchen.

James was leaning against the kitchen island eating another waffle.

"Are you hiding in here?" I asked with a laugh.

"That depends. Is Justin gone yet?"

"Yeah, he just left."

"He was hyper today."

"You riled him up with your choice of attire." My eyes landed on the outline of James' junk in his gray sweatpants.

"I don't think you can see anything…"

I outlined his length with my finger. "We've been over this before. You can see *everything*."

He laughed. "So that was why Justin was so hyped up?"

"That and I'm pretty sure he'd already had a lot of coffee before he even got here. And he's really perturbed by the whole two weeks thing."

James nodded. "There's another wedding at the country club that day, so we can't use the main ballroom. It's a pretty small wedding though, so the kitchen will be able to accommodate Rob's wedding too. Fingers crossed it's nice outside and we can do an outdoor thing. So we have a venue and catering. What's left?"

"Everything else."

He nodded. "We should leave them to it then. It's beautiful out. Let's go for a walk in the park."

"James, we have to help."

"You saw what happened in there," James said. "Rob didn't ask me to be his best man. Hell, he didn't even ask me to be a groomsman. I don't think they need our help."

I thought I'd imagined James looking a little jealous about the possibility of Rob asking Matt. But I definitely didn't imagine the hurt in his voice right now.

"I'm sure he's just going to ask you privately."

James shrugged. "Who cares."

"You care."

"No, not really."

I just stared at him. He clearly cared. "You're being silly. Rob said he was going to have three people in his wedding party. That's you, Matt, and Mason. You're in it."

James shrugged again.

"They're just busy with all the details." That was it. They were just too preoccupied to ask us to be in their wedding party. "You know what? You're right. Let's leave them alone with those binders for a bit and take that walk around Central Park." That's what we would have been doing if we were alone today. And I always craved alone time with him.

"That sounds great." He pulled me in for a kiss.

I smiled up at him. "But I have to go dress shopping with Daphne at 4."

"Did she ask you to be a bridesmaid?"

"No, but she asked if I'd go look at dresses with her."

"They're being very tight-lipped about their wedding parties."

"Come on, let's give them some time alone. They just need a moment to talk about it together before they ask us." I pulled James toward the door. "We'll be back in a bit!" I called to Rob and Daphne.

"Don't fuck on our dining room table," James said under his breath.

I laughed and pulled him out of our apartment.

***

It was a gorgeous day. Summer was trying to end quickly this year. Some trees were already starting to drop leaves. I remembered Justin's chant about droughts. This summer had been pretty dry. Maybe Rob and Daphne would get beautiful autumn colors in their wedding photos after all.

"The country club was a great idea," I said. "It's going to be beautiful this time of year."

James squeezed my hand. "It's definitely beautiful this time of year. Especially out on the golf course."

I felt my cheeks blushing. I knew what he was referring to. He'd taken me there in the fall. Our first real date. We'd done unspeakable things on that golf course. "Is it weird for them to get married there? Where we…you know."

"I'm sure they can put up an arch somewhere away from the mini-waterfall."

"And the willow tree," I added.

He smiled and stopped on the path, pulling me into him. "And the willow tree. I definitely didn't forget about that."

"How could you possibly?" He'd backed me up until my back hit the bark of the tree. The golf course had been deserted, but there'd still been this thrill around the possibility of getting caught. He'd had me screaming his name in minutes.

"Maybe after the ceremony we can sneak off and recreate a few things," he said. "I could definitely go for a round two against the tree."

"Pretty sure we'll be taking pictures after the ceremony."

"We're not in the wedding party, Penny."

"Rob is definitely going to ask you. He was your best man and you'll be his."

"Not necessarily."

"You're being very cute right now."

"I'm not being cute," James said.

"You're being a little cute."

His hands left my waist and cradled my face. And then he kissed me, his tongue sliding past my lips. Completely unraveling me. He kissed me like I was the only thing keeping him alive. Right there on the walking path. It was anything but cute. It was scandalous and had me digging my fingers into his back. God, what I'd do to be back on that golf course right now.

"I'm thinking of so many ways to seduce you right now," he whispered against my lips. "I'm really liking this five months of seduction thing."

"You're not supposed to be coming up with ideas. Since *I'm* seducing *you*." Although, I hadn't thought of what to do today. Which was ridiculous because it was only the second day. But all I could think about right this moment was grabbing lunch. Maybe I could do something with food. Or sparkles, since they were still all over me. "Are you hungry?"

"We just ate breakfast."

"I'm eating for two. I could really go for some pickles. What about you?"

He laughed. "No, I definitely don't want breakfast pickles. But let's go find you some. I'm not sure if any restaurants are open for lunch yet though."

"Oh, we also need another watermelon," I said. "I finished the last one off yesterday. Let's just go to the market."

"You mean the grocery store."

"No, the market."

He smiled down at me. "How many times are we going to debate this? A market is like a farmer's market with only fresh produce and stuff."

"No. It's another term for the grocery store. I swear. And I won't stop calling it that. It's what I've always called it and that's what my family calls it."

"But it's really confusing when you call it that. You've even accidentally sent Ellen to the farmer's market a few times and she's looked down at the list and couldn't get anything there. It's a grocery store, baby."

I shook my head. "He agrees with me," I said and put my hand on my stomach.

"You're teaming up on me with our unborn daughter?"

"Our unborn son."

He shook his head. "You fight dirty."

Dirty. Hm. That actually gave me an idea for tonight's seduction. Dirty and food? *Yum.* "I'm pretty sure you like it when I'm dirty." I winked at him. "Now please escort me to the market so I can eat some morning pickles."

"I'm pretty sure that's the most horrifying sentence you've ever spoken."

I laughed and lightly hit his arm. "Very funny. Oh my gosh, I almost forgot to call Bee. Give me one second." I pulled out my phone and tapped on Bee's name.

"Hey, Penny!" she said. "Last night was so much fun. I can't believe Rob is actually getting married. Do you think he'll stop calling you sexy all the time now?"

I laughed. "Probably not. Speaking of their wedding, Justin was here today. We have a million things we need to do to help them get everything ready in time."

"You know you can count me in. Wait. One second, Mason wants me to put you on speaker phone."

"I'll put you guys on speaker too so James can chime in." I hit speaker phone and held it in front of James and me.

"I have an idea," Mason said. "Probably the best idea ever. They need a venue, right? I'm thinking...Club Onyx."

James and I both looked at each other. I wasn't sure Mason's sex club was exactly the right vibe for 'I do's'.

"Good God," Bee said. "That's what you wanted to say? Why'd I even put it on speaker phone?" She groaned.

"Hear me out," Mason said. "We already have an altar..."

"It's a stage," Bee said.

"I'm not talking about the stage. That wouldn't be appropriate. I'm talking about the sex altar."

"That kind of altar is not the same thing!" Bee said.

"Of course it is. An altar is an altar whether it's for sex or a wedding ceremony. Same difference. Plus we have catering."

"I wouldn't call an abundance of alcohol catering," Bee added.

"Alcohol is more important than food at a wedding. And I can talk to Tanner to see if we can fast track the grand opening of the restaurant. Plus if they want dancers, we can provide that. We have tons of entertainment like that."

"Daphne is not going to want strippers at her wedding."

"Rob might," Mason said. "It would be a fun surprise for all the guests. Unexpected. And Rob likes throwing epic parties."

I looked over at James. Rob had used that exact word to describe his ideal wedding. *Epic.* What kind of crazy wedding was this going to be?

James just laughed in response.

"Penny, are you still there?" Bee asked. "Please tell my fiancé that one of his best friends does not want to get married at a sex club in front of a sex altar with exotic dancers."

"I'm going to have to side with Bee on this," I said.

"What?" Mason said. "I have so many great ideas. I was just getting started."

"I know, but as great as all that sounds, we already have a venue."

"Damn," Mason said. "I really wanted that to be my gift to the happy couple. I'll have to think of something else."

"Where is it going to be?" Bee asked.

"James' country club," I said.

"Our country club," James clarified, wrapping his arm around me.

It was still really weird saying things were *ours*. Especially when my personal bank account only had a few thousand dollars in it.

"Ah that's going to be so pretty!" Bee said. "So much better than Club Onyx."

"Yeah right," Mason said. "Club Onyx would have been sexy as hell."

"Sexy is not the right vibe for a wedding," Bee said. "We've been over this."

I laughed. Was that why they were taking so long to plan their wedding? Because Mason wanted to get married to Bee at a sex altar? *Probably.* "There's still a lot they need help with besides the venue, Mason. I'm sure you'll think of something that could help them out. Speaking of which, Bee, can you come to the bridal boutique at 4 today? Daphne wants us both there."

"Of course," she said. "And seriously, I can help with whatever she needs. Just keep me posted."

"I will. See you at 4."

"See you then." She hung up, but before she did I heard Mason talking about Club Onyx weddings again. "They're very different altars," Bee said and then the line went dead.

James kissed the side of my forehead. "And you were worried about Rob and Daphne getting married where we've banged. Just think about all the things that have happened on that stage or by that sex altar."

I laughed. "Very true." I wasn't exactly sure what a sex altar was. But I was hoping my surprise for James tonight would be so sexy that he'd be praying for more.

CHAPTER 10

Saturday

"So do you think this is a shotgun wedding?" Bee asked.

"What? No." Why did everyone keep saying that? I'd seen Rob and Daphne together. They were madly in love. It wasn't that crazy that they wanted to get married right away. And now I was seriously starting to wonder if people had thought I was pregnant when James proposed to me so quickly. It was just love.

"Then why rush it?"

"You heard Rob. He doesn't want to go another day without making Daphne his wife. It's very romantic."

"Or…he knocked her up." Bee took a sip of champagne as we waited for Daphne to come out in the first dress.

I laughed. "I don't think so. They would have told us."

Bee shrugged. "All I'm saying is that Daphne is super particular about things, and a quick wedding seems like her worst nightmare. There has to be a reason."

"Maybe that is the reason. A long engagement would mean indecision and headaches." I stared at her. "Speaking of which…what about you? When are you getting hitched?"

Bee looked down at her huge ring. It sparkled under the lights that made all the wedding dresses shimmer.

"Like normal level-headed people, Mason and I are just enjoying being engaged right now. Plus we barely have any free time to just relax, let alone enough time for wedding planning. And we've only been engaged a few months. We're the ones doing it right. This is insanity."

"So it has nothing to do with *where* Mason wants to get married?"

She laughed. "Well, I will say, it wasn't the first time I'd heard about Club Onyx being the perfect wedding venue. He's out of his mind if he thinks I want to say 'I do' in front of that sex altar."

"What happens at a sex altar exactly?"

"Use your imagination," she said with a laugh. "Whatever you're thinking, it's probably happened."

People worshipping each other's bodies. I actually kinda liked the sound of it. My plan for tonight was definitely going to be fun. A full sex altar display.

"Ah!" Bee exclaimed as Daphne walked out.

I shook away the thought of James worshipping my body and turned to Daphne. Her dress was…huge. There was so much fabric. It was drowning her.

The bridal consultant was holding the train of the dress, and even she looked overwhelmed by the material. I was pretty sure the consultant was a few seconds away from either tripping over it or being tangled up in it.

"This is all…too much, right?" Daphne asked as she stepped up onto the elevated portion in front of all the mirrors. "I want to make sure I can dance. And I can't dance in…this." She looked behind her at the train.

"Definitely not," Bee said. "But the train might be detachable."

The bridal consultant shook her head. "It actually clips up to the waist. Give me one second." She suddenly looked much more composed as she expertly folded the fabric, hooking it up on the rest of the dress, successfully making the whole thing look...even bulkier.

Yikes. This dress was so old fashioned, and not in a trendy vintage way. More like in a...burn it kind of way. The bridal consultant said there were only so many to choose from that could be altered in time. And now I was worried they were all hideous monster dresses that no one else would be caught dead in.

Daphne laughed. "This is so awful."

"I'm so glad you said so," I said with a laugh. "It's truly terrible. It's hard to look at."

"Hideous," Bee added. "Next!"

Daphne laughed. "I'm glad we know each other well enough to be honest. I can't even imagine what I'd do without you guys right now. I probably would have wound up purchasing a dress that should be taken out back and shot."

I laughed.

Daphne looked back to the bridal consultant. "Please get me out of this thing."

The consultant smiled, not at all offended by our comments. "No problem. Let's try a more fitted silhouette." They both walked back to the changing area.

"Are you a bridesmaid?" Bee asked me as she took another sip of champagne.

"No, she hasn't asked me. Has she asked you?"

Bee shook her head. "I know she has a few friends that don't live in the city anymore. I'm guessing she'll be asking them."

"Yeah, I guess." I pressed my lips together.

"Are you upset that she hasn't asked you?" Bee asked.

"I mean...no."

Bee raised her eyebrows at me.

"Fine, yes. I thought we've been getting close over the past couple of months. She's going to be my sister-in-law. I want her to like me."

"Even if she doesn't ask you, it doesn't mean she doesn't like you. She asked us here, didn't she?"

"Yeah."

"I get it," Bee said. "I thought she really liked us too. I'm not going to lie and pretend I'm not bummed she didn't ask us."

"Right? It's silly, but I'd always just assumed I'd be in Rob's wedding. He's one of my best friends. And you know he hasn't even asked James to be in it yet?"

"He hasn't asked Mason either."

Huh. "What about Matt?"

Bee shrugged. "I don't know."

Weird. "I'm sure James, Mason, and Matt will all be in it. As for us? I'm not so sure."

"It'll be fun to just get to relax and have fun at the wedding though. Being a bridesmaid is stressful business."

"Was my wedding really so stressful?"

"Um...do you not remember your husband getting shot?"

I shook my head. I didn't need to be reminded. The best day of my life had so quickly turned into a nightmare. I was lucky that James was still alive. I didn't take a second of that for granted. "That didn't have anything to do with bridesmaid duties."

"Still. Stressful AF."

"Touché." Hopefully this wedding wouldn't end so dramatically. Knowing Justin and Rob though...they were probably already planning something insane. I just hoped whatever it was wasn't dangerous.

"I have an idea," Bee said. "Stressful duties aside, I think we'll have more fun if we just act like we are bridesmaids. For at least this afternoon. Let's help Daphne find the most amazing dress ever. Let's have so much fun."

"Agreed." I lifted up my glass of water and tapped it against Bee's champagne flute. "Even if Daphne doesn't see it yet...we're one big family. And I'm happy she's going to be a part of it." *I just hope Daphne thinks so too.* We were going to be sisters.

Just then Daphne came back out. And it was like the whole boutique was hushed.

"That's it," Bee and I said at the same time.

Daphne's smile grew. "Really? You both like it?" She twirled around in front of the mirror. I had no idea what elaborate things Justin and Rob were planning, but none of that really mattered. This dress hugged Daphne in all the right places. It was like it was made for her body. It was simple and elegant, almost Grecian in its design. And you could just tell from her face that it was the one. She was glowing. And she looked beautiful.

"You look amazing." It was seriously perfect. Especially if Justin and Rob stuck with classic black and white elegance. Or sex party. Or whatever they decided on. She could make it work anywhere. It was like the dress was made for her and only her.

"Hot fire," Bee said.

Daphne turned back to us. "I think this is the fastest decision I've ever made."

I turned to Bee. *See. They're getting married fast because of the indecision thing.* This was the only way Daphne could have ever walked down the aisle. Quickly.

I was pretty sure Bee knew what I was thinking, because she rolled her eyes at me.

"Are you saying 'Yes to the Dress'?" the consultant asked.

I held my breath.

"Um…well…shouldn't I try on a few more?" Daphne asked. "You're not supposed to choose that quickly. I think…"

"Daphne, it's the one," I said. "It's made for you." I did not want this to turn into a her-ordering-food situation. Or else it would be the day of the wedding and we still wouldn't have a dress. I wasn't a bridesmaid, but right now she needed me to act like one. "It's perfect."

Daphne was beaming. "Yes! I'm saying yes to the dress! Ah! I'm getting hitched!"

***

I had completely forgotten that Justin had booked an appointment for bridesmaid dresses too. And I wasn't exactly sure what I was doing in this hideous poofy thing when Daphne hadn't even asked me.

I walked out of the changing room and Bee laughed at me.

"Stop it," I hissed.

"It really highlights your baby bump."

I swatted at her arm. But she was right. This dress made my little baby bump look way bigger. It was so unflattering. "Yours isn't any better."

Bee's dress was cut at an awkward angle that was somehow not a short dress or a long dress. It was just a weird dress that cut her off at the calves and somehow made her look squat. Which was weird because Bee was anything but squat.

Bee flipped her hair over her shoulder. "Are you trying to tell me I don't look sexy in this very formal number that was clearly designed for sasquatch's daughters?"

I couldn't help but laugh. "That's exactly what I'm saying."

"Rude. I'm suddenly feeling better about not being a bridesmaid."

Same. I was trying to be sexy for the next few months. This dress was the opposite of sexy. James would probably lose his sex drive if he saw me in all this poofiness.

"Hmm," The lady helping us said as Bee and I both walked back into the main room. "We'll definitely have to alter this to fit better," she said and cinched the fabric around my waist, somehow making it worse.

Screw you too.

She turned to Daphne. "But you said these ladies were just here to help. That your actual bridesmaids aren't pregnant so this area won't be as big of a deal." She pointed to my stomach.

I was going to cut a bitch.

Daphne shrugged. "I don't know. I'm...I have to make a few calls. I..."

"It's fine," she said. "We just need to land on the style right now. You can call us tonight with the exact sizes we'll need to rush order."

"Tonight?" Daphne bit her lip. She looked so stressed out.

The woman nodded. "So do you like either of these styles?"

Daphne stared at us. And then she tilted her head to the side like that would help.

Bee put her hand on her hip. "I promise you, whoever you choose to stand up there with you on your wedding day will seriously hate both these options."

Daphne laughed. "I think you're right. I just didn't want to say anything in case you guys loved them. I have an idea. How about you two pick out dresses you think might actually work? I trust your fashion sense way more than mine."

"Deal," Bee said. "We'll find something that'll work." Bee grabbed my hand and pulled me over to the rack of dresses. "Thank God."

I shifted past a few dresses. And then a few more and wandered over to another rack. "Oh, what about this one?" I said and pulled a dress off the rack that had a few simple straps in the back, mimicking the Grecian style of Daphne's wedding gown.

"You're a genius." Bee grabbed another one and we both went to go change.

My baby bump showed a little in this one too, but at least the fabric didn't highlight it. I turned to look at my back in the mirror. From the back you couldn't even tell I was pregnant. And it showed a lot of skin. This was perfect. My smile faltered. *Perfect for…whoever Daphne chose.*

Bee smiled as I walked out of the dressing room. "You look so hot."

"Same to you."

Bee did a little twirl. "Hopefully she'll like them. I can't wait to wear…" She cleared her throat. "I mean, I can't wait to see how they look on whoever wears them."

"Right."

Bee sighed. "Why hasn't she asked us yet? We've been having such a fun day. I really thought she'd ask."

I pressed my lips together. "Me too."

"Maybe when she sees how great we look she won't be able to resist making us bridesmaids." Bee grabbed my hand and we walked back out for Daphne to see us.

Daphne looked up from her phone and smiled. "You guys look great."

"Do we have a winner?" the consultant said. "And the black really is a perfect color. It'll look good on every skin tone."

Right, the skin tone of whoever Daphne chose. I was kinda sick of this consultant rubbing in the fact that Bee and I weren't good enough.

"Do you guys really like them?" Daphne asked. "I'm leaving this in your hands."

That sounded like bridesmaid power to me. But I knew it was actually just power Daphne was giving us because she was indecisive.

"I think they'll look really good with your dress," Bee said.

I nodded. "And they're understated so everyone's attention will be on you."

"Well, I'm sold," Daphne said.

"This is actually perfect," the consultant said. "We have a few of these in stock. As long as you don't mind using some of the sample dresses. You two take these off immediately before you mess them up for the actual bridesmaids."

Yeah, this lady freaking sucked. Whatever. I grabbed Bee's hand so we could go back to the changing rooms.

"That woman was very rude," Bee said.

"Right?"

"Does she think I'm sweating profusely or secretly dropping some timber under this thing?"

I laughed.

"Because now that she thinks I am…I kind of want to. I feel like I should go run a mile. Or squat in the corner and do my dirty business."

"You're ridiculous. Let's just get out of these dresses." I closed the door to my dressing room and took one more look at the dress. It really was perfect. I quickly turned away from the mirror and pulled the dress off. It would be perfect for someone else.

I changed back into my comfortable dress and sighed. This was much more my style recently anyway. The girl with the big tummy that shouldn't be a bridesmaid because I'd ruin the pictures or something.

Gah, stop it. I could still be sexy. And I'd prove it tonight. I was going to seduce the crap out of my husband. I shook my head. That reminded me of Bee's dropping timber comment. I was not going to seduce the crap out of my husband. I was just going to normal seduce him. Sex altar style.

CHAPTER 11

Saturday

There were many reasons why I was climbing onto the dining room table.

One – James had told Rob and Daphne not to have sex on it. And that reminded me that we never had.

Two – we'd picked up some fun stuff at the *market*.

Three – it had been a while since James and I had gotten messy.

Four – I'd be lying if I said I hadn't been thinking about sex altars all night.

I pulled off my dress and tossed it on the floor. I lay back, trying to strike a sexy pose. I had no idea if I was nailing it or not. My baby bump was not making it any easier. I turned to my side. Nope, that was worse. I moved to my back again and arched it. It made my baby bump protrude more, but I knew James loved when I arched my back.

I lifted up the bottle of chocolate syrup and drizzled some between my breasts. It slid down, leaving a trail that pooled in my bellybutton. Perfect. The scene was set. Now I just needed James to get his sexy butt down here.

I sent him a quick text. One I'd planned out perfectly. It was witty and full of sexual innuendo. At least…it would be when he saw me. "Dessert is on me tonight. And it's delicious."

His text came back almost immediately. "Where are you? I went to the bathroom and you disappeared."

Tonight hadn't gone exactly as I had planned. I got back late from Daphne's dress appointments. And then James and I fell asleep watching TV.

Not that falling asleep with James was bad. It was actually perfect. I loved falling asleep snuggled up next to him. But it wasn't exactly sexy. And I was not going to let today slip us by without a proper seduction. So when he went to get ready for bed I'd snuck down here, stripped, and sauced myself up. It was the perfect plan.

I texted him back: "I thought you might like a midnight snack." *That's right. Come devour me on our makeshift sex altar.*

"I'm good. I'll be in bed."

What? No. He had to come down here. He needed to lick this syrup off me like he was starving. I needed it. I'd been daydreaming about this all day. How could I get him to come down here? I needed to lure him with something that only he could do for me.

Got it. "But I need help opening something," I texted back. Wow that did not sound sexy at all. I'd been so good with the innuendo up until that text. I quickly typed out another text. "I mean…I just need help with something." There that was better. Kind of. God, why was I so bad at this? The *dessert is on me* line was so perfect. Because the chocolate syrup was literally on me. And now he just thought I needed help opening a jar of peanut butter or something. Peanut butter was not sexy.

I heard his feet on the steps and arched my back again. I could still recover. I heard him pause in the kitchen.

"Penny?" he called.

"In here!"

I bit my lip and tried to look as seductive as possible when I saw him through the archway. Instead of walking into the room, he paused, leaning against the doorjamb.

His eyes raked over my body. "So what do you need help opening exactly?"

Gah. "I didn't mean to send that text. I meant I need help with...something."

"And what pray tell does my wife need help with?"

I really liked when he called me his wife. It made me feel all warm and fuzzy inside. "I need help...coming." It was the first thing I could think of. I cleared my throat. "I mean, I made a mess and I need help cleaning it up." I shook my head. "What I really meant was *dessert is on me.*" *See. It's literally on me.*

He pushed himself off the doorjamb and walked over to me. "So let me get this straight. You need help cleaning up?" He dipped his finger into the chocolate syrup and spread it around, leaving a trail of deliciousness around my left nipple.

I swallowed hard and nodded.

"You need help coming?" he was holding back a smirk.

"Yes."

"And my dessert is *on* you?" His finger was still swirling around my nipple. "Or you are my dessert?"

"Both."

"Well you texted the right guy." He put his finger that had been circling my nipple into his mouth. "I can help you with all of those things."

"Good." I arched my back a little more.

"But my services aren't free."

SEDUCTION

I really hadn't thought this scenario through. I was completely naked on the table. I didn't have any cash on me. "My purse is in the other room."

"Not cash." He grabbed my hands and pulled me backward until my head was dangling from the edge of the table. He traced his fingers through the chocolate syrup between my breasts and lowered his pajama bottoms. And then he pumped his hand up and down his thick erection, spreading the syrup all over him. "You can pay me with your mouth."

Before I could even think of a smart reply he thrust himself into my mouth. God, he tasted like chocolatey goodness. I wasn't even hungry, but now I was dying for more.

I tried to reach out and grab his ass, but he was pressing the backs of my hands down on the table. I was completely at his mercy.

"Just like that, baby," he said. "Take every inch and maybe I'll do what you asked."

I moaned.

"You're soaking wet right now, aren't you? You love ending the night with my cock in your mouth. It's the only dessert you crave."

God yes. I tightened my lips around him and he groaned.

He thrust forward, shoving his length down my throat. Choking me. And I loved every second of it.

He leaned over, licking the chocolate off my nipple and lightly tugging on it.

Jesus. And just like that, he'd flipped the script. I wasn't seducing him. He was seducing me. He was always the one in control, even when I thought I was holding all the cards.

He ran his tongue down the center of my chest and over my stomach, tracing the trail I'd left.

Cleaning up the mess? *Check.*

Eating his dessert? *Check.*

Fucking my mouth? *An unexpected check.*

And I had no doubt he'd make me come. Hell, I could probably come just like this. I loved making him groan as he buried his cock in my throat. And it was an added bonus that he tasted like chocolate. I'm pretty sure I was about to add chocolate to my list of cravings along with pickles and watermelon. But I think I preferred my chocolate delivered this way.

He thrust his hips faster. And I tightened my lips around him again.

I heard the squirt of the bottle and felt a glob of chocolate fall against my clit.

Oh my God.

"Keep sucking me or I'll stop," he said. His breath was warm against my thigh.

I didn't need him to explain. I bobbed my head and he thrust his tongue deep inside of me.

I felt my back arch again as he circled his tongue around me. "Delicious," he whispered against my clit. He let go of my hands as he leaned forward, burying his tongue in my wetness.

I immediately grabbed his ass to help guide his thrusts into my mouth.

He pushed his thumbs against my lips, spreading my pussy for him. And he feasted. He licked, and sucked, and drove his tongue madly in and out. Circles. Deeper.

I moaned his name but it was lost around his erection thrusting into my mouth.

God, I was so close. *So fucking close.*

He spread my lips farther, like he needed more. More of me. More of everything. And he shoved his tongue farther, circling my wetness.

So close.

I was pretty sure I was whimpering now.

"Baby, I could eat you all night," he said and moved his lips back to my clit. He lightly sucked.

Yeah, I was definitely whimpering.

And then he sucked harder. He groaned around my clit, the movement of his lips pushing me over the edge. He kept his lips on my clit until my legs stopped quivering around his head.

He slowly pulled out of my mouth, even though he hadn't come yet.

"Wait..." I reached out for him. I wanted to taste him. My new craving for chocolate and cum was stronger than I thought it would be.

"I don't want to cum in your mouth tonight," he said. His eyes were dark and full of lust.

"Where did you want to come?"

His eyes raked down my body.

Ah, he thought since I was already messy that I wouldn't mind a bigger mess. Well, he was right. I grabbed the bottle of chocolate syrup and squeezed it as hard as I could. I actually meant to pour more on myself. But when I squeezed the bottle, my other hand that was propping me up slipped in the syrupy mess behind me.

And a big glob of syrup hit James' cheek.

As soon as I saw the shocked expression on his face, I squeezed the bottle again, shooting it at his chest.

The smile on his face was contagious. "Oh, you're going to get it," he said.

I squealed as he reached out for me. I slid back on the table and jumped off the side. He grabbed the bottle I'd abandoned on the table and squirted it toward me, a glob of chocolatey goodness hitting my left tit.

I didn't mind one bit. I was already sticky.

He chased me around the side of the table and I switched directions, running back around the table the other way. I wiped some of the chocolate off my breast and flung it toward him. This was now a full-fledged food fight.

He grabbed the bottle again, squirting more at me. It was so on. I pushed some into my hand off the table and flung it at him again. He dodged it and it landed with a squishy noise somewhere on the floor. And he took my moment of distraction to lunge across the table to get to me. I screamed again as I made a run for it. I made it to the foyer before I felt his strong hands.

He caught me around the waist, pulling my naked back to his strong chest.

I laughed as I tried to squirm away, but I couldn't get far. Our bodies were practically sticking together.

"Are you running away from me?" he whispered in my ear.

I squirmed in this grip again. His erection pressed against my ass. He knew just how to make me horny all over again. His lips fell to my neck, and I could feel chocolate smearing onto me.

We were making a terrible mess. But I didn't even care.

"I don't like when you run from me," he said, his voice rumbling in my ear. "Now press your hands against the wall. Right now. I'm ready for the rest of my payment."

I had no idea how he was still stuck in roleplaying mode. I'd abandoned it as soon as he shoved his cock in the back of my throat. But I followed his instructions. I felt myself practically dripping. I didn't know if it was me or the chocolate sauce, but I knew I needed him.

"I cleaned up your mess." He pressed down on my back, arching it. "I ate your dessert." His fingers slid down to my wetness, circling me. "And I made you come." His hands slid to my hips. "Now you're going to take my cock and scream my name."

He thrust inside of me hard.

"James!"

His fingers dug into my hips as he slammed into me again and again.

I pressed against the wall, trying to match his thrusts. This was the second time in two days we'd somehow wound up in the foyer fucking each other's brains out. If this was our new normal, I'd take it. I didn't just want five months of seduction. I wanted a lifetime of it. Just like this. With his cock deep inside of me and me screaming his name

"Get on your knees," he said.

What? I pushed back against him, making him groan.

He pulled out of me, and put his hand on my shoulder, gently shoving me to the ground.

"Touch yourself," he said.

I reached down between my legs, filling the spot he'd abandoned with my fingers.

He wrapped his hand around his erection. He moved his hand slowly up and down, using my juices as lube.

"Rub your clit," he said. "I want you to come when I drench you."

Fuck. I slid my fingers out of my pussy, swirling the wetness over my clit. I loved when he told me what to do. I loved when he jerked off above me. The sight of him losing control over me turned me on even more.

"Faster," he said as he stroked his cock, moving his hand up and down quicker.

I moved my fingers in faster circles, the pressure on my clit making my pussy clench.

He could tell. He could see it in my face. And as soon as I came, he exploded all over my chest.

I moaned again and his next shot landed in my mouth. His last one landed on my drenched pussy. He'd claimed every inch of me.

My hand stopped moving.

And his hand fell from his cock. His chest rose and fell as he stared down at me. I was drenched in his cum. "You're so fucking sexy, Penny."

I licked his cum off my lips in response.

He groaned. "We should get cleaned up."

I was about to stand, but he leaned down and lifted me into his arms. I should have protested. He was still recovering from his injuries. But I loved when he took care of me.

He carried me through the kitchen and up the stairs. "So what made you decide on this tonight?" he asked, cradling me against his chest.

I looked up at him. "The whole sex altar thing at Club Onyx."

"Hm."

"Hm what?"

"Baby, if you want to know what happens on a sex altar, all you had to do was ask."

I swallowed hard. "Okay." I stared up at him. His expression wasn't giving anything away. "I'm asking now."

"Let's just say, tomorrow is going to be fun."

God, I was already wet again just thinking about it. What was he planning on doing to me tomorrow?

CHAPTER 12
Sunday

Ian was driving us all down to the Hunter Creek Country Club. Our SUV sped past the other cars on the highway. We were all laughing and having a great time. And by we all, I meant all of us but Matt.

James turned around from the passenger seat and smiled at me. Somehow we were the only couple who hadn't gotten to sit together. Rob and Daphne were in the middle seats and I was scrunched in the back with Bee and Mason.

And I didn't want to tell anyone, but I really had to pee. I'd already made them stop once and I didn't want to have to make them stop again. *We're almost there, we're almost there*, I chanted silently to myself.

I needed to distract myself. "Did you say why Matt wasn't coming today?" I asked. I had my suspicions that maybe Rob had asked Matt to be his best man. And that Matt wasn't here today because it would be awkward since none of the rest of us were in the wedding party. Yeah, I was still a little bitter. More for James than myself. Rob had been James' best man. And James wasn't even good enough to be a groomsman for Rob? It was a slap in the face to James. Daphne could slap me in the face all she wanted, but I didn't expect that from Rob.

Rob shrugged. "Matt had other plans."

Other secret best man plans? "What other plans?"

"I don't want to talk about it." He folded his arms across his chest and looked out the window.

Um...okay. That didn't seem like best man duty stuff. Rob seemed a little pissed. Or maybe Matt had messed up something with the plans? "Are you mad at him?"

Rob turned around to face me. "Why would I be mad that one of my best friends isn't coming to help scope out my wedding venue and giving me his full attention when I need it most?"

"I think all of us will give you plenty of help."

Rob shook his head.

"You're being a bit of a groomzilla," I said.

Bee laughed.

Rob was about to open his mouth when Daphne put her hand on top of his. "You really are," she said. "Matt had other plans that he made before we announced our engagement. You can't expect him to be able to drop everything just because we're being spontaneous."

"Oh yes I can," Rob said.

"Groomzilla," Bee whispered to me. She cleared her throat. "So where is Matt? What very important business did he have that he couldn't be here?"

"It's not business. Business I would understand," Rob said. "He's hanging out with another friend."

"Tanner?" I asked.

"Don't say his name in this vehicle," Rob said.

I laughed. "Seriously, Rob, what is your deal with Tanner?" I'd met him a few times and he seemed perfectly nice. Matt had been hanging out with him more and more because...well...he was the last of our friends that was single. I got it. Being the seventh wheel constantly couldn't have felt great.

"He's weird," Rob said.

That was kind of rude. "Aren't we all a little weird?"

"I'm not weird," Rob said. "I'm normal. He's not a normal person. He's something...else."

I laughed. "Something other than human?"

"That's not what I said. But...maybe." He rubbed his chin like he was actually considering the idea that Tanner was some supernatural being.

"It's not Halloween yet. You're getting a little ahead of yourself."

"I just think that when your best friend is getting married you should ditch your other, lesser friends."

"I think it's nice that Matt still has a single friend to hang out with." I looked out the window and willed myself not to pee my pants.

"I don't," Rob said.

Mason laughed. "Dude, you can't be Matt's wingman anymore. And every single guy needs a wingman."

"I could still be his wingman. Daphne wouldn't mind, would you?" he asked.

She just stared at him. "Seriously? Yeah, I think I'd mind a little."

"Huh. Interesting. I wouldn't actually be flirting with anyone. Just pumping up Matt."

James laughed.

"What?" Rob said.

"I'm sorry, that just sounded really sexual. Pumping Matt."

Rob laughed. "Yeah, I guess it did. And now Tanner is pumping him up instead of me." He grabbed Daphne's hand. "So much has changed."

"You'll live."

He leaned over and kissed her.

Ian pulled up in front of the country club. A parking attendant rushed over to open up the doors for us.

"Is Justin already here?" Rob asked.

"Yeah he's been here for hours getting some stuff ready," I said. I'd offered to let him drive down with us but when he said he wanted to leave at 4 am I politely retracted my offer. 4 am? Was he mad?

"Should we start with a tour of the outside?" Rob asked. "When Daphne and I had dinner here, it was dark. I'd love to see the golf course."

"You can start wherever you want," I said and climbed out of the car. "I'm going to the restroom."

"You just went to the bathroom at that rest stop."

"Yeah, which was over an hour ago."

He just stared at me.

"You try being pregnant."

He laughed. "No thanks. I like scotch too much."

Very funny. I left everyone behind as I rushed into the country club. I waved to the hostess but didn't hear anything she said as I went toward the bathrooms.

I pushed into the women's room and sighed when I reached a stall. My poor bladder. I really needed to stop eating so much watermelon. It never stayed with me for long. Especially now that I was pregnant.

I heard the door open and close right before I flushed the toilet. I waited a beat for whoever it was to go into a stall. Despite having years of experience socializing at events I attended with James, I still hated small talk. I waited a few seconds before stepping out of the stall.

"What are you doing?" I asked. "This is the women's room."

James smiled. "Like we weren't just making out in a restroom a couple nights ago."

"Don't remind me of the Parrot Palace." I washed my hands and grabbed a paper towel.

He stepped up to me, brushing a loose strand of hair behind my ear. "If you needed to use the restroom, why didn't you just tell Ian to stop somewhere?"

"Because I already made you guys stop at a rest stop and I could tell everyone thought it was annoying." Children were the ones that were supposed to demand a road trip stop every hour. Not a grown ass woman.

"So you just held it?"

"Yes." I knew it was silly.

"On the way back I'll make sure we stop twice, okay? I'll say it's me."

"They're going to think you have a bladder infection."

"I don't care what they think. I need to make sure my pregnant wife doesn't accidentally pee her pants."

It was such a ridiculous statement to come out of my husband's mouth. I would have laughed if it also wasn't super sweet. "So did you follow me into the bathroom to tell me I'm silly? Or did you have something else in mind?" My eyes fell to his lips. I was pretty sure my sex drive was out of control. James didn't seem to mind though.

"As tempting as that is…I think we should save the fun for the sex altar tonight."

"Oh we're actually doing that?"

"Of course."

"So what exactly is it again?"

"I told you, you're going to have to wait to find out."

Damn it, I really needed to find out what happened on a sex altar. Bee would know. "Should we join everyone else?"

James put his arm out for me.

I wrapped my hand around his bicep and let him guide me out of the restroom. He didn't seem at all perturbed by the fact that a few club members gave us weird looks when we walked out of the women's restroom together. But I sure felt my cheeks turning red. Really...how did he never get embarrassed? I looked up at him as he escorted us outside.

"You're so handsome," I said.

He smiled down at me. "And you get more beautiful every day."

"You mean larger."

"That is definitely not what I just said."

"But it's true." I put my hand on my stomach. "Where do you think they wandered off too?"

"It's not true," he said, ignoring me. "You're not getting larger. You're growing a little human. And you look beautiful doing it."

"Try taking me on a sex altar in four months and you might think differently."

"If you like tonight, I'll absolutely take you on a sex altar again in four months. And five months. And right after the baby is born. Well...whenever you can have sex again after that." He pressed his lips together. "How long do we have to wait?"

"I'm actually not sure." I had done very little research about stages of pregnancy beyond the one I was on. I was worried I'd see something and freak out. I really didn't want to know anything about the actual birth. It was just going to drive me insane. Just the thought of a head coming out of me already made me shiver.

"Well, now I'm curious." He pulled out his phone.

I laughed. "Come on, we need to go find everyone else." I grabbed his arm and started walking. They weren't by the tennis courts or the pool. Or at the outside bar, which I was a little surprised about. I thought for sure they would have stopped there. *Where are they?*

"A month," James said. "Six weeks at the most. That's not that bad." But his face said otherwise.

"Not that bad? What is the longest we've gone without having sex?"

"I don't know…a few days?"

"Six weeks is a lot longer than a few days."

He smiled, one of his cocky grins that made my knees weak. "Well, it doesn't say anything about your mouth."

I laughed and hit his arm. "So you expect me to pop out a baby and then fill our nights with me giving you tons of head?"

"That doesn't sound so bad to me."

"Hm." Honestly it didn't sound that bad to me either. Especially if I could cover him in chocolate syrup again. Speaking of which…I had not done a great job of cleaning up the mess we'd made. Ellen was definitely going to be suspicious when she came to work tomorrow. But it wasn't my fault that I was bad at cleaning. She never let me touch a mop when she was around.

I should have confessed to James that giving him head for six weeks didn't sound that bad to me. Instead I just smiled up at him. "I guess we'll see how you behave."

He laughed. "And when have I ever behaved badly?"

"Oh, I don't know. You made a pretty big mess last night."

"If I recall, I actually cleaned up your mess." His eyes trailed down my body.

I laughed. "And then proceeded to cover the rest of our dining room in chocolate syrup."

"That was not my fault. You started it."

"You started it." Wait…had he? I actually didn't remember who squirted who first.

"We can agree to disagree." His phone buzzed and he looked down at it. "Apparently they found the spot they want to get married," James said. "They're out back on the golf course."

"Awesome." I walked over to a golf cart and climbed into the driver's seat.

"You're driving, huh?"

I couldn't even remember the last time I drove a car. Ian usually drove us everywhere, and when he didn't, James was always behind the wheel. And I'd never driven a golf cart. But I had five months to live it up. I wasn't going to waste a second of it. I smiled up at him, trying to raise my eyebrow like he always did. "Unless you want to race me."

"They don't go that fast, baby."

"Scared?"

"No. But you should be." He climbed into an adjacent golf cart and started the engine.

I turned on mine too. There was no roar of an engine. If anything it was more of a sputter. I looked over at James' golf cart and realized it was a much newer looking model. I was just about to protest when James yelled, "Eat my dust!" He pressed down hard on the gas and sped off.

"Hey! Cheater!" I pressed down on the gas too and lurched forward. I made a sharp turn to follow him on the cement path. What the hell did he mean that these things didn't go fast? The wind was whipping through my hair as I swerved again to chase him down. James was used to his fancy cars with zero-to-whatever horsepower in two seconds or something. This was plenty fast for me.

The golf course was hilly and every time I took a turn, I felt like the golf cart was going to flip over. But James was in front of me and his never flipped. So I had to be safe…right? Damn, how was he still ahead of me? I was freaking flying.

I pressed down harder on the gas and finally managed to pull up next to him. James had to shift right so I wouldn't slam into the side of his golf cart.

"Are you trying to push me off the course?" he yelled through the whipping wind.

I actually wasn't. I just wasn't great at driving this thing. But that's what he got for not letting me drive for the past couple of years. I almost sideswiped him again and he veered off into the grass to escape my onslaught.

"Where are you going?!" I turned off onto the green too and tried to catch up to him again.

"Shortcut!" he yelled back to me with a laugh.

What shortcut? We hadn't even decided on where we were racing. Wait, where were we going? Had Rob said which spot they'd chosen? Damn it, James had tricked me. He probably knew where Rob and Daphne were.

I sped up again, but there wasn't really any point. I had no idea where the end of our race was.

"Where are we going?!" I yelled at him.

He didn't respond. But he did turn around and wink at me.

That dirty scoundrel.

His golf cart came to a stop and I almost drove right into the side of it. I swerved left to avoid totaling both the golf carts.

"You cheated," I said and stepped out. "You didn't count down from three to start, then you veered off the course like a crazy person, and you didn't tell me where the stopping point was."

"Sore loser."

"You can't be a sore loser if your opponent is a cheat."

He stepped forward, his breath hot in my ear. "We'll see if you keep backtalking me tonight when you're tied down on the altar, completely at my mercy." His warm breath tickled my skin. Or maybe I had goosebumps because of what he said.

He was going to tie me up on the altar? I really needed answers from Bee. I looked to my right and saw all our friends staring at us. They looked surprised by our spur of the moment drag race. But probably not as surprised as I looked. Because they were standing right by a very familiar looking willow tree. Our freaking sex tree!

CHAPTER 13

Sunday

"They're by the willow tree," I whispered to James.

"Yeah. We probably should have been out here to steer them away from that spot."

You think? "We had sex there," I hissed. "They can't get married right there. It's practically a sex altar."

"Hardly. I'm not sure we're going to have much of a say in this, though. Daphne looks so happy."

He was not being helpful. I hurried over to them. My eyes glanced over to the little waterfall. I remembered stripping right there for James. Right before he took me under that willow tree and pressed my naked back against the bark and fucked me. I'm pretty sure I had yelled 'Professor Hunter' loudly enough for people to hear us on the terrace. This golf course was huge. What the hell were they doing right here? Why? Seriously...*why?!*

I cleared my throat. "Hey guys. Just starting the tour? That's fun. Thanks for waiting for us. Let's go this way. I think you'll like what's going on by hole 6." I tried to get them to start walking. And it wasn't a complete lie. There was a cute little bridge by hole 6. They could get married on that. Far, far away from our sex tree.

"No, we chose the spot," Daphne said. "Isn't it beautiful? The willow tree is going to look amazing in the pictures. We just knew it as soon as we saw this spot. And isn't that waterfall so cute?"

"No. It's...loud." Yup, that made sense. "The water is definitely too loud for the ceremony. The guests won't be able to hear your vows. That would be a travesty. Right, Rob? Because I bet you're planning some hilarious vows."

"Of course I am," Rob said. "And I can hear you just fine right now. The water isn't that loud, Penny."

"It'll be louder with all the people though. The voices carrying, mixing with that super loud water? No way. It won't work. Where is Justin? He'll have something to say about this."

"He's taking pictures." Daphne pointed to where Justin was. He'd just immerged from underneath the willow tree. He was snapping tons of pictures with his phone while somehow also balancing a planner and taking notes.

"It's so big under there," Justin said and looked up from his planner. "Depending on the number of RSVPs, we might be able to have the ceremony under the tree."

Good God, no.

"Wouldn't that be amazing?" Justin said. "We could cover it with fairy lights. It'll be magical and romantic."

"I'm allergic," I said. "I'm terribly allergic to willow trees." I started scratching the inside of my wrist.

"I didn't realize you had any allergies," Bee said.

"Just this one. And it's terrible. My face gets all red and puffy when I breathe in willow tree air."

Mason tilted his head to the side as he looked at me. "You look okay right now, Penny."

I tried not to glare at him. *Thanks, Mason.* Was there a way to make my face look red and puffy right now to make my point? I couldn't think of anything. "That's be-cause…I'm not right next to it." *Smooth.*

Justin sighed. "You're ruining my vision with images of red puffy faces." He shook his head. "Not under the tree then. We don't want anyone's face blowing up. And we probably will have too many guests anyway. But we can make a beautiful arch right here." He stepped to the side and waved his hand through the air. "That should be far enough away. And you, Penny, can take an antihistamine just in case."

Shit. That was a good fix. *Damn you, Justin, for being so good at your job.* "But what about the terrace? Have you guys seen that? I was thinking that would be really nice. And it's already covered in case it rains. There's a cute little firepit and everything."

"A firepit?" Justin said. "Stop it with your backyard shenanigans. No, no, no." He stepped forward. "If we put the arch right here, the beautiful couple will be able to look down the aisle and see that little waterfall." Justin walked down the aisle he was imagining in his head. "It's utterly divine. Pure perfection." He spun back around. "I can see it. It's happening, people!"

Daphne smiled and Rob pulled her into his side. They both looked so happy.

I swallowed down the lump in my throat. I didn't want to mess up their happiness. So what if James and I had had sex right there years ago? No one needed to know.

"Allergic to willow trees?" James whispered as he wrapped his arms around me. "That would have been such a good save if allergy medicine wasn't a thing."

I sighed. "Do you think we should tell them? That might make them change their minds. I don't want it to accidentally come out in a few years and for them to be pissed that we didn't mention it."

"Do you really think Rob cares if we've had sex right there? He's not exactly ashamed of sex. He'll probably just high-five you."

He was right. Rob wouldn't care. "What about Daphne?"

"Look how happy she is."

Daphne and Rob had started dancing. He dipped her and then pulled her back up, her laughter flitting through the air.

I sighed. I didn't want to ruin anything for them. "Okay, fine. But the bridge at hole 6 would have been perfect if you ask me."

"Where would you get married if you were having your wedding here?" James asked.

I looked up at the beautiful willow tree. "Right here. But that's because we have history with this tree." I had very fond memories of us getting down and dirty here.

"Really? Or is it because it's the most beautiful spot on the golf course? There's a reason we stopped here that night. The fireflies lit up the water. Don't you remember? It was perfect. It was almost magical."

It really was perfect. And it was a beautiful spot to get married. I nodded. I could easily picture Justin's vision. Rob and Daphne were going to be so happy here on their wedding day.

"Besides," James whispered. "We had sex *under* the tree. And you saved us from having the ceremony right at the spot."

That was true. This could have been so much worse. Instead I'd just be staring at the tree during the whole wedding, biting my lip, remembering James thrusting inside of me. I swallowed hard.

"About that firepit," Justin said and walked over to us. "We need to see it. Because if there is already covering on the terrace, it could be a good place for the reception."

I smiled. "Not too backyard for you?"

"We shall see, won't we. Oh my, I do see your face turning red."

What? I touched my cheek. I was pretty sure I was blushing thinking about having sex with James under the willow tree. *Sold it!*

"Let's get you away from this tree. If you'll excuse me, I'll be driving back to the terrace with Rob and Daphne. James' driving is too rugged for my delicate sensibilities. And yours too, Penny." He spun around and hurried over to the happy couple's golf cart.

I laughed. At least he wasn't calling Daphne a barbarian anymore. I looked up at James. It was so tempting to wait behind and pull him under the tree. But he said we were waiting for sex tonight. So...I stood up on my tiptoes, leaning in for a kiss. But at the very last moment I paused. "Race you back!" I yelled, leaving him hanging. I hopped into his golf cart, thinking that it was faster than mine.

"Who's the cheater now!" he yelled after me.

***

The weather was perfect today. There wasn't even a chill in the air as we all sat out on the terrace sampling tray after tray of appetizers. It was like I'd died and gone to pregnancy heaven. All. The. Food. And I was putting it away. I was made for taste-testing right now. I grabbed my second quiche and sighed. If this wasn't on the menu, I was going to sneak into the kitchen on the wedding day and demand some. *So freaking good.*

Justin had never experienced Daphne around food before. I was pretty sure he was horrified, but he was being cool about it. Although his eye definitely twitched after she shoved away her twelfth sample.

"So what was wrong with the quiche again?" Justin asked while making rapid-fire notes. "It looked like you liked that one."

Daphne shook her head. "Well I loved the spinach, but what kind of cheese was in there?"

Justin looked down at the menu. "Swiss."

"I'm not a fan of Swiss cheese," Daphne said. "Do you think we can start making substitutions?"

"You can make whatever substitutions you want. But that requires you to actually be able to make a choice about *what* you're substituting."

"I'm making choices. I want there to be cheddar in the quiches. Wait. No! How about provolone? God, I love provolone. But does it pair well with spinach?"

"Swiss and spinach are a perfect pairing. Cheddar or provolone would send the whole quiche off balance. How about we put them down as a maybe?"

Daphne shook her head. "Nope. No to the quiches then."

Darn. I agreed with Justin. Swiss and spinach were a perfect pairing. For being so particular about her food, Daphne was making terrible choices. Or rather...no choices at all.

"But you've said no to everything on the first three trays," Justin said.

"Let's hope the fourth tray is better," Daphne said.

IVY SMOAK

"My girl knows what she likes," Rob said and wrapped his arm behind her back.

"There is no fourth tray," Justin said. "That was all the appetizers on the list for your package."

"Then let's try the cheaper appetizers," Daphne said.

"That is highly unusual."

She shrugged. "Let's just try those. I didn't really love any of the expensive ones. Maybe the other list will be better."

"That's definitely not how that works."

Daphne just stared at him.

Justin didn't look calm anymore. It looked like his head was about to explode. He waved over the waiter that was helping us with this train wreck of a food sampling. "Can we try everything on this menu too?"

"Yeah, I'm sure we can arrange for that. Our chef will need a few minutes though. Are we going for the cheaper package then? I'll have to notify the chef if we want the other samples for the main course and desserts."

Justin looked over at Daphne.

"Can we just try all of it?" asked Daphne. "All that you have to offer? Please."

"Very well," the waiter said. "Give me a few minutes and I'll get those other appetizers out for you."

"Please keep the alcohol coming," Justin said.

I laughed.

Justin stared daggers at me as the waiter walked away. "Penny, a word?" He set down the menus and walked off.

It seemed like I was in a lot of trouble. I looked over at James. He shrugged. But I could tell he was thinking the same thing I was. That Justin was royally pissed.

Yeah, I was definitely in trouble. I excused myself and followed Justin. He'd walked back inside and was pacing in the restaurant.

"How are you doing?" I asked as the doors closed behind me.

"What the actual hell?!" he shrieked.

"So…not good then?"

"You owe me more than just a few favors, missy. You knew this barbaric woman. You knew she was weird about food. Don't you lie to me. You knew she'd be a nightmare." He pointed a sassy finger at me.

I guess he was back to calling Daphne a barbarian. "I'm sorry, Justin. But she's only weird about food…"

"Food is half the wedding!"

"That's not true. There's fancy clothes and dancing and a beautiful ceremony."

"A ceremony followed by lots of food! We've been sampling appetizers for 30 minutes and she hasn't chosen one. Not a single one!" He grabbed a folded cloth napkin off a nearby table and threw it on the ground.

"Justin…"

"How is she ever going to decide on a band or a DJ? Or when she wants the ceremony to start? Or what kind of flowers she wants for her bouquet or for the arch! There's a million more decisions to make and she doesn't like Swiss and spinach together!"

"I get it. I'm with you. Swiss and spinach is a wonderful combination."

"Then talk some sense into her. We don't have all day to sample food. I need them to make decisions about more stuff."

"I'm telling you, she's only bad with decisions about food. She's already picked out her dress. And the bridesmaid dresses. And she's chosen the location. We're checking things off left and right."

"We're going to be talking about appetizers for hours!"

"I'm sure you've had bridezillas before."

"This is not bridezilla behavior. It's barbarian behavior."

"Justin…"

"I have more contingencies now."

"Justin. You already agreed to do the wedding."

He huffed. "I did not agree to…that." He pointed to the window. I looked out to see Daphne, her nose scrunched up after she bit into an appetizer that I'm sure was freaking delicious.

I nodded. He had a point. "Okay. What are your new contingencies?"

"Every single person you know that gets engaged…you send them to me. Immediately. Right after you see someone drop to one knee you butt in there and recommend me. You owe me."

"Okay, done." I was going to do that anyway. Minus the whole butting into the proposal thing. "What else?"

"Get all the girls to drive back to the city in my car. And let me be chauffeured with the gentleman." He lifted his chin in the air.

"Um. Okay, I guess I can make that work." I wasn't sure how James was going to feel about that. Not just because we didn't like being apart. But because Justin got handsy the more he drank. And he'd just stolen a glass of something from a passing waiter.

He drank it down in one gulp. "And there's more contingencies that I haven't even thought of yet."

"Okay. If they're reasonable, I'll make them happen."

"Oh, like Daphne is reasonable?"

"Fine, even if they're unreasonable I'll make them happen. Come on, let's go back out there. I'm sure Daphne has found a handful of appetizers she likes and we can move on to soups and salads."

He groaned. "Thank God it's my cheat day. Because I'm eating all the carbs. I can't handle this stress!"

CHAPTER 14

Sunday

"It's a tad too spicy, don't you think?" Daphne said and looked at Rob. She fanned her mouth like she'd just eaten a jalapeno instead of a creamy chowder.

Rob had just lifted another spoonful. "Oh. Um. Yeah, babe. Definitely too spicy." He plopped his spoon down into the bowl.

I swore I saw Justin's nostrils flare.

"There's no spice," Justin said calmly. "It's a crab and corn chowder. There's seriously nothing else in it but cream and a few seasonings."

Daphne lifted a spoonful and sniffed it. "Are you sure? There is definitely something spicy in there."

"Garlic perhaps?" Justin asked. "That hardly counts as spicy."

"That's probably it. Do you think they could remove that?"

"It'll be flavorless, but…"

I lightly hit my foot against Justin's shin.

He yelped at the top of his lungs. "Penny Hunter, I love you to death, but did you just strike me? What in heaven's name have I done to deserve that?"

James gave me a weird look.

"I…" my voice trailed off. I'd barely tapped him. What was he screaming about? "I was just trying to get your attention because you mentioned to me in the dining area that the chef here is really good at substitutions like that."

He glared at me. Because he had absolutely not said that to me. But he had promised to be calm.

"Don't you remember?" I asked.

"Yes." He turned back to Daphne. "Is that a yes to the chowder if the garlic is removed?" He shook his head like it pained him to ask.

"It's my favorite of the ten," Daphne said.

"So...yes?"

"Without all that spice, yes."

Justin wrote it down, but I didn't see him write anything about the garlic. "She'll be too busy on her wedding day to even eat any of this," he said under his breath.

I didn't think Daphne heard, so it was fine. And he was right. I barely remembered even sitting down at my own wedding. Daphne probably wouldn't be eating the soup. She'd be too busy greeting everyone and receiving congratulations. But...it was her day. And she was allowed to have bland soup if she wanted.

"Justin," I said, using my most authoritative voice.

He looked up at me.

"No garlic," I said and pointed to his menu that was all crossed out in different colors.

"Right, how could I forget?" He wrote 'no garlic' next to the chowder and circled it in bright red. "Happy?"

As a matter of fact, I was. I'd feel personally responsible if this wedding was a disaster. I'd recommended Justin to them. So this had to go seamlessly. I took another spoonful of the delicious chowder, the way it was meant to be. Daphne really was missing out. It was freaking amazing.

Daphne started trying the salads, but I was pretty content with my soup. I looked over at Bee across the table. I needed to trade seats with Mason for a few minutes. Because I was dying to ask her about the sex altar thing again. I needed to know what my husband was planning for me tonight.

I contemplated how to get Mason to move. Maybe I could tell him there was a sex party out by hole 6 or something. I smiled to myself. That would probably work. Although he'd take Bee with him. They were the kinkiest couple I knew. *Hell, maybe I should just ask Mason.*

I took my last bite of chowder. And then my stomach churned. *Damn morning sickness.* In the afternoon. I was getting really tired of all the lies I'd been told about pregnancy. I excused myself and hurried off the terrace.

The restaurant was practically empty right now, the afternoon crowd gone and the evening crowd still an hour off. Which was good. Because I wasn't going to make it to the bathroom.

I pushed through the doors of the private room just in time and threw up right into a bucket filled with champagne and ice.

James didn't have to say anything. I could feel him as soon as he entered the room. His hands were warm on my neck as they pulled my hair out of my face. He kept my hair in one hand as he rubbed my back with the other.

I leaned over and threw up the rest of the food I'd sampled.

James moved his free hand to my hand. He rubbed my palm in that way that made my stomach feel better. "Maybe the chowder was bad."

I laughed. "It was delicious." I grabbed one of the linen napkins and wiped off my mouth before turning to him. "I hate this."

He sat down in one of the chairs so that he'd be eye-level with my stomach. "Hey, sweet girl," he said and put his hand on my stomach.

"Boy," I corrected.

James shook his head and spread his fingers over my belly. "Do you think maybe you could be a little easier on your mom?"

It was the first time James had referred to me as *mom*. Something about hearing that word made me feel nauseous all over again. I was so excited to be a mom. And yet…a mom? I was too young to be a mom. I still called my own mom *mom*. Was I supposed to stop that when I became a mom? I didn't know how any of this worked. I'd only read one of the books that Rob had given us when we found out we were expecting. I had so much research I needed to do.

James leaned forward and placed a kiss on my stomach.

"I'm going to be a mom," I whispered. The dam broke and tears spilled down my cheeks.

He looked up at me. "Yeah, one of those sexy ones that all the other moms hate."

I smiled. The nervous energy dissipated as soon as our eyes locked. It wasn't like I was doing this alone. James was going to be the world's best dad to our baby. We did everything as a team. And we'd do this together too. "I love you." I straddled his lap.

He ran his thumbs beneath my eyes, removing my tears. "I love you too. Please don't cry. You know how much it pains me when you cry."

I leaned forward and ran the tip of my nose down the length of his. "It's just the hormones," I said.

"Are you sure?"

"Yes." I wasn't sad. Honestly, straddling him like this? I was more horny than anything else. "Do you remember the first time we were in this room?"

James didn't look around, but his hands settled on my waist. "I remember."

I laughed, remembering how our waiter had almost seen my panties around my ankles. "We were wild."

"We're still wild."

"James, can you please just tell me what a sex altar is?"

"You'll find out soon." He looked down at his watch. "Actually, it's probably almost set up. I wonder how much longer this food tasting will take?"

"What do you mean almost set up? Who's setting it up?"

James just smiled.

"What are you planning?"

He leaned forward, whispering in my ear. "Sinful things, baby."

I swallowed hard.

"And if I didn't have the best night ever planned, I'd take you right here, right now." He lightly bit down on my earlobe.

God. I take back what I thought earlier– Mason and Bee weren't the kinkiest couple we knew. We were. But I needed to know what I was walking into. And what kind of setup was he referring to? "We should probably get back. I bet they've moved on to the dinner course."

James groaned. "This is taking forever."

I climbed off his lap. "We're halfway through. And Daphne is less particular about desserts."

"Is she?"

"Mhm. One time when we were out, she took ten minutes ordering dinner. But for dessert she didn't have any substitutions or anything. She just ordered directly off the menu."

"Really?"

"Yup." But that was just one time. I'd seen her eviscerate a dessert menu too. Hopefully this would be more like the former. "Either way, I'm starving."

James laughed and stood up. "Well, no one's going to want this now. Might as well make the rest of this afternoon fun." He pulled out the champagne from the bucket and wiped it off with a napkin.

"Gross."

"What? It didn't get inside the bottle."

"Well, either way, you can't drink. Because I kinda sorta promised Justin he could ride back with just the guys."

"Wait, what?"

"And Mason drives too fast and Rob isn't great at paying attention, so I'd really prefer if you were driving."

"I'm driving back with you," he said.

"Unfortunately not. There are a lot of contingencies to Justin planning this last-minute wedding. He's been very particular."

"He put driving with us into his contract?"

"Not exactly…we don't even have a contract."

James laughed. "So you've been negotiating with him just for fun? Because it really seems like he's committed to this wedding."

"Yes?" *Damn, Justin was tricky.* There was no way he was going to pull out of this. He loved a challenge. He'd been playing me. Acting all dramatic and stuff. Although…I don't think that was acting.

James laughed. "You're a terrible negotiator." He grabbed my hand and led us out of the private room. "How about you come get me next time he wants to add a contingency. I'll take care of it."

"If you say so. Maybe just give that champagne right to Justin to calm him down."

"Alcohol does not calm that man down."

I laughed, but my laughter died in my throat as we reached the window that looked out on the terrace. I watched in horror as Justin stood up, picked up a plate, and threw it on the ground. It shattered into a million little pieces. And then he grabbed two glasses off the table and did the same.

What is he doing? Had he lost his freaking mind? I pushed out the doors and was about to open my mouth when Daphne clapped.

"Yes, just like that," Daphne said. "I know neither one of us is Jewish, but I've always wanted to smash plates and glasses."

Justin stomped down onto the shattered glass for good measure. "I can definitely get behind this idea. It's quite satisfying." He grabbed another plate and threw it on the ground. "Mazel tov!"

Okay then. I'd thought he was throwing a tantrum. I should have known better. Justin was a professional. He was really only showing me his sassy side because we were friends.

I stood on my tiptoes and kissed James' cheek. "I'll be right back. I need to ask Bee something." I hurried off before he could ask me if I was going to question her about sex altars. He knew me too well.

"Hey, Mason," I said. "Could I switch places with you real quick?"

"Trouble in paradise?"

I laughed. "No. I just need to ask Bee about sex altars." *Oh my God.* Had I just said that out loud? These hormones had turned my brain to mush.

Mason laughed. "Well, Bee knows plenty about those."

Bee lightly slapped his arm before he stood up.

Mason winked at me and walked around the table, plopping into the chair beside James. They started laughing about something.

Probably me. But hopefully not. I turned to Bee as I sat down. "So tell me everything. What happens at a sex altar?" I started eating the crab cake that had just been served. I didn't care that I was using Mason's fork. Bee looked surprised, but she didn't know what it was like to be this hungry. My baby boy was insatiable.

She laughed. "Oh. I thought you were joking. I figured you just wanted to sit with me so we could talk about how all this food is perfect and Daphne is a psychopath."

"Well that too, yeah."

Daphne had just turned up her nose at the crab cakes. She truly was insane. These were award-winning crab cakes. I added them to my mental list of things to sneak off and eat during her wedding.

"So are you planning on creating a sex altar for James?"

"No, he's setting one up for me. I think. I don't really know how any of that works."

"It's not very complex. You know the altars at church-es?"

I nodded. "The table where they pour the wine and all that."

"Right. So it's like that. But instead of blessing the food...James will be blessing your body. Worshipping it really."

"Worshipping it?"

"Yeah."

"How exactly?"

"However he feels like. You'll be tied up, so you're kind of at his mercy. His mouth, his cock, toys, other stuff. One time Mason used candle wax on me and I freaking loved it."

I take it back again – Bee and Mason were kinkier. "Didn't that hurt?"

"Don't tell me that a little pain doesn't make the pleasure that much better."

I nodded. I really loved when James spanked me. I pictured the slap of his palm and then how soothing it felt when he gently rubbed the tender skin. Every time he did that I ended up practically dripping with desire.

"But it's like...fun?" I asked.

"Oh, it's the most fun. I definitely recommend silk re-straints though. The metal really bites into your skin if you know what I mean. Rope is pretty painful too."

I laughed.

"No, I'm serious." She grabbed her wrist. "One time I had bruises for a week. Worth it though." She winked at me. "You know what? Now you've got me wanting to do a sex altar thing tonight too. Lord knows we've earned it after this torture. I'll do one tonight too and we'll have lunch tomorrow and talk about all the sexy things our men did to us. Deal?"

"Um…"

She put her hand out.

I shook her hand without even thinking about what I was agreeing to. *Damn, I really am terrible at negotiating.*

"Get ready for the night of your life," Bee said.

CHAPTER 15
Sunday

Ian drove us girls back in Justin's car. Another thing Justin insisted on. He wanted to drive in James' car. And...apparently I gave him whatever he wanted all the time. James really did need to handle negotiations from here on out.

Ian dropped off Daphne and then Bee.

"See you tomorrow," Bee said and hopped out of the car. "I can't wait to hear all about it."

Ian pulled away from the curb and I wondered if he had any idea what Bee was referring to. I'd be absolutely mortified if he knew I was about to experience a sex altar tonight with James. I'd be mortified if anyone other than Bee knew. Or maybe Mason. But only because they did stuff like this all the time. Anyone else...nope. Mortifying.

Ian and I were both quiet on the drive home. Which was unusual for us. Which made my stomach twist with knots. *Good God, he knows!* I cleared my throat. "So...what's up, Ian?"

His eyes glanced in the rearview mirror, connecting with mine for a second before moving back to the road. "Nothing."

Nothing? Really? He definitely knows. And then I remembered something terrible. James had said the sex altar was almost set up. Which meant...someone else had set it up.

SEDUCTION

And there were only so many people who could have done that because Ian was with us. "What have Briggs and Porter been up to today?"

"Working."

How vague. Working on what? I bit the inside of my lip. If I was lucky, James was just messing with me and hadn't actually asked for anyone to help with it. But that didn't mean Briggs and Porter wouldn't know about it soon. "Have Briggs and Porter already gone home for the evening?" There were cameras all over our house. I didn't love the idea of anyone watching our sex altar-ness.

"You know one of them stays at all times, Penny."

Oh, right. "Maybe they should both go home tonight. Give them the night off. They've earned it. You too."

He looked at me in the rearview mirror again. "You know I can't do that."

I did know that. James and his crazy rules. We were safe and happy. We didn't need three security guards. But I also refused to let any of them go because they were all wonderful guys. Maybe we just needed fewer cameras. Or maybe James had set up the sex altar in the bathroom where there weren't as many cameras. Although a sex altar over a toilet didn't exactly sound very sexy.

"Is everything alright?" Ian asked.

"Mhm." *Nope.* "Did James mention anything to you about…tonight?"

"No, what about tonight?"

Did he actually not know? Maybe I was just overacting. I mean…who the heck would James let in our house to set up something crazy like that? No one. That would be way too awkward. Which meant Ian was being quiet for another reason. "Is everything alright with you?"

"Just lost in thought."

"About what?" I held my breath, half expecting him to say sex altars.

"Nothing."

He was being so weird tonight. "Are you mad at me or something?"

"No, not at all. I love working for you guys."

Okay. I was about to ask another question when he pulled up to our apartment building.

"I gotta get this car to Justin's place. I'll be back in a bit."

I'd have to question him another time. "Thanks for driving."

"Always," he said with a smile.

There was the friendly face of Ian I'd grown to love. I opened up the door and stepped out before he could do something silly like open the door for me. I was capable of opening doors myself. I walked into our apartment building, waved to the concierge, and stepped onto the elevator.

The doors dinged and I stepped off. I looked down the hall at the security door. I wondered whether it was Briggs or Porter who was watching us tonight. One of them was certainly in for a treat.

I opened up our door. "James, I'm home!" I dropped my keys on the kitchen counter.

There was no response.

"James?"

No response.

We must have beat them back. Which was good because that meant that James was driving carefully. I eyed the fridge. It was super tempting to have some watermelon. Or a pickle. Oh, or both. I was just about to grab the handle to the fridge when I thought I heard a noise up-stairs.

I froze. "James?" I whispered this time.

No response. But I hadn't really expected one. He wasn't home yet. It must have just been my imagination playing tricks on me.

But then I heard another sound. Almost like a banging noise. I grabbed a knife out of the knife block. I have no idea why. I barely liked cutting up raw chicken. There was no way I was about to stab an intruder. But I still found myself tiptoeing toward the stairs.

"Penny?"

I screamed at the top of my lungs and spun around.

Briggs was standing there with his hands out, like he was worried about what I was doing with a knife.

"Briggs?"

"What are you doing?" he asked.

"I heard a noise."

"So you grabbed a knife instead of calling me?" He stepped forward and grabbed it out of my hand. He opened his mouth and then closed it, like he knew whatever had been about to come out was inappropriate. He was probably wondering what the hell I'd been thinking.

But I hadn't been. I was just scared. "I'm sorry, I heard a noise upstairs. And James isn't back yet."

"Well, please call me next time, okay?" He looked a little calmer now.

"Can you go check?"

He smiled down at me. Like I was a silly kid asking him to check under my bed for monsters. "It's just Matt and Tanner."

"What?"

"Yeah, they came to set something up."

"Set what up?" I swear I stopped breathing.

"I don't know." He shrugged and put the knife back in the knife block.

But I knew what they were doing. *Good God, no! No!* Matt and Tanner were setting up the sex altar. *Why?* Why on earth would James do this to me? I'd never able to face either of them again. But…maybe I was early enough to stop them. Maybe they hadn't seen what they were about to set up yet.

"Um…if you'll excuse me." I was about to hurry up the stairs, but Matt and Tanner had just appeared at the top of them. Looking like they'd just finished a hard project.

Tanner ran his fingers through his long hair that had gotten sweaty on his forehead. And he was wearing a fucking construction belt!

No.

And Matt wiped some sawdust off his cheek before he saw me and winked.

No!

They started walking down the stairs.

"I'll leave you to it," Briggs said from behind me and left. How badly I wished I could run after him. I wanted to hide. I wanted to do anything other than face Matt and Tanner.

"Nice to see you again, Penny," Tanner said. He grabbed my hand and drew it up to his lips. He placed a soft kiss against the back of my hand. I'd seen so many movies about old fashioned gentlemen, but Tanner was the only one I'd ever met in person. We hadn't hung out that much, but every time I saw him, I liked him more and more. I had no idea why Rob hated him so much. He was so nice.

"So...um...hi," I said. I didn't really know what else to say.

Tanner smiled and dropped my hand. "You're blushing."

Yeah, that made sense.

"How was food tasting with Daphne?" Matt asked and opened up the fridge. He pulled out two beers and tossed one to Tanner.

Tanner caught the bottle in one hand and then flicked the top of it off with just his thumb.

How the heck did he do that? Did he have the world's strongest thumbs or something? That was an oddly particular and impressive talent. "You know how Daphne is," I said and turned to Matt. "Is that why you didn't come today?" I was thankful for the change of topic. *Let's talk about Daphne and how she should be banned from all restaurants.*

"Nah. I just already had plans to hang out with Tanner."

"In my house?" I asked. *Damn it, why did I just redirect the conversation to the awkwardness?*

Matt laughed. "No, we were on our way to the bar around the corner when James called me."

They were on their way to pick up chicks at a bar. And James diverted them here for...*God.* I looked back and forth between him and Tanner.

Tanner took a long sip from his bottle. "I owed James a favor," he offered.

"Oh. Okay. Cool." I scratched the back of my neck. I had suddenly forgotten what to do with my hands. "Do either of you want some watermelon?" I couldn't embarrass myself if I had a mouthful of watermelon.

"I'm quite alright," Tanner said. "Thank you for offering. But you might want to rethink that. The last thing you want is to need to pee while you're all tied up. Unless James is into watersports…"

I closed my eyes and pretended like this wasn't happening. But when I opened my eyes Matt and Tanner were still standing there smiling at me. "If you'll excuse me. I'm just going to go kill myself."

Matt laughed. "It's fine, Penny. We had nothing to do today anyway. And it's not like neither of us has set one of these up before."

How kinky were all my friends? I was beginning to think I was the only woman on earth who hadn't been worshipped at a sex altar.

"I have one permanently mounted in my apartment," Tanner said. "Or two, depending on the day."

"See?" Matt gestured to Tanner. "Nothing to be embarrassed about." But then he looked back at Tanner. "Wait, do you really?" He laughed. "Where are they?"

"In my sex dungeon of course," Tanner said and then turned his attention back to me. "Well, we should probably get out of your hair, Penny. Your husband just got back and I have a feeling he'll want you all to himself. But if you'd like an audience, I'm free all night. I can even arrange for an entire gallery if you'd like."

A gallery?! Was that the official term for a group of perverts? I looked over my shoulder. James hadn't come in yet. "No gallery. And how do you know he's back?" I turned back to Tanner.

"He wrote to me." Tanner coughed. "Texted me, I mean." He pulled out his phone almost as if he needed to prove to me that he had one.

Okay. Tanner really was a nice guy. Hell, he'd just done James a huge awkward favor in his spare time. But Rob did maybe have a point…Tanner was a bit strange.

"Oh, I almost forgot my houseboy," Tanner said. He walked to the bottom of the stairs. "We're leaving!" he yelled.

Wait, was there someone else involved in this ridiculousness?

A short little man in a butler's outfit ran down the stairs. "Sorry, Master Tanner," he said. "I was just putting the finishing touches on the altar."

No! I didn't even know this man and he knew about the sex altar? I cleared my throat, hoping that would be the end of that. "I'm sorry, I don't think we've met. I'm Penny."

"Oh, don't mind Nigel," Tanner said. "He's my houseboy. He likes it when you ignore him. Just pretend he's a piece of furniture. Let him blend in."

I looked at Nigel and then back at Tanner. "I don't really understand anything that you just said."

Tanner laughed. "I get that a lot. Well, we're off. Enjoy yourself," Tanner said. "I'll see you again at the wedding."

I waved goodbye to him and Nigel, but then caught Matt's arm. "You invited him to the wedding?" I whispered. "Rob's going to kill you. And who the hell is that weird little man?"

Matt laughed. "Tanner's houseboy. He literally just told you that." He lowered his voice. "Nigel is super creepy, right? He really likes to stare."

We both glanced toward the door, where Tanner and Nigel were waiting for Matt. Tanner was looking at his phone but Nigel was staring directly at us. Or…rather…at Matt. He was definitely just staring at Matt.

"Anyway," Matt said. "Every single guy needs a wingman at a wedding. It's bro-code. Rob will understand."

"Will he? Because he was pretty upset today that you were hanging out with Tanner instead of going to the tasting."

"Rob will be so busy on his wedding day that he won't notice. Trust me."

I did not trust him. Rob had basically thrown a hissy fit in the car. "Matt…"

"Don't say you don't trust me," he said. "You trusted me to set up a freaking sex altar in your apartment. Have fun, Penny." He kissed my cheek and then left with Tanner.

My stomach was uneasy from the fact that Matt was inviting Tanner to Rob's wedding. And even more uneasy because there was a sex altar waiting for me upstairs that two of my friends plus Nigel had just built. Was James trying to mortify me? Was that part of it? A religious shaming thing? Because I'd had enough of that growing up in a Catholic church.

I didn't know whether to run upstairs to look at it or stand by the door and freak out at James when he came in.

I didn't have to decide, because right then, James walked in. He was smiling, not a care in the world.

"James Hunter, did you seriously ask our friends and Nigel to build a sex altar for us upstairs?"

"Who's Nigel?" James asked.

I ignored the question. Nigel was the least of our concerns. "Do you have any idea how mortifying that is? I'll never be able to look at Matt or Tanner or Nigel ever again without thinking about that."

"Well, hopefully after tonight you'll only be thinking about me when you think of sex altars."

"It's not funny," I said and lightly slapped his arm. "This is so embarrassing."

"I love when you blush."

"Don't flirt with me! You are in so much trouble."

He flashed me his perfect smile.

"I will slap that smile off your face."

"Well it's a good thing that's not what they were doing then."

I just stared at him. "Wait...what?"

"I asked Tanner and Matt to just pretend they'd been setting up a sex altar. To distract you from the real surprise. And really...who is Nigel?"

"Tanner's houseboy. Forget about Nigel. This is important. So...they weren't setting up sex stuff?"

"Nope." He didn't offer any more information.

"So what were they doing?"

He smiled again. "I wanted to surprise you. They were really setting up the nursery."

My mouth dropped. "Are you serious?" I hit his arm again. "I'm going to kill you. That was so not funny."

"It was a little funny."

Fine. Maybe a little. But I wasn't going to tell him that. I'd been worried about who knew all day. And to find out no one did? Was he trying to send me into labor early?

"Come on. You're going to love it." He grabbed my hand and pulled me toward the stairs.

I didn't say a word. I was still coming down from that evil trick. "They thought that I thought it was a sex thing."

James laughed.

I groaned.

James smiled outside the door to one of our spare bedrooms. We'd decided that this would be the nursery. But that was as far as we'd gotten with our plans because we couldn't decide on a color. It had to be something neutral because we didn't know if we were having a girl or a boy. And James did not like that I kept insisting on shades of blue.

"You're going to love it," James said and put his hand on the doorknob.

I shook my head, trying to rid the tension from my body. It was a dirty trick. But the fact that the nursery was finished was actually really sweet.

James opened the door and I gasped. This was not a nursery. What was it that Tanner said he had in his house? This was a freaking sex dungeon!

But before I could say a word, James put a bag over my head.

CHAPTER 16

Sunday

I screamed at the top of my lungs. I was still all jittery from when I thought someone was trespassing.

James ignored my scream and lifted me over his shoulder like a sack of potatoes.

"You're such a liar," I said. *God.* Matt and Tanner did know. *Noooooo.* I would have slapped James' perfect butt, but my arms were locked in place and I couldn't see a damn thing.

"I was just trying to calm you down," James said. "Tonight is supposed to be erotic. And you seemed a little...tense."

"Would you please put me down and take off this bag?"

"I can do one of those things." He laid me down on something cold and hard. And then I felt metal surround my wrist.

I heard the click of a handcuff. "Bee said to use silk instead of metal."

"So you talked to Bee about this but you're horrified that I talked to Matt and Tanner?"

"Yes." I knew I was a hypocrite, but that's just how my mind worked.

"You know, Penny." He grabbed my other wrist and shackled it. "You act like no one knows we have sex. But my baby is inside of you."

I swallowed hard. "I know people know we have sex." I tried to move my arms but quickly realized that these weren't handcuffs at all. I couldn't move even an inch. It was like these were bolted down to the sex altar thing. "But they probably assume we have normal sex. Not whatever this is."

"No, I don't think so. A sweet girl like you? Everyone knows you're kinky as hell."

Do they? Am I? I closed my eyes even though there was a bag on my head covering my face. *Fine.* It wasn't like this was the first time we'd used restraints and toys and stuff. And just because Bee didn't like the feeling of metal digging into her skin? I kind of liked it. I especially liked these. Usually with handcuffs you could wiggle around a bit. But these restraints had me completely at his mercy.

"The last time I restrained you, I remember you begging me to fuck you harder." He put his hand on the side of my throat. "And when I spank you, you thrust your ass out farther so I can spank you again."

God, I was getting wet just thinking about him spanking me.

"So don't pretend for a second that you're not excited about this." He grabbed the front of my strapless dress and pulled it down.

I felt my nipples harden from the cold.

"Or that you don't secretly love the idea of my friends knowing what I'm about to do to you. Because they know. They're probably picturing it right now. Wishing they were me." He grabbed my exposed breasts and I moaned.

He chuckled and removed his hands. "This is going to be fun."

"This is completely inappropriate, James. Our baby is going to sleep here."

"So it's only appropriate that we christen this room now instead of later, don't you think?"

Well, he had a point there. It was better that we fucked in here now instead of when the baby was born. "Fine, but we're not keeping the walls black." Our baby would not be sleeping in a sex dungeon.

James laughed. "Of course not. But before we paint it whatever blue you decide on, we're going to make the most of this room."

"This sex dungeon."

"If that's what you want to call it," he said. He pulled my dress lower and I heard the fabric rip. Yeah, there was no way he was getting that over my pregnant belly or hips.

"Did you just rip my dress?"

He didn't respond, but he grabbed my ankle and cuffed it into something just like he had with my wrists.

"James, just unshackle me so I can get undressed."

"That won't be necessary." He grabbed my other ankle and shackled it. "Your dress was strapless and you weren't wearing a bra." He grabbed the sides of my thong and ripped the material off. "You're already naked, baby."

"Stop ripping my clothes!"

"Don't make me put a gag in your mouth."

Would he? I pressed my lips together. And more importantly...would I like it?

"Good girl," he said.

I'd barely gotten a good look at the nursery sex dungeon, but there must have been speakers put in, because suddenly we were surrounded by the sounds of mumbled chants. It wasn't sexy. It was creepy. "James, what the hell is that?"

"Worshippers. We're in a temple. You grew up going to a Catholic church. Don't tell me you never thought about your priest taking you into a confessional booth and having his way with you."

"The priests at my church were old and bald."

"Hmm. Well, imagine if one of them looked like me. Would you have pictured it then?"

Of course I would have.

It's like he knew what I was thinking. Because even though I didn't respond, he lightly brushed a finger against my clit. "Imagine me eye-fucking you from the altar."

I swallowed hard.

"Waiting till I could get you alone for a moment after the sermon." His thumb slid lower, brushing against my wetness.

Mmm.

"I think you'd linger in the pew once everyone left. Hoping we'd have a moment alone."

His thumb slid inside of me, his fingers digging into my ass cheek. "I think you would have dreamt of what we'd do if we were ever alone, without a whole congregation watching our every move. Isn't that right?"

"Yes." My voice came out breathless and weird. But I could picture it. I could envision him up there, completely forbidden. I just wanted one taste. Was that how he'd pictured me when I was his student? Like I was forbidden fruit? Just one little taste.

"Could you imagine the rumors that would spread if we started an affair? A priest taking advantage of one of his flock? It's sinful." He slowly circled his thumb inside of me.

Jesus. I would have moved, but the restraints kept me spread eagle on the table.

"Well, it never would have happened. Because we can't be alone." His thumb fell from my skin.

Wait, what?

"So I just invited you up here during a normal sermon." He turned up the sounds of chanting. "And I don't give a fuck what anyone says. I'm going to worship your body like you're my one and only goddess. And everyone's going to watch."

I could actually picture the altar at my church. The hundreds of people in the pews. The chants growing louder. I'd never considered my church erotic. It was rather boring and dull. But picturing it now while I was spread out on this altar and James was saying sinful things to me? I'd never pictured anything sexier in my life.

"Open your mouth, baby." His thumb pulled down my lip as I obliged. "Suck," he said.

I expected him to shove his cock in my mouth, but instead he slipped in something small and rubbery. Some kind of toy, I think.

He pulled it out of my mouth. I was just about to ask him what it was, when something burning hot hit my skin.

I screamed out, but my scream died in my throat when James slid his finger back inside of my wetness. No, not his finger. Because it was vibrating like crazy. It must have been the toy I'd just sucked on. *Holy shit.* I swore my back would have arched if I could move. Instead, the metal bit into my skin as I tried to move.

"Let's see how many sins we can commit tonight, baby."

I felt more hot liquid drip between my breasts. That must have been the hot wax that Bee mentioned. It definitely burned, but it wasn't as painful as I thought it would be. Probably because the toy inside of me and James gently kissing my breasts had me on the verge of coming.

But it was like he knew I was about to cum, because I felt his finger slide in next to the toy and the vibrations suddenly slowed down.

I moaned.

"Did you think I was going to let you come that quickly? I've been dreaming about this moment for months. It'll be my cock that will have you screaming. Do you understand me?"

God, I loved when he used that commanding tone with me. I nodded and then screamed again when he poured more hot wax on my skin. This time on my inner thigh. It dipped dangerously close to where his finger had just been.

He wouldn't pour it *there*, would he?

He kissed my inner thigh, tracing the path of the wax with his lips. "Baby," he groaned. "You're soaked."

I knew that.

"You're dripping on the altar. Everyone can see it."

I clenched around the toy. God, I needed to come. "Please," I moaned.

"You love that everyone is watching." His breath was hot against my skin. "Tell me you can't wait for everyone to see me bury my cock in your tight pussy."

"James…"

His finger slipped in beside the toy again. For a second it started buzzing faster. But then it slowed down even more. To barely vibrating.

I wanted to cry. I was so fucking close.

I felt his hot breath on my skin, skipping over my aching pussy. Past my stomach. He paused between my breasts. And then his tongue slowly swirled around one of my hard nipples.

"Someone in the front pew just pulled out his cock," James whispered. "He's hard for you. He's wishing he was up here feasting on your body."

I whimpered. This roleplay was twisted. And I fucking loved it.

"Someone else is jerking off watching you. Do you like that? That you're making other people sin?"

"Yes."

"A woman just spread her legs in the pew to the left. Her fingers are trailing up her leg as she watches you squirm. Do you think it's me she wants?" His tongue slowly swirled around my nipple again. "Or do you think she wishes she was me?"

Yup, this was definitely twisted. And I could picture it all perfectly. A woman in the pew staring at us. Her fingers pulsing inside of her. How badly I wished I could touch myself right now. The low vibrations of the toy and James' words were driving me mad.

"I think she's imagining her tongue swirling around your nipple instead of mine. I think she's wishing it was your tongue sliding into her pussy instead of her own fingers. I think she wishes she was the one about to fuck you." He lightly bit down on my nipple.

I moaned.

"Sinner."

I didn't know if he was talking about me or the fake woman in the pew. But I was right there with him. Picturing the people watching us. Loving this. Wanting to be us and with us.

"You like that, you dirty girl?" he whispered before lowering his mouth to my throat. His teeth lightly bit into the side of my neck before sucking on the skin. "Do you want me to invite someone else up here to fuck you while I watch?"

"No. I want you."

"I'm celibate. I made a vow. I can't fuck you."

I groaned. "You just said I couldn't come because I was going to come on your cock."

"You want me to break my vow?" He poured more hot wax on me.

I screamed and moaned at the same time. I felt crazy. I just need him to touch me. Lick me. Fuck me. Anything. "Please."

"You want me to be a sinner like you, you little slut?"

I felt like a slut. I felt exposed and needy and ready for anything to fill me. "Fuck. Me."

"Hm." His fingers trailed over my breast and down my stomach. "But I'm not done worshipping you yet." He slid a finger inside of me.

I swore I almost exploded just then, but he pulled the toy out.

"Delicious," he said.

Was he seriously licking the toy instead of me? He was driving me mad. "Fuck me," I said again.

I finally felt his hot breath between my thighs. "I'd lose everything if I fucked you."

"I'm worth it."

He groaned. "Oh, I don't doubt it for a second. One taste and I've lost all reason." He thrust his tongue inside of me.

"James!"

But it was like my plea did the opposite of spurring him on. His tongue was so slow. Lightly dipping in and out like he was lazily licking an ice cream cone and savoring it. I didn't want him to savor me. I wanted him to fucking devour me.

I tried to move my legs so I could wrap my thighs around his face. But the metal dug into my ankles. "I swear to God…"

"You really shouldn't swear to God," he said. "We're in a place of worship."

God damn it, fuck me! "I'm a dirty slut," I said. "I've been eye-fucking my priest for months. I've wanted him so badly I came up here in front of everyone to finally get his cock rammed so far up my pussy that I'll never forget the feeling. Right here. Right now. Fuck me or I…"

"Patience is a virtue." He thrust his tongue deep inside of me.

Yes! For what felt like the millionth time, I was seconds away from coming when he poured a shit ton of hot wax down my chest. The pain caused my brain to scramble, pulling me away from my impending orgasm. "I'm going to fucking kill you, James."

"Killing is a sin. One of many you're committing right now."

"Please," I begged. "I'll do anything."

"Anything?"

"Anything!" I sounded desperate, but I didn't come.

"Fine. I'll break my vow. But only if I get to baptize you when I'm finished fucking you."

"Yes!" I had no idea what I was agreeing to, but it didn't matter. All I heard was that he was eventually going to be finished fucking me. Which meant he had to start.

I felt the table shake and suddenly my knees were bent up and my legs were spread even wider. I tried to move, but I was still shackled. There must have been some mechanical feature that spread my legs so that he could...*Fuck!* I moaned as he finally thrust into me.

"Goddess," James groaned. "My fucking goddess." He slammed into me so hard I felt his balls hit my ass. Again and again. Fucking me relentlessly.

"Everyone's watching, you little slut."

"James," I moaned.

"Are you going to come while everyone can see? Are you my filthy sinner?"

"Yes!"

"Confess that you're a sinner. Ask for forgiveness. Beg me for it. Beg me." He groaned.

My body started to tremble. "Forgive me father, for I have sinned!"

His thumb brushed against my clit and I was a goner. My body shook as my pussy clenched. The metal bit into my skin but I didn't even care. The pleasure was intense and fast and mind numbing.

He slid out of me and tore the bag off my head.

He was kneeling over me, his thick cock in his hand. God, he was so sexy. Yeah, if he'd been my priest I would have definitely had sinful dreams about him. Hell be damned.

"You shall be baptized and your sins will wash away."
He groaned as a shot of his cum hit my cheek. "Bathe in
me." Another shot. "Sinner." Another shot hit my chest,
soothing the burn of the hot wax. He groaned once more,
drenching me in his cum.

I was panting as I stared up at him. I'd never been so
turned on in my life. I was still stretched out and shackled
and I swore I was already ready for round two.

"That was fucking hot," he said. He dipped his thumb
in the cum on my cheek, trailing it down to my lips. He
pressed his thumb into my mouth.

I swirled my tongue around his thumb.

He groaned and slowly let his thumb fall from my
mouth.

"So that's what a sex altar is?" I said, still trying to
catch my breath.

He smiled. "I have no idea what the fuck a sex altar
is." But then he paused. "Actually, I vaguely remember
something about one in college. I think. My time at Har-
vard is all really hazy."

I just stared at him. "Seriously?"

He laughed. "Sorry. I really don't remember. But I figured Tanner would know, so I called him to set it up. I
could tell you wanted to try it. I think I might have gone a
little more religious than I was supposed to."

I laughed. "I really liked it. You're so much hotter than
any priest I've ever met. Am I allowed to tie you up on this
thing?" I tried to move, but I was still shackled down.

"I don't think so."

"What? Why?"

"Oh, baby, you wouldn't have any idea what to do
with me. I'm in control, remember?"

Was that a challenge? Because I could bag him and get him on this table too. I probably just needed some help. That's what my girls were for. *Challenge accepted, James.* I just needed to get unchained first.

CHAPTER 17

Monday

"You're already blushing," Bee said. "Tell me everything."

"It was really intense."

"Good intense?"

I nodded. Really good intense.

She smiled. "Same. Although it looks like you guys decided on metal instead of silk." She nodded toward my wrists.

I was wearing a watch and lots of bangles, but you could still see the red marks on my wrists. James had kissed my wrists and ankles and every inch where the hot wax had landed before we'd fallen asleep last night. But it didn't hurt. The whole experience was...wow. I shrugged. "I didn't mind the metal."

"You kinky bitch."

I laughed. "The hot wax was fun too."

"Did you use nipple clamps?"

"No."

"Oh. You should. They're fun." She took a bite of her cheeseburger. "God this is so good."

The mention of God made me smile. I'd gone to bed thinking of all the ways I could sin next and have James punish me. Which was silly. I didn't need to do anything bad for James to punish me. All I needed to do was put on a mini skirt and ask him to spank me. I tried to hide my smile around a bite of cheeseburger.

Mmm, this cheeseburger was almost as good as sex. Almost. Unlike James, this burger couldn't claim me and drench me in cum. I almost laughed out loud. James and I had a great sex life. We had sex most days. But something about these five months of seduction was really getting to my head. It was like all I could think about was straddling his face.

"You know…" Bee said. "You two could always come to Club Onyx sometime. Just to check it out."

I laughed. "No need. Club Onyx came to us."

"What does that mean?"

"We have a sex dungeon now."

"Fancy," Bee said. "I'm pretty sure my bedroom is just classified as a sex dungeon."

I laughed.

"Still," she said. "You should think about it. It's loads of fun."

I nodded, even though I was pretty sure that was a big no from me. I didn't need to go to some crazy sex club. My sex drive was plenty high. Besides, I'd barely even explored my new sex dungeon yet. I'd been bagged most of last night. And James and I hadn't left the bed this morning until it was time for me to come here. I needed to explore and figure out a way to get James up on that table.

"It's cool that James set up a sex dungeon," Bee said. "That's super kinky."

"Actually Tanner and Matt set it up." The truth just fell out of me. But I immediately wished I could take it back.

"Seriously? Even kinkier. I bet that drove Matt mad."

I groaned. "Would you quit it? Matt does not have a crush on me. We've been over this."

"Well if he didn't before, he definitely does now. Guys love girls who can get freaky in bed. And…on sex altars."

I threw a French fry at her.

"Hey." She swatted it away. "Stop it, I just got a blow-out." She fixed her hair and then took another bite of her cheeseburger.

"Speaking of getting your hair done…any word from Daphne today?"

Bee shook her head.

"Yeah, me either." I guess my fill-in bridesmaid duties were done. I sighed.

"It's going to be fine," Bee said. "Think about how much more fun a wedding is when you're just a guest and not in the wedding party. We can get drunk and dance the night away with no responsibility."

I raised my eyebrows.

"Sorry," she said. "*I* can get drunk. But we can both dance the night away."

"Deal."

"Do you know if they have a hotel picked out yet? I want to grab a suite before they're all gone. Maybe I'll snake the presidential suite from Rob and Daphne just because I'm bitter about not being asked to be a brides-maid."

I laughed. "I'm not sure. I kinda figured James and I would just stay at his old apartment." It was close to the country club and it had been ages since we'd been there. I loved visiting campus. It reminded me of being young and in love. I looked down at my stomach. It reminded me of not getting bigger and bigger each and every day.

"Well if you change your mind, grab a suite too. Maybe we can hold the suites ransom until Rob at least asks Mason and James to be in the wedding. Really…who else is he going to ask? I'm so confused."

"Well…Matt."

"Yeah, but didn't you say he was gonna have three groomsmen? Matt, Mason, and James. Boom. Done. In another life I should have been a wedding planner. Just kidding. I could not handle the stress of Justin's job."

"Me either." I picked up a fry. "I have a question for you. Do you think Rob will be pissed if Tanner comes to the wedding?"

"Yes."

"Yeah, I thought so. Matt's inviting him as his plus one. Something about bro-code and needing a wingman at a wedding."

"Oh…Rob's going to be so pissed."

"Do you think I should tell him?"

"Absolutely not!" Bee said. "That's Matt's drama, not yours. If he's crazy enough to bring Rob's enemy to the wedding, that's on him."

"True. But as a good bridesmaid…I'd tell Daphne."

Bee rolled her eyes. "It's not happening."

I sighed. "Yeah. I know." I ate my fry and then lifted my glass of water. "To being normal guests at the wedding and having the time of our lives."

"You know it," Bee said and tapped her glass against mine. "Shit, is that the time?" She looked at her watch. "I gotta run! I have a meeting in ten." She grabbed her wallet out of her purse.

"Go. I got this."

"You sure?"

"Positive." I waved her goodbye. Then I sat there awkwardly eating alone for a few minutes before pulling out my phone. I shot Daphne a quick text: "Need any help with any wedding planning today?"

It only took a minute for her one-word response to come back: "Nope."

Bee was right. None of us were going to be in this wedding.

***

I had to wait for James to go to work the next day in order to get a proper look at our new sex dungeon. It was way more intense than I'd even imagined. There were drawers lined with all sorts of toys. I lifted up what I thought might be the nipple clamps that Bee had mentioned at lunch yesterday. They looked very painful. I tossed them back in the drawer and closed it.

I ran my hand along the wooden altar. The craftsmanship on this thing was masterful. I'd compliment Matt on it, but I was literally never going to mention him knowing about this ever again. Hopefully he'd never mention it again either. *Fingers crossed.* I wasn't ready to die, and I'd definitely die of embarrassment if he ever brought this up again.

The room was pretty straightforward. I didn't know what all the toys were for. Or the chains hanging from the ceiling. But I was sure I'd find out soon. I couldn't help but laugh. In a few months we'd have a crib in here. I put my hand on my stomach. "What do you think, little dude? Are you a fan of the aesthetic?" I shook my head. "I didn't think so."

I sat down on the altar. "What do you think is going on with Uncle Rob and Aunt Daphne?" I looked down at my stomach, like he could actually respond to me. I need-ed some advice. Daphne was pretty much ghosting me. And Rob was ghosting James. We'd both offered to help since we had the time, and they'd both refused. Maybe I'd insulted Daphne somehow? I had kind of shoved Justin on them. But I was trying to help. And Rob loved Justin. That couldn't be it.

We'd also shoved the Hunter Creek Country Club on them. It was probably the combination of that and Justin. But I was just trying to help my future sister-in-law. Rob was one of my best friends, it was silly that we were being iced out of this.

"Maybe I should surprise them by bringing them din-ner or something? They're probably crazy stressed, right?"

No reply from my belly.

"Yeah, I thought it was a good idea too. Let's get to it." I groaned as I stood up. I was sore from the other night. And this extra weight wasn't doing me any favors. I kind of just wanted to take a nap. But…I had to make sure Rob and Daphne didn't hate us for some reason.

I wandered into the kitchen and opened the fridge.

"What are you searching for, honey?" Ellen asked.

I smiled. "I was thinking of making dinner for Rob and Daphne. I can drop it off so they have time for wed-ding planning stuff tonight. Do you know if we have any chicken?"

Ellen waved her hand through the air. "I've got it. And what a lovely idea." She practically pushed me out of the way.

"I can make it, Ellen."

"Nonsense. Just relax. Relaxation is good for the ba-by."

Relaxation was boring for me and the baby. But I knew Ellen wouldn't let me help. "Thanks, Ellen." I wandered into the family room. Actually…I was pretty tired. Maybe just a quick nap. I yawned and lay down on the couch.

***

"Penny," James said, his fingers brushing through my hair.

I slowly opened my eyes. "You're home early."

He raised his eyebrow. "No, I'm actually late. It's past 6."

"What?" I quickly sat up. Wow, I must have really been out. "We have to go. We're taking dinner to Rob and Daphne's place."

"We are?"

"Mhm. To make sure they know we're not meddling and just trying to help. And then Rob will ask you to be his best man and everything will be wonderful."

James smiled. "That sounds like meddling."

"No way. It's dinner. And it's just for them. We won't even stay."

He raised his left eyebrow again.

"Stop it," I said with a laugh. "I'm not meddling."

"Rob can choose whoever he wants in his wedding party. Daphne too."

"I know that." But Rob was certainly in the wrong for not asking James. And I was going to fix it. Meddling be damned. "Let's get going."

"Or…we could stay in just the two of us," James said. "I think Tanner and Matt left a lot of surprises in the nursery."

"If you ever mention Matt or Tanner again in the same sentence as nursery or sex dungeon, I'm going to lose my mind."

He laughed.

"I'm totally serious," I said. "I'll have to tie you up and torture you sexually as punishment."

He laughed again.

Which was appropriate. Because in my snooping I definitely hadn't found a way to overpower him and get him shackled. The sex dungeon was clearly designed by men. *Hmph.* I knew I could ask Bee to help me plan something out. But I kind of wanted to include Daphne too. To make her feel like she was part of the family. Not that a sex dungeon screamed "welcome to the family." Oh well. It would certainly be a bonding experience.

"Let's head over," I said and stood up. "We're on a mission."

"Meddling," James coughed.

"I am not."

He stood up and pulled me in closer. "You are." He pressed his lips against mine, barely holding back his smile. "Meddle away. I love watching you try to fix everything. It's very cute."

"I promise you'll be thanking me in thirty minutes when Rob asks you to be his best man."

"Mhm."

I was right about this. Rob was just stressed out by all the last-minute stuff. He'd relax with a homecooked meal and remember to pop the question to James. Easy peasy.

CHAPTER 18

Tuesday

Rob had only recently moved back to town. And just like everything Rob did…he didn't think twice about his living arrangements. He'd moved right in with Daphne.

I loved their place. But I knew Rob was already checking out new real estate. The place felt like Daphne. It did not feel at all like Rob. Rob was more of a penthouse kind of guy. Not a basement apartment kind of guy.

James and I made our way down the steps of the duplex. Which, I guess was actually a triplex since the basement had been converted into their apartment? Was a triplex even a thing? Either way, it was super cute.

"Do you think she's pregnant?" James asked at the exact same time I rang their doorbell.

"No. And keep your voice down." Their apartment was tiny. And I bet the walls were perfectly fine, but not exactly thick.

"I think he probably knocked her up."

"Why does everyone keep saying that?"

James smiled. "Who else is saying it?"

"Justin. He won't let it go. Bee too. Rob does everything spontaneously, including proposing. He just loves her."

"And the baby he put inside of her."

I laughed. "You're ridiculous."

"Wanna bet?"

I looked up at him. "On whether or not this is a shot-gun wedding or that you're ridiculous?" I shifted the casserole dish in my arms.

"The shotgun wedding thing. I'm not ridiculous in the slightest." He grabbed the casserole dish from me.

I glanced at the door. I never backed down from a bet. But...I was sure they were just about to open the door. And the last thing I wanted them to overhear when they were already stressed out was that people thought they were getting married out of obligation. "Oh, it's so on. But drop it right now." I nodded toward the door.

James put his finger on the doorbell. I could hear the ring throughout their apartment. Yup, thin walls.

But no one came to the door.

"I guess they're not home," James said. "Which is good, because I'm hungry and I really want to eat this." He lifted the foil on the edge.

I swatted his hand off it. "We'll just leave it for them."

James looked down. "There's probably rats here. We can't just leave a dish of food. It'll attract more of them."

"You are just as bad as your brother. This apartment is so cute. Just because you're used to high-end everything doesn't mean this place has rats!"

Daphne opened up the door just at that moment. A frown cut across her face.

Oh, fuck. I was defending her apartment, but I was pretty sure the end of my sentence was just: "This place has rats!" I cleared my throat. "Hey! I was just telling James how much I love your apartment."

She nodded, but I could tell she looked hurt.

"I mean it," I said. "You heard the end of my sentence, but I was actually saying that your place doesn't have rats."

"It's true," James said. "I think you may have just heard the end of what she said and it was completely out of context. I was the one that thought there might be rats if we left this dish on your doorstep." He lifted up the casserole dish. "We brought you dinner. We know you must be crazy busy with all the planning."

"Oh." She smiled, immediately believing him. "How thoughtful of you."

Not how thoughtful of *you guys*. Just James. *Gah*. Yeah, I was definitely not going to be a bridesmaid.

"Shit," Rob said and groaned.

I peered over Daphne's shoulder. Rob had just hit his elbow on a doorjamb as he was pulling on a shirt.

Okay, wow, we'd definitely just interrupted them banging.

"Anyway," I said. "We just wanted to drop this off and get out of your hair. Unless you needed help with anything?"

"Hey, guys," Rob said. "Did Ellen make that or did you?" he said and looked at me.

"Ellen."

Rob smiled and grabbed it out of James' hands.

"I'm not a bad cook," I said.

"I didn't say you were." He peeled back the foil and reached somewhere to the right and suddenly had a spoon.

Yes, their apartment was tiny. But cute, I swear it!

"I just really love Ellen's cooking," he said and ate a spoonful of the chicken pot pie. "So freaking good. It's actually perfect, because we just depleted a whole lot of energy." He winked at Daphne and her face turned crimson.

James cleared his throat. "Okay, well, enjoy. Catch you guys later."

"Unless you need help with anything," I added. "Wedding related or...anything. We're always here for you."

"Nope, we've got it all handled. We'll see you this weekend though. I think it's Mason's turn to pick the place."

It was Tuesday. They weren't planning on seeing us for four more days? They really didn't want our help? It felt like my stomach dropped. *Daphne hates me.* I just nodded. "Sounds good. See you this weekend, guys."

"Thanks again," Daphne said with a wave and a smile before the door slammed in my face.

I felt tears welling in my eyes. I quickly ran up the stairs and back to the sidewalk. Ian was parked, waiting for us, but I just needed a minute. So I walked straight past the car.

The autumn night air was finally chilly. So I could feel the hot tears slide down my cheeks. I quickly wiped them away.

"Penny, where are you going?" James said and caught my wrist.

"I looked like a complete ass."

"I love your ass." His hand squeezed one of my butt cheeks.

"Very funny. Daphne hates me."

"That's definitely not it." He touched the side of my face. "Penny, are you crying?"

"I love her apartment. And she thinks I'm an elitist monster. And I'm not. I just want to be her friend. And I freaking hate being hormonal. I'm acting like a crazy person. People don't get along with their sisters-in-law all over the world and I'm acting like it's a huge problem. God, I *am* elitist!"

"Baby." He pulled me in closer. "Everything is going to work out. I promise."

"What if we never see Rob anymore because she turns evil and keeps him away?"

James laughed. "They come to every hangout we have and every party we host. They're family. We're all family. Nothing will change that. Just don't scream 'rats' next time you see her."

I punched his arm.

"Ow," he said with a laugh. "Wow, mothers really do gain super-human strength."

I laughed too.

He cradled my face in his hands. "No more tears. Not over this, anyway. If they want us in their wedding party, they'll ask. If they don't, that's fine too. But you will not shed another tear on someone else's opinion of you. Especially someone who doesn't even really know you yet. Once she gets to know you, she'll love you. I promise. How could she not? You're amazing, baby."

God, he was so sweet. "I just…I like when people like me."

The corner of his mouth ticked up. "I think that's normal. But you're a Hunter now. And a lot of people hate us." He leaned forward and whispered in my ear. "Because we're elitist monsters."

I laughed. "You're not. I didn't mean that. You're really not." I wound my arms behind his neck and stared into his dark brown eyes. "But...there is this new restaurant and the reviews look really good..."

"So you're saying you want to get out of this rat-infested borough and use my last name to score us a table at the last minute?"

I smiled. "Exactly."

He turned to go back to the car, but I grabbed his hand.

"We can walk," I said.

He raised his eyebrow. "So we're not leaving this borough?"

"Don't you trust me?"

He shrugged. "Whatever, I'm starving."

We started walking down the block.

"Here it is," I said after a few minutes.

He looked up at the glowing neon sign. "Baby, I don't think you need a reservation here." He smiled down at me. "There aren't even any tables inside."

"I know."

"What were the rave reviews even about?"

I tried to hide my smile, but I couldn't. "Apparently they have really great pickles."

He laughed. "Let's go get you some pickles then." He pulled me inside the restaurant that was indeed new, but not at all high-end.

***

"Just a fair warning...you're going to have to pee all night." He climbed back into bed with the bowl of watermelon he'd just fetched me from downstairs.

"It's worth it." I pulled the bowl to my chest like the little watermelon gremlin that I was.

"Just like eating ten huge pickles on the sidewalk of Manhattan was worth it?"

"Mhm. But it was only five." I took a bite of watermelon. *Holy summery goodness.* I was glad we could still find watermelon now that it was fall. I'd been very worried about that. And I half suspected that James had paid our local market to keep them in stock. "Thank you," I quickly added. He had gone all the way downstairs to get it because I said I was too cold to leave our bed.

"You know I do whatever you ask when you distract me with those." His gaze wandered down to my exposed breasts.

We'd been in bed together ever since coming back from the restaurant. And I'd decided I no longer liked wearing clothing. Pregnancy changed people, right? I was now a nudist. A watermelon eating nudist. I took another bite and a little juice fell on one of my breasts.

James leaned down and licked it off, his eyes locking on mine.

I bit my lip. I wasn't sure which thing I wanted more right now. Another bite of watermelon or more of James' tongue. *Just kidding.* I wanted him. I was about to put the bowl down on the nightstand when James shifted lower.

Yes, please. Would it be acceptable to eat watermelon while James went down on me? I thought about it for a second. Nope, it was too weird.

But then he stopped far too soon and kissed my stomach. "Hey, baby girl." He put his hand on my stomach, splaying his fingers. "How are you doing in there?"

I smiled down at him.

"Good, good," he said. "You know...I feel like we should probably tell you...you're going to have a niece or nephew soon too."

I laughed. "James, Daphne isn't pregnant."

He smiled up at me. "I don't know...it sounds like our daughter agrees with me."

"We're having a boy."

"I think we need to bet on both of those things. What do I get if we have a girl? And what do I get if Daphne is knocked up?"

I laughed. "Good move separating them. Because it would have been a lot harder to win if you lumped them together."

"I'm the good negotiator in our family, remember?" He lifted his left eyebrow.

I made a few concessions to be nice to Justin and now I was a terrible negotiator? *No way.* I put my bowl of watermelon down. I needed to focus. "Okay, if I'm right about our son..." my voice trailed off. "You have to get another tattoo. Because your heart will beat for him too."

He smiled and kissed my stomach. "Your mother is terrible at this. I was already going to do that."

Damn it. "And if Daphne isn't pregnant...you have to use your charm to make her like me. Because I still really want her to like me even though you said it'll all work out."

He shook his head. "That was some truly awful negotiating, Penny. I was already going to do that too. Why'd you think I said it was all going to work out?"

I picked up a pillow and threw it at him.

He caught it before it hit him and laughed.

"Let me change my rewards then," I said.

"No way. You're locked in."

I stuck my tongue out at him.

"You better put that away unless you want it on my cock."

I kept it out.

He reached out and tapped on the tip of my tongue with his hand.

I laughed. "What do you want if you win?"

"I haven't decided yet. When I win, I'll just ask for whatever I want."

"What? You made me say mine. You have to tell me yours."

"Yeah…not happening, baby."

God, he was so tricky! "Well I want that too. I want to ask for whatever I want when I win. It's only fair."

He grabbed my ankle and pulled me down, dragging me across our sheets until he was looking down at me. "Fine…I'll allow it. If I get something right now in return."

"What do you want?"

He looked down at my stomach. "I was thinking it might be fun…over the next few months…" He looked a little embarrassed.

"What are you thinking?"

"I thought we could read Harry Potter to her. While she's still cooking in there. So she comes out loving it too."

I had no idea why, but my eyes started watering again. "I freaking love that idea."

"Yeah?"

"Let me go grab it." I was about to climb out of bed when he put his hand back on my stomach.

"I've got it." He reached over and pulled his old copy out of his nightstand.

I smiled. How long had he been waiting to ask me this? Because I definitely remembered that copy being in the library downstairs.

He pulled out a sheet of paper that was marking a page and crumpled it in his fist before tossing it to the side.

"We won't be needing that, will we?" he said and kissed my stomach.

Tears pooled in my eyes. I knew what was on that paper. It was an emancipation letter to his parents. He'd felt trapped. Lost. I put my hand on top of his on my stomach. No, our son or daughter would never feel that way. I already loved our baby with all my heart. And I knew James did too.

He smiled at me and then cleared his throat and started reading.

It was probably the most adorable thing I'd ever seen him do. Lying in bed on his stomach, his feet in the air, reading.

And I suddenly got the strangest image in my head of our son doing exactly that one day. Because we were having a boy. And he was going to come out loving Harry Potter. And looking just like James.

I picked my watermelon bowl back up and started eating as I listened to the familiar words. I didn't know it was possible, but I fell even more in love with James. Especially when he started doing different voices for the characters. And extra especially when he'd stop every now and then and kiss my baby bump.

Tonight it was easy not to be afraid of change. Because things were already changing and I was happier than ever. Plus, now I knew exactly what I wanted to be for Halloween this year. I couldn't wait for the Caldwell Halloween party.

CHAPTER 19

Saturday

"Interesting choice," I said to Mason as I sat down next to him in the crowded pub.

"Me?" He laughed. "Rob chose the place."

Honestly that made a lot more sense. It wasn't Rob's favorite restaurant with the busty waitresses, but the barmaids definitely screamed Rob. So did the fact that he'd chosen a pub. With high top tables that were super uncomfortable to sit at. My feet dangled off the edge of my stool. "But he chose last week."

"Yeah, he called us and asked us to switch with him," Bee said. She looked over at one of the barmaids. "Figures."

I laughed. "When Rob called you guys to switch, did he mention anything else at all?"

Mason took a sip of his beer. "And by anything else at all do you mean…"

"Yes, I mean did he ask you to be a groomsman?" James and I hadn't heard from Rob or Daphne since we'd dropped off their surprise dinner. And I couldn't help it…it was seriously bugging me.

James laughed as he slid into the seat next to mine. He handed me my glass of water. "You gotta let it go," he said.

"It's fine if Daphne doesn't ask Bee and me. I completely understand. But you and Mason? Rob said he was going to have three groomsmen. It's crazy if you guys aren't included."

"Maybe it's some guys from work," Bee offered.

Mason just shrugged.

There was no way Rob had found a best friend at Hunter Tech. He'd only been working there a couple of months and he'd known these guys his whole life. "It seriously doesn't bother you?" I asked him.

"Rob's like a little brother to me," Mason said. "And like my actual little brother...I may have tormented him a bit when we were both kids. Maybe he's still holding a grudge from that time I tossed him in the trashcan and closed the lid."

I laughed. "But that was forever ago."

"Hey." He smiled down at me. "It wasn't that long ago. You act like James and I are ancient."

"I do not."

"You kind of do," James said.

"Well, in my defense, when I was in..." my voice trailed off as I quickly did the math in my head. "When I was in middle school you guys were graduating from high school."

"Cradle robbers," Bee coughed into her hand.

I reached across Mason to high-five her.

"I think that says a lot more about the two of you than it does about me and James."

"Oh really?"

"Yup. Two words – daddy issues."

Bee slapped his arm and he laughed.

I rolled my eyes and turned toward my husband. "I do not have daddy issues."

"Your dad is great, but I don't want you thinking about him while we're in bed. As kinky as it sounds, I don't love the idea of you calling me daddy. Well...at least until you pop out my daughter. Maybe I'll get used to it then."

I smiled at him.

"Or maybe it's a sugar daddy thing," Mason said.

"Do not make me throw this in your face," Bee said and lifted her glass in the air, tilting it dangerously close to Mason's suit.

He leaned over and kissed her on the cheek.

"Sorry we're late," Rob said. He pulled out a stool for Daphne and then plopped down beside her. "What did we miss?"

"We were just talking about how all our girls are into sugar daddies," Mason said.

I smiled to myself. Mostly because it seemed like Mason was trying to push Rob's buttons. Because maybe, just maybe, he cared more about being a groomsman than he wanted to admit.

"Maybe your girls," Rob said and gave him a hard stare.

I cleared my throat. "So...this was your choice?" I asked. "Are you going to do another proposal tonight?"

He laughed. "No. That would be weird and unexpected. Right?"

At first I thought it was a rhetorical question, but based on the way he was staring at me, he definitely wanted an answer.

"Um...yeah," I said. "It would be weird."

"Good."

I just stared at him. "Good?"

"Yup, good."

Daphne was looking around the restaurant instead of at any of us.

I wondered if she was still upset about the rat comment. If I could just explain myself...

"Where's Matt?" Rob asked.

"I don't know," Mason said and pulled out his phone. "I haven't heard from him at all today. Actually, I haven't heard from him in a few days."

Me either. I hadn't heard from him since I caught him setting up a sex altar in my house. And honestly I was a little relieved that I didn't have to face him right now. Because I was still a little mortified about that.

Rob sighed. "He's probably with that annoying guy."

Mason just shook his head.

"What was his weird friend's name again? I can't quite remember," Rob said, although I was 100% sure he knew it.

"Tanner," I offered.

"Ah yes. What kind of name is that, anyway?"

"A pretty normal one."

"Psh."

"Speaking of Tanner," I said. "Have you guys ever met Nigel?"

Rob shook his head. "Who's Nigel?"

"His houseboy."

"Isn't that like a sex slave?" Mason asked.

I laughed, even though it looked like Mason was being serious. "No. It's like a servant. He was this cute little man in a butler's outfit."

"Yeah, that's a sex slave."

"No. He wasn't. More like an assistant I think."

"I knew it," Rob said. "That explains everything. Well…some things. Not all of it. Tanner's gay."

I laughed. "No. Definitely not. Almost every time I see him at events he's with at least one woman. Sometimes two."

"For show," Rob said. "He's overcompensating."

"Don't be jealous just because he's better at picking up women than you are," Mason said.

Yup, Mason was definitely a little bitter about this groomsmen thing.

Rob put his arm around Daphne's shoulders. "I have the most beautiful woman in every room," he said. Daphne smiled up at him.

"Speaking of Tanner," I said. "On a scale of one to ten, how upset would you be if Matt invited him as his plus one to your wedding?"

"Ten is the most upset?"

I nodded.

"A seventeen then. But I don't have to worry about that. Because Matt would never do that to me. We're best friends."

I bit the inside of my lip. Did he really not realize that by me asking I was confirming that it was in fact happening? "What if Matt needs a wingman at your wedding though?"

Rob laughed. "That's my job."

"But you'll be the groom."

"I can multitask."

Okay then. I really needed to talk to Matt. Or…not. Because I was still uncomfortable about the sex altar thing.

Fuck my life. My stomach churned. And for the first time in months it wasn't from morning sickness. I hadn't thrown up in a couple days and I was hoping it was gone for good this time. But I really hated secrets. I didn't want Matt to accidentally ruin Rob's wedding.

"Maybe we can set Tanner up with Justin," Rob said.

Everyone at our table just laughed.

"Rob, Tanner definitely isn't gay," James said. "Jealousy doesn't look good on you."

"I'm not jealous of Tanner or his butler boy."

"That sentence sounded jealous."

"Forget about Tanner. Who I don't care about at all. I'm just pissed because I'm getting married in one week and my best friend isn't here."

It was weird that Matt wasn't here. He wasn't usually late for our weekly hangouts. But he'd been off last week after the proposal. He'd almost gone home early instead of celebrating with us. Then he'd skipped out on the food tasting. And now he was a no-show. What was going on with him?

But my train of thought came to a stop as Matt walked up to our table. And walked may have been a little generous. It was more of a stumble. He was clearly drunk out of his mind.

"Hey," he said and collapsed into a seat. "What did I miss?"

"Where have you been?" Rob asked.

"I was right over there." He pointed to the bar.

Had he actually been sitting over there the whole time? All alone? Getting completely shitfaced instead of hanging out with us?

Rob pushed some breadsticks in front of him. "Well, sober up, buddy. It's going to be a night to remember."

That was the second weird thing he'd said. The first was about a second proposal. What was he up to?

Rob rolled up his sleeve to check his watch.

Yup. The watch was back. Which meant he was definitely up to something again.

He cleared his throat. "Oh, I forgot to tell you guys. Brendan's coming up for the wedding. I asked him to be a groomsman."

We all just stared at him.

"Brendan?" I asked. "The guy who lived in James' old apartment building on campus?"

"Good, you do remember. Yeah, he's one of my best friends. We got super close when I lived on campus. Figured he had to be one of my groomsmen. And I'm so glad he said yes."

I'm sorry, what? "You asked Brendan? Brendan whose last name I don't even know to be one of your *three* groomsmen?"

"Yeah, he's a great guy."

What the actual fuck was wrong with him! That meant that either James, Mason, or Matt was out of the wedding party. Or maybe all three of them. I wasn't even one of them and it felt like a slap in my face.

"Penny, didn't you make out with Brendan once or twice?" Matt asked as he took a huge sip of beer.

Thanks, drunk Matt. I really appreciate you bringing that up.

James lowered his eyebrows as he glared at Matt.

James excused himself from the table to go get another round of drinks. Mason went with him to help. And

Rob and Daphne wandered off to discuss something in the corner of the bar.

"Are you okay?" Bee asked Matt.

"Oh, I'm great," Matt said.

Bee reached out and grabbed his hand. "Really? Because you're not acting great."

"I'm fucking fantastic. You know, you don't have to pretend to care about me just because you're screwing my brother."

Bee removed her hand. "We're engaged," she said.

"Like that means anything."

Bee shook her head. "I'm going to go get you some water." She excused herself from the table.

Matt and I just sat there in silence for a moment.

Something was definitely bothering him. But I was a little scared to ask since he'd just bitten Bee's head off.

"Did you have fun in that room the other night?" he finally asked, breaking the silence. "Not as innocent as you look, huh?"

I could feel my face turning red. "You're in a destructive mood today."

"Yeah." He looked down at his half empty glass. "I hate weddings."

It was the first thing he'd said tonight that sounded sincere. "Why?"

He blinked and didn't answer.

"Why do you hate weddings, Matt?"

He shrugged, playing with the condensation on his glass.

I got it. Weddings kind of sucked when you were single. He was the last of our single friends. But that didn't mean he had to lash out at all of us. I'd been planning to tell him not to bring Tanner tonight. But I was pretty sure if he didn't bring Tanner this might be the version of Matt that showed up at Rob's wedding. And no one wanted that. I'd keep that tidbit of information to myself. Even though I hated secrets. A secret for one week wasn't so bad though.

"I'm here you know," I said. "If you ever want to talk about it."

"There's nothing to talk about."

It kind of seemed like there was...

"I gotta get out of here," he said. He downed the rest of his glass and slammed it on the table. "Later, Penny."

"Matt." I grabbed his hand before he could walk out.

He looked down at my hand and then back up to my face. His pupils were dilated. And I was worried it wasn't just alcohol in his system. I didn't care that he was being a jerk. I just needed to make sure he was okay.

"You shouldn't spend the night alone. Come back to our place."

For just a second his eyes fell to my lips.

I knew he was drunk. I knew he wouldn't remember any of this in the morning. But I immediately let go of his hand. I wasn't inviting Matt into my bed. I was offering him one of the guest rooms.

"I got him," Mason said and put his arm around his little brother's shoulders. "He can crash at our place tonight. Right, Bee?"

Bee nodded. Even though Matt had just been incredibly rude to her. But that's what family did.

"I need another drink," Matt said.

"No, you most definitely do not," Mason said. "Sorry, guys, we're going to cut out early. We'll see you later..."

"Wait!" Rob yelled. "One second." He cursed under his breath and stared back at the bar. "If you can just wait another minute…"

"This is ridiculous," Daphne said. "Just ask them."

"But…"

"I've been so stressed out about this all week. Enough is enough." She turned toward us. "I'm so sorry, guys. Justin told us that everyone is asking people to be in their bridal parties in elaborate ways these days. Like promposals and baby gender reveals. But we don't need barmaids to dance and fireworks to go off and for everyone in the bar to get a round on us. You guys are our best friends. And I'm so sorry it's such late notice, because everything is last minute with this wedding. But we'd be incredibly honored if you'd be in our bridal party. I'm sorry we didn't just ask you right away like normal people."

Rob laughed. "Eh. Who wants to be normal anyway? Besides, that was actually right on time. Great job, babe."

Music started blaring and all the barmaids stopped what they were doing. They climbed up on top of the bar and started doing some kind of dance where they swung each other around a lot. I wasn't sure how they didn't fall off.

I nudged James' side. "They asked."

He smiled down at me. "All of us."

"Wait, what about Brendan?" I yelled over the music blaring.

Rob put his arm around me. "Daphne wanted to ask her friends Kristen and Alina too. So I needed a fourth. What, you thought I was replacing one of my best friends or something?"

"Yes, actually," I said with a laugh.

"Never, Penny. I couldn't get married without all of you by my side." He kissed the top of my head. "Another round on me!" he screamed to the whole bar.

"Huzzah!" Matt yelled.

"Nope, we're going home," Mason said.

"But…"

"It's going to be a rough week," Mason said under his breath. He gave Rob a hug before guiding Matt out of the restaurant.

"We're going to be bridesmaids!" Bee squealed and hugged me. "I called it."

"You did not. You were just as worried as I was."

"Nah. O ye of little faith, Penny."

I laughed as she gave Daphne a hug too.

"I'm actually really curious about those fireworks now," James said. "Are those still happening? And if so…is it safer for us to get out of the bar before they go off?"

"Shit," Rob said. "I saved the best for last! Follow me!" He ran out of the bar.

All of us followed him out into the chilly fall air. But it felt more summery tonight. Because fireworks were going off in the distance in Central Park.

"Those are really for this?" James asked. "That's definitely elaborate."

"They're for you actually," Rob said. He dropped to his knee. "Be my best man, big bro?"

James laughed. "I already have my speech planned. My little brother's getting married!" he yelled to some people watching us on the sidewalk.

I laughed. It was the most ridiculous thing I'd ever seen in my life. Everyone around us definitely would have thought James and Rob were engaged if James hadn't clarified that his little brother was getting married. Or maybe now they just thought it was gay incest…

"Men," Daphne said. "I swear I wanted to tell you guys right away, but Rob swore me to secrecy and I'm bad at keeping secrets. So then I didn't want to hang out with you guys until we got to tell you because it was making me all nervous and I'm already nervous because of the wedding."

"I'm just glad you don't hate me," I said.

"Hate you? Penny, I've never met anyone more welcoming in my life. You already feel like the sister I never had.

I started blinking away tears.

"Don't cry…"

"It's my hormones, I swear. But Daphne, you feel like the sister I never had too."

She gave me a big hug. "Thank you. For all your help. And for making me feel like I'm already part of the family."

I was sobbing now. Because I was so happy. And relieved. Not just for myself. But for all my friends. This wedding was going to be freaking spectacular.

CHAPTER 20

Sunday

I glanced at the alarm clock. It was 3 in the morning. But James and I had forgotten to have sex before he fell asleep. It was the first day we'd missed since starting our five months of seduction. We'd stayed out so late with Rob and Daphne celebrating. I was pretty sure I'd gotten second-hand intoxicated just from the smell of booze in the air.

I knew James was exhausted. Or else he wouldn't have fallen asleep as soon as his head touched his pillow. But my blood was pumping faster than usual. It was like my body needed him. Like I couldn't sleep without him inside of me first.

For a second I just stared at him in the darkness. I wasn't sure I'd ever get sick of staring at him. I hoped I never would.

I wondered if this was how it would be once the baby was born. Being up in the middle of the night. James exhausted. I smiled to myself. If this was how our life would be once my son arrived, I'd take it. I'd wake up in the middle of the night countless times if it meant seeing James like this. He looked so at peace when he was sleeping.

It hadn't always been that way. He used to barely sleep at all before we met. He'd told me once that he had the best sleep of his life when he was beside me.

So maybe it was wrong to disturb him. But I couldn't sleep until I made good on my promises.

"James," I whispered.

He groaned.

It was tempting to wander into the sex dungeon and find something to tie him up with. But I wasn't sure if he'd love waking up to that. I knew he'd love waking up to this though. "I forgot to seduce you today."

He slowly opened his eyes, his eyelids heavy.

"I need you," I whispered.

"Come here." He reached out and pulled me closer. Turning me so that my back was to his front. He kissed the side of my neck, soft and slow. Torturously slow.

I tried to turn, but he grabbed my hip, keeping me in place.

"Baby, if you're going to wake me up in the middle of the night, you'll have to do whatever I was dreaming of." His fingers lazily bushed across my clit. "Mmm, you're so fucking wet."

I arched my back into him

He groaned.

"And what were you dreaming of?" I asked. Because if it was this…I was definitely okay with that. I could already feel how hard he was against my ass. Apparently I wasn't the only one that needed something before bed.

"You on all fours." His fingers brushed across my clit again. "Me fucking you from behind. Your back arched just like this." He buried his face in my hair like he was breathing me in.

I could give him that fantasy. Easily. This time when I moved he let me. I slowly pulled off his baggy t-shirt that I was sleeping in and positioned myself in the middle of the bed. I locked eyes with him. The way he was staring at me made me feel alive. I arched my back and bit my bottom lip.

He grabbed another pillow and propped it behind his head as he watched me.

That was not the reaction I was expecting. "What are you doing?" I laughed.

"Taking you in."

I tried to arch my brow and failed.

"God you're sexy."

I loved that he found me sexy even when I wasn't doing something quite right. I jutted my ass farther into the air and he groaned. At least I could do this.

"Put your hands on the headboard," he said, his eyes trailing over my ass. "You're going to want something to hold on to."

"Yes, Daddy." I tried to hold in my laughter. I'd been trying to figure out the perfect way to tease him about his comment earlier. This seemed like the perfect opportunity.

He laughed. "Yeah, definitely not my kink."

"If you say so, Daddy."

He laughed again. "Penny, put your hands on the headboard now. And if you call me Daddy one more time I'll have no choice but to spank you."

I pressed my lips together as I crawled forward. I wrapped my hands around the bedpost. "Better, Daddy?"

His palm gently ran over my ass, caressing me. "You know perfectly well that I prefer when you call me professor." He slapped my ass hard.

I gasped.

He slapped me again and then massaged my sore ass cheek. "Now, let's try this again. Do you have something to say to me?"

"I'm sorry, Professor Hunter."

He groaned, his fingers digging into my ass cheek. "I'm a sick fuck, you know that right? You married a man who gets hard as soon as you call me that."

I looked at him over my shoulder. "I'm pretty sure we were made for each other. Because I'm soaking wet just thinking about my professor fucking me."

"Your husband," he corrected, massaging my ass again. "You're dripping at the thought of your husband fucking you so hard that you won't be able to walk tomorrow."

"Is that a promise?"

"Oh, Penny. You know better than to question me." He slammed into me from behind.

I moaned. When I'd awakened him, I'd been expecting him to make love to me, barely awake. Slow and lazy. I had no idea why I'd expected that. James never fucked me slow and lazy. Well, sometimes slow. When he made love to every inch of my body. But never lazy.

He pulled my hair, making me arch my back even more.

Oh God.

CHAPTER 21

Friday

"That's what you're wearing?" James asked, his eyes landing on my breasts.

Every day I had a harder time hiding my little baby bump. So tonight I was embracing it. But I knew everyone else at this thing was going to be dressed sexy. I knew I'd fit right in with my super low-cut dress and push-up bra. I loved torturing my husband. "You don't like it?" I asked as I pulled on high heels.

He lowered his eyebrows. "Change. Now."

I laughed.

"I'm serious, Penny."

"I don't fit in anything else. This dress is stretchy."

"What about the dress you wore last weekend?"

I stared at him. "Exactly. I just wore it last weekend."

He shook his head. "I'll buy you a million stretchy dresses tomorrow."

I loved when he was overprotective of me. This jealous side of him made me want him all over again. And we'd literally just had sex an hour ago. I grabbed his face in my hands and tilted it down toward me. "It's just a silly bachelorette party. People do stuff at bachelorette parties they regret because they drink too much." I let go of his face and touched my stomach. "I'm pregnant. So I won't be partaking in that. Which means you have nothing to worry about. I'm the one that should be worried about you."

He smiled down at me. "Nothing could ever tempt me away from you."

"Are there going to be strippers?"

He laughed. "Probably. It's Rob."

So true. If Rob went that over the top for the proposal and the bridal party-posal, he was definitely going to have strippers at his bachelor party. "See. I'm the one that should be nervous."

"You don't think there will be strippers at the bachelorette party too? You are adorably, naïve, Penny."

I laughed. "Daphne doesn't seem like the stripper type."

"Doesn't Justin though?"

I pressed my lips together. He had a really good point there. "I still don't know why Justin wanted to come to this. You'd think partying the night before the wedding would just make tomorrow more stressful. Aren't there last-minute things he should be doing?"

"When I talked to Rob yesterday, he said everything was already set. They really pulled this shotgun wedding off."

I laughed. "Daphne isn't pregnant. They're just in love."

"Oh, she's definitely pregnant."

"No way. I'm winning that bet. Although...I said if you won that you'd have to use your charm to make her like me. And clearly she already likes me. So I get to change my terms."

"I don't know..."

I slapped his arm. "Yes I do. And I get to tell you what I want later, just like you do."

"None of that matters. Because my soon-to-be sister-in-law is most definitely knocked up."

"You're ridiculous."

"Maybe so." He pulled me in close. "I'm going to miss you tonight."

I'm pretty sure the last night I spent alone without him was the night before our wedding a few months ago. I'd had a little slumber party with my bridesmaids. Daphne had so much fun at mine that she wanted to do it all over again. So I wouldn't get to sleep in my husband's arms tonight. "I'm going to miss you too. Maybe we can sneak away like we did the night before our wedding."

"Hmm…" he leaned down and placed a soft kiss against my lips. "Keep your phone on you. I'll figure something out. But I have to get going…the limo is probably already downstairs."

"You never told me what you planned for tonight," I said as James pulled on his leather jacket. God, I loved that jacket. And I hated any woman who saw him in it tonight. He was droolworthy.

"That's because I didn't plan it."

"But you're the best man…"

"I know. But Justin called me and insisted he had the whole thing already planned out. He just said to get in the limo and the itinerary would be waiting for me."

"Why the heck would Justin want to plan the bachelor party but attend the bachelorette party?"

James shrugged. "Because he likes male strippers."

True. "Either way, it's extra impressive that he was able to plan the wedding, the bachelor party, and the bachelorette party all in record time. I was a little worried since Alina isn't as familiar with the city, but he took the bachelorette party right off her maid-of-honor plate."

"That was nice of him."

"Well, Justin is the best. Which is good. Since he's throwing our baby shower."

"He is?"

"Mhm. Part of my stellar negotiating skills that you're mad jealous of."

James laughed. His phone buzzed in his pocket and he pulled it out. "The limo is waiting. I'll text you later if I can get away, okay?" He leaned down and kissed me. "And you should probably change," he added before walking out of the bedroom.

I glanced at the clock. My friends would be here any minute. I didn't have time to change. Besides, I was a bridesmaid tonight. And bridesmaids were supposed to dress like this. I walked over to the floor-length mirror. Hmm. Maybe it was a little too low-cut. I guess I could change real quick...

My phone started ringing.

Too late now.

***

I climbed into the limo. Justin was the only one inside so far. He downed his glass of champagne and then hugged me.

"Get ready for the night of your life!" he screamed.

Wow, he was already very drunk. "Shouldn't you be saying that to Daphne?"

The limo pulled back into the NYC traffic.

"Penny." He put his hand on his chest. "What do you take me for? Tonight will be each and every one of your favorite nights ever. I'm a party planner. And I've aced it. It's the bachelorette party to end all bachelorette parties."

I laughed. "Well, I can't wait. What are we doing?"

"It's a surprise, baby doll. Champagne?" He started pouring himself another glass.

"I'm pregnant."

He laughed. "I thought you were allowed to drink a little on special occasions."

"I'm not sure that's a thing."

"Well, darn. Don't worry though. This will still be fun sober. I think. I don't really know. It all came together last minute."

"But you just said it was the bachelorette party to end all bachelorette parties."

"Yeah. It should be. But there are so many moving pieces. And I had a whole bachelor party to plan too because James absolutely insisted on it."

Did he though?

"And getting everyone super drunk was part of how I was pulling it all off. I'm running on empty. I have the biggest wedding of the season tomorrow and I haven't slept in three days."

"Justin…that's…not good. Maybe you should take a nap?"

"Nonsense. I'll sleep when I'm dead."

I was starting to realize that Justin lived off of caffeine and champagne. And…stress. I didn't know how he did it. I wanted a nap and I'd already taken one this afternoon.

We pulled to a stop in front of Bee's place.

She was dressed just like I thought she'd be. A sparkly mini-dress with sky high heels. The kind of dress I would have 100% worn if I wasn't pregnant.

She climbed into the limo. "Your tits look amazing," she said to me. "And Justin, you look divine as always."

Justin smiled. "I love you. You know that right? I'm obsessed. When do I get to plan your wedding to that handsome lover of yours?"

Bee laughed and plopped down on the seat between us. "I think we've had enough weddings this year. But I'll keep you updated."

"You better." He handed her a glass of champagne.

"So what are we doing tonight?" Bee asked.

"It's a surprise." He tilted her drink up so that she'd have to take a sip. "Drink, drink, drink!"

Bee laughed.

If he was trying to get everyone shitfaced before we even arrived anywhere...I was starting to wonder if all Justin had planned was this limo ride.

Honestly that sounded kind of good to me. The limo screeched to a stop at a red light. I put my hand on my stomach. Sudden stops like that over the past few months had always made me nauseous. But tonight...I felt fine. I breathed a sigh of relief. I was really happy that I hadn't had morning sickness all week. It was like a wedding miracle. For a minute there, I'd been wondering how to hide a brown paper bag in a bouquet. But now I had nothing to worry about. *I hope.*

The limo came to another stop in front of Daphne's place. Two girls I didn't recognize climbed into the limo.

"You must be Alina and Kristen," I said and put out my hand. I didn't know them, but I'd heard fun stories. Daphne had been friends with them in college. But I definitely didn't know which one was which. Had Daphne said Kristen was the taller one?

And then it hit me. I'd been so consumed thinking about James, the baby, and the wedding, that I didn't put it together that this was Kristen. *Kristen Kristen!* Daphne's friend that used to stalk my husband when they were all in college. At least, that's how James put it. He'd almost had to issue a restraining order against her. And she'd been at James' bachelor party at the Blue Parrot Resort too. Where Rob and Daphne had met. Had she hit on my husband there too?

"It's so nice to meet you. I'm Alina," the blonde one said and shook my hand.

So that meant Kristen was the taller one with brown hair. I thought about maybe saying something about Kristen's silly crush from ages ago. To just laugh off the whole situation right away so nothing would be awkward. But maybe it was better if they didn't know that I knew. Right? I put out my hand for Kristen. "Nice to meet you." Yup, this was a better way to handle it. Just pretend I didn't know her.

Kristen high-fived me instead of shaking my hand. "Thank you so much, all of you, for helping our girl out like this at the last minute."

"Speaking of our girl...where is Daphne?" Justin asked. "We're already running late!"

Someone needed to take away his champagne.

Kristen laughed. "You know Daphne...she was having trouble deciding on an outfit."

"I thought she only had trouble deciding on menu items," Justin said.

She laughed. "Where did you get that idea? She's indecisive about everything."

Justin stared daggers at me.

Okay, fine. Daphne was a little indecisive about some other things. But not the same way she was with food. I hadn't lied. I'd just...sugar coated the truth. Sue me. "I'm sure she'll be out any minute."

"So I have to ask," Kristen said and turned back to me. "What's it like being married to Professor James Hunter?"

Alina kicked her shin.

"Ow! I wasn't being bad. I was just asking a question."

"Ignore her," Alina said. "Kristen had a crush on James in college. But it's over now. Because she has an incredibly sweet boyfriend."

Kristen shrugged and grabbed a glass of champagne. "Tim is wonderful. And perfect in every way. Including how he understands the need for hall passes."

Alina kicked her again.

"Stop it," Kristen said and grabbed her shin. "I was joking. Obviously I'm not going to try to sleep with Penny's husband. That would be inappropriate. Unless she were to give me permission. Oh! Maybe we could swap."

There was an awkward silence.

I was certainly not going to give this crazy woman permission to sleep with my husband. Besides, James wasn't into tall, tan girls, with big breasts and pretty faces. I swallowed hard. He wasn't. I was just getting in my head because my tummy was growing and I looked short and squat next to these volleyball players.

I cleared my throat. "I'm going to go check on Daphne." I climbed out of the limo. I knocked on Daphne's door but no one answered. I slowly opened it. "Daphne?" I called.

Still no response.

I walked into her place and wandered into the back where her bedroom was. She was sitting on her bed in the middle of about 50 dresses.

"The one I wanted to wear doesn't fit."

"That's okay."

"I'm fat! For my wedding!"

I laughed. "Daphne, you look amazing. I'm the one that's going to be fat for your wedding." I pointed to my baby bump.

She finally smiled. "There's a difference between pregnant and fat. You're glowing."

"I don't know about that. I feel huge." I plopped down next to her on the bed. "Especially next to Kristen. I really wish I never knew about her crush on James."

"Oh my gosh." She grabbed my hand. "Please just ignore anything Kristen says tonight. She and Alina were pre-gaming and I swear she's already drunk. And when she's drunk she…"

"Talks inappropriately about my husband?"

"Bingo. I'm so sorry. She's incorrigible."

"It's fine. I'm used to women wanting to sleep with James."

Daphne laughed. And then she groaned. "Wait, it doesn't go away once you're married? Because I could seriously knock some girls out the way they look at Rob."

"No, it doesn't go away."

"I guess that's what we get for marrying the Hunter brothers."

I smiled. "It's worth it though."

"So worth it." Daphne grabbed one of the dresses off her bed and pulled it on. "Thank you. For calming me down."

"Hey, that's what sisters are for."

She smiled at me. And then tears started to well in her eyes.

"Daphne, don't cry. You look beautiful." And she did. If I thought Bee's dress was sparkly, this thing was off the charts. And she looked perfectly skinny.

"It's not that." She quickly wiped under her eyes so her mascara wouldn't run. "I just...I really...I always pictured my brother would be here for my wedding. For all the important stuff, you know?" Her lower lip started trembling. "All the big things."

Oh, Daphne. My heart ached for her. I stepped forward and hugged her. Because it was all I could do. Suddenly her freak out made a whole lot more sense. She wasn't nervous about marrying Rob. Or worried she was getting fat.

"I wanted him here," she said, a few of her tears landing on my shoulder. "How did he not know how much I wanted him beside me?"

"He knew." I hugged her tighter as I blinked back my own tears. She was missing her brother because tomorrow was one of the most important days of her life. And she wished he was still around to see it. He'd had addiction problems like James. But his story had ended in tragedy.

"I miss him most on holidays. And things like this." She sighed and hugged me back. "You should see me on Christmas. Literally every Christmas since he passed. I'm a mess."

"I know it's not the same at all but...I do understand. When I almost lost James? It was like a piece of my heart shattered. And I don't know what I would have done if he never woke up. You're so strong, Daphne. But you don't have to be strong alone anymore. Because we're you're family now too. And I promise, we're not going anywhere."

She laughed even though it was tinged with sadness. "You know?" she said as she stepped back. "If you haven't noticed…I can be a little indecisive."

"Oh? Really?"

She laughed. "Don't even with me."

I laughed.

"I thought I'd be second guessing this crazy wedding by now. I fell in love with Rob so hard and so fast, you know? But all of you guys made it easy for me to be sure I made the right choice. I think I needed this more than I ever realized. A big family."

"And now you have it." I smiled at her. "How about we go get this insane bachelorette party over with so we can get you down the aisle."

"Deal." She wiped under her eyes once more. "Let's go party in style!"

"That's my girl."

She laughed and looped her arm through mine.

I wasn't sure why I ever thought she hated me. She'd quickly become one of my very best friends.

CHAPTER 22

Friday

The music was so loud that I could feel it vibrating through my whole body. I always loved dancing. But I loved it significantly more when my husband was here. And when my feet weren't swollen. And when I wasn't worried that my baby would now pop out addicted to techno music. I slid onto a stool at the bar.

Justin was jumping up and down in the middle of the dance floor.

"What are you drinking?" the guy next to me at the bar asked.

I put my left hand on top of my baby bump and turned to him. My engagement and wedding bands shimmered under the lights. "I'm not. But thanks."

"What are you doing in a place like this?"

"One of my friends is getting married tomorrow." I turned on my stool back toward the dance floor. "Right there." I pointed to Daphne who was now wearing a shimmery tiara and a bright pink sash that read: "Bride-to-be."

"Are any of them single?"

I was about to say 'no,' but pressed my lips together. Kristen had made a few more comments about my husband. And honestly, I'd rather her be drooling over someone else. Like this guy. "See that tall one with brown hair?"

"Yeah." He smiled.

"She's the only single one."

"Noted. Thanks." He disappeared into the crowd.

Payback was a bitch. Not that it was really payback. Kristen could just tell him I was mistaken. That she was happily dating someone. But knowing what little I knew about Kristen, she'd probably spend the rest of her night grinding against him. I didn't care what she did, as long as she didn't do it with James.

Speaking of which…I pulled out my phone, hoping I'd have a text from him. I really wanted to meet up with him later. But I only had one text and it was from Melissa: "Call me."

I looked back at my friends. They were all still dancing. I grabbed my purse and headed out the doors to an alley. I walked a little farther until I couldn't hear the music and called Melissa.

"Oh my God, you won't even believe what happened today!" she screamed.

I laughed. "It can't be as crazy as my day. I can't believe I haven't talked to you in a couple weeks. So much has happened."

"You first," Melissa said. "Because my news is going to blow your mind and we won't be able to talk about anything else."

"Well…I'm at Daphne's bachelorette party. Because she and Rob are getting married tomorrow."

"Tomorrow? When did that happen?"

"They planned the whole thing in two weeks."

"Oh, so she's pregnant?"

I laughed. "Everyone has been saying that. But no…they're just in love."

"Well, good for him. I never thought he'd settle down. How is my niece or nephew?"

I looked down at my stomach. "He doesn't like techno music." I hope.

Melissa laughed.

"Wait. Melissa, isn't it like…almost 5 am there?" She was on an extended work trip in London.

"Yes it is."

"What are you doing up?"

"That's what I wanted to tell you! You won't even believe who I ran into at my dinner meeting tonight."

I honestly had no idea. "Who?"

"Josh."

"Josh? As in college Josh?"

"Yes. What are the odds that we'd run into each other in London of all places?"

"So slim."

"I know. It's fate, right? We spent the whole night just talking and walking around the city. It was amazing. And he just dropped me off at my hotel." She sighed and I could picture her falling backward onto her bed. "I think I'm still in love with him."

I opened my mouth and then closed it again. "Really?"

"It felt like the very first night I hung out with him all over again. We caught up and just talked the night away. I still remember that first night I hung out with him perfectly. I had this feeling in my bones that it would be my best year ever. And in so many ways it was. Until everything crumbled at the end of spring semester."

Melissa had not taken that breakup well. It was probably one of the reasons why she'd ended up in Rob's bed. "So the spark is still there?"

"Girl, it's not a spark. It's freaking fireworks!"

I leaned against the wall of the club. "I'm so happy for you."

"But he goes back to Texas tomorrow night. We're supposed to hang out all day tomorrow and I...I don't know how I'm going to walk away again."

"Who says you have to walk away?"

"Because I still have work here. And as soon as it's done I'm flying back to NYC."

"I thought your job had offices in Texas?"

"Stop it," Melissa said. "I can't drop everything and move to Texas just because I felt a dumb spark."

"Nope. Fireworks. Don't change your words on me."

She groaned. And then she was quiet for a long moment. "I really never stopped, you know? I was so focused on school and then finding a job and I just...never really processed it. I never stopped to think about how much I freaking missed him."

"I know." I'd felt so awful knowing they'd broken up, knowing that I wasn't in town to be there for her. She'd had little flings with Rob, Matt, and Tyler. But they were just that. Flings. Because she'd never gotten over Josh. And all those guys hadn't been looking for something serious either. "This could be your second chance to do it right."

"Just for the record, you're encouraging insanity, Penny."

"I'm just a believer in love."

She slowly exhaled. "I'm going to marry him this time."

I smiled. "I don't doubt it. All I have is one question. Did he kiss you goodnight?"

"Yes. And it was even better than I remembered."

"Well, you have your answer. He's feeling it too. I think you have to go for it, Melissa."

She squealed and I held the phone away from my ear.

"Keep me updated, okay? I gotta get back inside."

"Love you!" she said.

"Love you back." I ended the call and looked down at my phone. Talking to her reminded me of Tyler. I hadn't heard from him in weeks either. But I also wasn't going to call him. Because I was giving him the space he needed to be happy. I hoped he and Hailey were doing well. And I hoped that one day they'd move back to the city. I had this silly idea in my head that our children could grow up together.

I looked down at my stomach. "That's silly, right?"

My belly did not respond.

"Who knows, little guy. Maybe Tyler and Hailey will have a little girl and the two of you will live happily ever after."

No response.

"I can already see it," I said. "I can already picture you coming into this world and making it so much brighter." I smiled to myself. I knew I looked insane in this back alley talking to no one at all. And yet...I was really freaking happy tonight.

I turned to go back inside, but thought better of it. A few more minutes of fresh air would be nice. I shot James a quick text: "Hopefully we're heading back to the hotel soon. Do you know when you guys will be there?"

I waited a few seconds for his response, but none came. They'd probably be another hour at least. Hopefully my friends would wrap it up soon. I was exhausted.

But still happy. How could I not be? Two of my best friends were getting married tomorrow. Melissa was happy. James and I were expecting a baby. How could things get any better than this?

I turned around to go back inside the club, and someone threw a bag over my head.

CHAPTER 23

Friday

I screamed at the top of my lungs.

The man who bagged me responded by lifting me off the ground and throwing me over his shoulder.

"Let me down!" I screamed.

He started moving.

"Help!" I started thrashing around, but he caught my arms in one hand and put his other arm firmly around the back of my thighs so I couldn't knee his dick.

Damn it! Why hadn't I gone right for his nuts? What was wrong with me?

The only thing I could manage to do was kick my feet. He didn't seem to have any regard for the safety of his shins. Or maybe he did, because he just shifted me. I thought he was going to drop me on my head. Instead, I was just hanging down farther on his back so he could wrap his hands around my ankles.

I had the use of my hands back, but I was completely disoriented and...*Oh no.* Please, for the love of God don't let the morning sickness come back right now! I swallowed hard, hoping to somehow manage not to throw up. I took a deep breath.

"Help!" I screamed again.

But I'd been alone in the alley. And the club music was too loud. *Oh God.* I'd jinxed myself terribly. I'd just said how amazing everything was and now I was going to be murdered on the city streets.

There would be no wedding. I'd never get to see Melissa be happy. And this baby?

No. No fucking way. I would not let anything happen to my baby. "Help me!" I yelled even louder. I started hitting the back of his legs with my fists. "Help!" I was not going to be murdered today. Because it wasn't just me I had to protect. I thought about my baby and the little boy I'd imagined him becoming. Brown eyes just like his father's. The little goblin running around our living room. Long afternoons watching cartoons and snuggling.

"Put me down!" I screamed, tears trailing down my cheeks. But that strategy wasn't working. And now I was choking, trying not to puke everywhere. So I stopped hitting him. "Please. I won't tell anyone what happened. Just let me down. Do you want money? You can have anything you want in my purse. Please just let me go."

He didn't respond.

"Someone help me! I'm pregnant! He's hurting my baby!" I slammed my fist into the back of his leg. For a second, I thought he was going to fall over. Instead, he just shifted me again.

And my belly lurched.

No.

I tried to swallow it down, but I couldn't. I morning sickness-ed myself all over the stupid bag on my head. And then I just kept throwing up because of the smell. And...

"Gross," the guy said. "I did not sign up for this."

My stomach lurched again.

I heard a car door open.

"I don't think you want her in there," the man said. "She just…threw up."

He wasn't going to throw me in the back of a car and murder me?

"What?! Why'd you make her vom?!"

I'd recognize Justin's voice anywhere. "Justin? What the hell!" He was a dead man. I reached out like I could strangle him, even though I couldn't see him.

He yelped. "I was just trying to get everyone's hearts racing before the main event!" He tore the bag off my head and screamed at the top of his lungs as the bag and some vomit splattered onto the sidewalk.

I just stared at the city sidewalk from my upside-down vantage point and tried not to throw up again. I groaned.

"Put her down!" Justin demanded.

Now that I knew I was safe, I didn't want to be put down. "No," I groaned. Because being put down meant turning right side up. And right side up meant my stomach churning again and the vomit going on me instead of the sidewalk. Not that it mattered. I could see it in the tips of my hair.

I'd been scared to death. And then relieved. And now so gross. I started crying.

"Justin, what the hell?" Daphne said as she climbed out of the limo, holding a clean bag that must have been on her head.

"Oh my God, Penny, are you okay?" Bee said and stumbled out of the limo next to Daphne.

"Here, let me see if I can help," Daphne said. "If we put this bag around her hair…"

"No, I've got this," said Justin. "Get that bag back on your head and your bachelorette butt back in the car!" He turned to Bee. "You too you blonde Goddess."

And then he tore his shirt off, one of the buttons almost hitting my eye. He wrapped up my hair, turban style, before the big strong kidnapper man set me down on my feet. Justin reached into my turban and pulled out a fancy satin scarf. He dotted my face with it.

"You okay?" he asked.

"No!" I slapped his hand away. "Not even a little. What the heck were you thinking?"

"I was thinking exactly what I said…that I wanted to get everyone's hearts racing before the main event."

I just stared at him. "And what's the main event?"

"A surprise." He put his hands out to the side and waved his fingers.

"Jazz hands don't make everything better."

"I know. And it's freezing out here." He put his hands over his nips.

He was being ridiculous. He wasn't even shirtless. He was wearing some kind of shiny black mesh tank top thing. Sure…it didn't look warm. But at least he wasn't covered in vomit.

"Can I please just go home?" I asked.

"What? No! Never! The night has barely even begun."

"It's almost midnight."

"Exactly. Midnight is when the fun truly begins. Here's what we're going to do. We're going to climb back in that limo and drive you home so you can freshen up and we can both change. James won't mind if I borrow a shirt, right?" he asked, even though I knew he wasn't really asking. Because he climbed back into the car without waiting for a response.

I groaned. How had the night barely even begun and I already looked like I was a hungover mess? I didn't really have a choice here though. I was at Justin's mercy. So I climbed into the limo.

Everyone was quiet.

The cologne wafting off Justin's shirt smelled amazing. But I was pretty sure nothing could mask the stench on me. I had somehow managed not to get anything on my dress, but once vomit was near anything…it all smelled the same.

"Are you okay?" Bee asked.

I shook my head. I wanted to be a trooper. I really did. But it was really hard when I was focusing so hard on not vomiting again.

Alina hiccupped and took another sip of champagne. "This is officially the craziest night ever. Well, one of the craziest nights. How do I always get in these crazy situations?" She tossed her bag to the side.

Kristen laughed. "Because you hang out with me."

"Okay…um…" Daphne looked at me. "I think we should call it a night, right? It's getting late anyway and…"

"Nonsense," Justin said. "We're just making a short pit stop at James and Penny's place. And then the night will continue as planned. Driver! Take me to destination #2!"

"Wait!" I turned to Justin. "You just said I could go home. I can't go anywhere like this." I gestured to my whole body. I was a fucking mess. I needed a shower or five. And a change of clothes. And I needed a whole tube of toothpaste in my mouth.

"Yeah." He looked confused. "We're going to your place," he said. "I just said that."

"No, you said destination #2."

He just blinked at me. "Did I? I'm pretty sure I said go to Penny's place."

"You did not."

His eyes started darting everywhere but at me.

"So let me get this clear. *My apartment* is destination #2 on the itinerary for tonight?"

His eyes grew round like he'd gotten caught in a lie. He downed his glass of champagne. "I named everyone's homes a destination number. For practical reasons. In case something crazy unexpected like this happened. I'm a planner, Penny."

I turned back to the driver. "What destination number is Daphne's apartment?"

He looked at Justin and then at me. "Um…"

I turned back to Justin. "Liar."

"Me?" He gasped. "Never."

But he still wasn't looking at me. And he was acting like a big fat liar. "Justin, I swear to God. Did you seriously have this planned?!"

He pressed his lips together and then gave me a saucy little smile. "I'm sorry, Penny. But you know I love exploring people's closets. You can learn so much about them. And I knew if I asked if I could sit in James' closet for thirty minutes you'd freak. Much like you are right at this exact moment. So technically I was right and we should just move on."

"You…you knew I'd get sick?"

"I suspected. You're four or so months along, right? So…morning sickness."

"A few hours ago you didn't even know if pregnant women could drink. How do you know so much about morning sickness?"

"I was putting on a show so you wouldn't suspect me. Clearly I did a good job."

"So let me get this straight. You planned out this night in part to explore my husband's closet?"

"Sounds fun to me!" Kristen said.

I shot her a death glare and turned back to Justin. "Not okay, man."

"I think everything is working out perfectly, actually," he said. "Destination #2!" he told the driver again.

The limo pulled away from the curb.

"I'm so excited to see his closet," Kristen said.

"Girl, same," Justin said and squealed.

"I am so sorry," Daphne said.

Bee started laughing. And once Bee started laughing after a few glasses of champagne, she rarely ever stopped. Eventually she had me laughing too.

"I thought I was going to die," I said through my laughter.

"Because of the smell?" Bee asked.

"No!" I started laughing harder. "Because of the whole getting bagged and thrown over someone's shoulder thing. Who were those guys?"

"Strippers," Justin said.

Bee started choking on her champagne. "Then why were they kidnapping us instead of stripping for us?"

"Because I paid double. Raphael is going to be very upset about all the kicking though." He gave me a hard stare. "His body is his livelihood, Penny. That was incredibly rude of you to do all that squirming. I hope you're planning on leaving him a big tip. Because he looked pissed with a capital P."

"Me?" I laughed. "I think *you* owe him a big tip. Who pays strippers to be kidnappers?"

"Well I don't know how to hire actual kidnappers. I'm a party planner. Not a murderer," Justin said. "You're welcome, ladies. It's fun to be manhandled by hotties, right? Besides, it was pretty obvious it was part of a thing."

"For us," Bee said. "Because we saw them coming through the crowd and they bagged us all together. But Penny was outside. She must have been fucking terrified."

"Hmm," Justin said. "I hadn't thought about that. You thought you were actually being kidnapped?"

"Yes! Why do you think I morning-sickness-ed all over myself?"

"Because I told Raphael to be extra shaky with you. So I could get into your husband's closet. We already talked about all this. New topic. Which Hunter brother is packing the most?"

"How are we supposed to know that?" Daphne said. "I've never seen James naked."

"Here's how we do it." He put his hands close together and slowly started moving them apart. "Tell me when to stop." He kept going. "Holy anaconda!" He kept going. "Good Lord, girl how do you fit that inside of you?" he asked when his hands were two feet apart.

"I'm sorry...what is happening right now?" Daphne asked.

"He wants you to tell him how big Rob is," Bee said. "You have to tell him when to stop." She gestured back to Justin's hands which were still moving farther apart.

"Oh." Daphne laughed. "Right around when you said Holy anaconda. But are you talking flaccid or erect? Because if you mean erect…"

Justin pretended to faint. "How can he be a grower *and* a shower? I think I'm in love!"

I laughed.

"Your turn," he said to me and started moving his hands apart again.

"Justin, you're literally about to go through James' underwear drawer. I think that's enough of an intrusion for one evening."

"Oh, so he's smaller than anaconda boy?"

"I definitely didn't say that."

Justin smiled. "I'm satisfied with that answer." He turned to Bee. "Your turn. And also have you seen the little one's?"

"I'm sorry…what?" Bee asked. "Mason does not have a little penis."

Justin laughed. "Oh, I don't doubt that. I meant the little Caldwell's member. Whatever his name is. I always forget because he's not important to me. It doesn't matter. Let's focus on Mason's. And go." He started moving his hands farther and farther apart until the whole limo was laughing.

CHAPTER 24

Friday

I knew everyone was waiting for me, so I wrung out my hair one more time. Part of me wanted to slap Justin for planning out this destination #2 crap. I thought we were friends. I took a deep breath. But honestly it didn't matter how disheveled I looked. Tonight wasn't about me. And I didn't want to delay Daphne's bachelorette party any longer.

I pulled on the dress I'd grabbed from the closet. This one was even more inappropriate than my first dress. James would not have been happy if he saw me leave the house in this. But it was one of my only dresses that still fit. I froze. Wait, had James somehow planned this fiasco with Justin? In hopes that I'd have to come change into something with less cleavage showing?

No, that was ridiculous. My husband was a little controlling, but I don't think he'd ever purposely make me get sick. This was all Justin. Yeah, I still wanted to slap him.

When I left the bathroom, everyone was jumping on my bed hitting each other with pillows.

Oh God. How did they have so much energy? All I wanted to do was climb into that bed and fall asleep. Honestly, the thought of sleeping at a hotel instead of here made me sigh. I wanted to be wrapped in my own comforter and James' arms. I didn't need a night out. I just wanted to be home with James.

Justin slid out of James' closet in a totally new outfit. "What about this one?" he asked as he spun in a circle.

Everyone stopped jumping and turned toward him.

"It's an A from me," Kristen said, in a sultry voice that I think she thought sounded like James.

Spoiler alert…it did not.

"A plus!" Bee yelled.

I laughed and threw a pillow at her.

She caught it and jumped off the bed. "Tonight is so fun!" she said and gave me a big, drunken hug.

Is it though? I literally just spent the last twenty minutes scrubbing vomit out of my hair. We had very different definitions of fun.

"Justin, you said you were just borrowing a shirt," I said. Why was he in a whole new ensemble?

"Yeah, but these pants were slim cut and way in the back of the closet. And every good party needs an outfit change. Besides, I've never seen James wear them before. He won't miss them." He adjusted his new V-neck shirt in the mirror.

He was acting like he saw my husband all the time instead of only at fancy events.

"Whatever you say," I said. Yeah, I was a terrible negotiator. "Is that all you took? The shirt and the pants?" I felt like I'd have some explaining to do to my husband.

Justin turned to me. "What do you think?" He gave me a wink.

"What else did you take?"

"You said I could have free reign in his underwear drawer."

- 227 -

"I didn't say that exactly…"

"Too late now. My tight little booty has already slid into a pair of very sexy briefs. And they're a little loose in the you-know-where region. I think James wins."

I laughed.

"Okay, ladies!" Justin said and clapped his hands to get everyone's attention. "If you think tonight has been fun…"

I don't.

"…then just wait until you see the surprise event of the evening. Time for destination #3! Come with me!" He sprinted out of the room.

"He has so much energy," Daphne said. "I need to get on his level." She cheered and jumped off the bed. "I'm pumped for whatever the surprise is. I mean, it has to be better than the getting bagged and escorted into James' closet thing." She looped her arm through mine.

"Oh, you mean your ideal bachelorette party didn't involve perving around in your soon-to-be brother-in-law's closet?"

She laughed. "Honestly, I should have guessed that we'd wind up here at some point since Kristen and Justin are both involved."

"Party time!" Kristen said and hopped off the bed. "I hope you don't mind…but I took something from the closet too." She held up one of James' ties.

I was just about to tell her that I most certainly *did* mind, but she sprinted out of the room so fast.

I was really starting to hate athletes. Especially ones with long tan legs, brown hair, and flat unpregnant bellies. *God, she's actually going to try to steal James from me, isn't she?* But if she thought James wanted to be tied up, she was mistaken. He was more the one to do the tying. And he certainly didn't want to tie anyone down but me. *I hope.* I thought about her stupid long legs again and tan skin. Sometimes being a short, pasty redhead really sucked.

"I'm so sorry," Daphne said, apologizing for Kristen for the millionth time.

"She's not actually going to try to sleep with my husband, is she?"

"No," Alina said, but bit her lip. "I mean…I don't think so. That would be totally inappropriate."

Daphne laughed. "I don't know if Kristen understands the meaning of inappropriate."

"We'll shove Matt in front of her tomorrow at the wedding," Bee said. "Surely that will be distracting enough. What's up with Justin acting like he doesn't know Matt, by the way? It's so weird."

I shrugged. Honestly a lot of things Justin did were weird. Like the fact that he was wearing my husband's clothes right now. And I was too tired to question any of it.

***

"This is not a good part of town," Bee said as the limo turned down another empty street.

We were passing by all these dilapidated buildings. Each one looked more rundown than the last.

"Where are we?" Daphne asked.

"Near the pier," Justin said. "Isn't it wonderful?"

"Um…no," Daphne said. "It's horrifying, actually."

"Getting those hearts racing again!" Justin said.

"Justin, are you trying to actually murder us now? Instead of just pretending to?"

"Bwahaha! Could you imagine? Moi? A murderer? Nonsense."

"Honestly the evil laughter right before that wasn't very convincing," I said.

"Bwahaha!" he said again.

"Justin, it's only September. If you're planning something Halloween related, it's a little too early for that. Save it for the Caldwell Halloween party."

He squealed. "Did you just invite me to the annual Caldwell Halloween party? It's the talk of the town that they're bringing it back. I'm so excited!" He screamed at the top of his lungs and I winced.

I hadn't technically invited him. But...what could I say now? "I'm sure I can get you an invite."

"I knew I loved you." He gave me a big kiss on the cheek. "You smell a million times better by the way. Almost as good as me in your husband's clothes. What cologne does he wear?" He lifted up a zip-up hoodie that I hadn't seen him take from James' closet and gave it a big sniff. He sighed.

"Justin, you can't have that."

He looked up from his sniffing. "What? This ratty thing?"

"It's...you can't have that one." James had worn it that night when he'd driven me home from my terrible date with Austin. The night it had started pouring. The first night he had kissed me.

"I know, it belongs in the trash. That's why I took it. I figured it was going there soon anyway."

"It's not trash." I grabbed it out of his hands. He was right. James' cologne wafted off of the fabric, making me feel dizzy. It was like I was transported back to that night. "It's my favorite."

"If you say so. You can have it back as long as I can keep everything else." He gave me a smile that showed me he knew exactly what he had done. Stolen a sentimental hoodie for negotiation purposes.

Didn't he know I was a terrible negotiator? I would have let him keep all the stuff anyway. "Yeah, of course. Those clothes are yours now." I pulled the hoodie to my chest. But this was mine. I couldn't imagine it ever being thrown away.

"So…back to the Caldwell Halloween party. Is it clothing optional?" he asked.

I laughed. "I think it's costume required."

"That doesn't answer my question."

Doesn't it though?

"You guys…this really feels like we just entered a horror film," Daphne said as she stared out the window.

"Don't worry, ladies. Destination #3 isn't Halloween themed. It's sex themed."

"Oh, are the stripper kidnappers coming back?" Kristen asked.

"No. I already utilized my stripper budget."

Kristen laughed. "Oh, you're serious?" Her face fell. "But what is a bachelorette party without strippers?"

"Sounds fine to me," Daphne said. "That would have been super awkward to tell Rob about tomorrow morning. Wait…do you think there were strippers at his bachelor party?" She turned to me. "Did James say anything about strippers?"

I held up my hands. "James didn't plan it. Justin did."

"What?"

Justin's saucy smile was back.

"Are there strippers at his?" she asked him.

"What happens at a bachelor party stays at a bachelor party. Look, we're here!" He pointed out the window.

Our limo had just stopped outside a very rundown warehouse. Just looking at it made me shiver.

"Yeah...I'm not going in there," I said. "That has tetanus written all over it. And I'm not sure if it's safe to get a shot while I'm pregnant."

"Me too," Daphne said. She immediately shook her head. "Not about the pregnancy thing of course. I'm not pregnant. I just meant...I don't want tetanus either. And that place looks rusty AF."

I laughed.

"This isn't a debate," Justin said and opened the door. "All of you will go into the haunted warehouse right this instant. Don't make me call Raphael to drag your asses inside."

"Technically...you said you already spent your stripper budget," Daphne said. "So you can't get Raphael here to do that."

"Money isn't the only way to pay people, missy. Now OUT!" He pointed toward the warehouse with all the authority in the world.

"He seems pissed," Alina said and climbed out. "I'm sure it's safe, right?"

"It sounds like something really sexy is about to happen," Kristen said. "I'm definitely in!" She joined Alina and Justin.

Bee shrugged. "He's not going to kill me. He wants to plan my wedding. I'm probably the safest one here." She patted my knee and climbed out of the limo.

Daphne and I looked at each other.

"He's not going to kill me the night before my wedding, right?" She laughed, but it sounded forced. "Although…he does kind of hate me. Maybe this is where he murders me and tries to steal Rob for himself. I should have lied and said Rob's penis was only this big." She held up her pinky finger.

I laughed. "Justin doesn't hate you." At least…I thought he had stopped hating her. It had been a little touch and go there for a minute. But he'd stopped calling her a barbarian, which was definitely a step in the right direction. "I'm pretty sure he'd have a hard time getting another wedding gig if he murdered a bride-to-be."

"Fair point." She nodded like she was encouraging herself. "Let's do this thing." She climbed out of the limo.

It was true. It would be career suicide for Justin to murder Daphne or Bee. But me? He'd already planned my wedding. Maybe he was trying to get out of the baby shower he'd promised to throw me. If this were a horror movie, I'd kill Kristen first. Just because I'd want to. And then Alina, only because I didn't know her as well.

But this wasn't my crazy plan. Justin was the evil mastermind here. He'd probably kill Kristen and Alina first too, just because he didn't know them. But then it would be me because he'd already planned my wedding. He'd keep Daphne alive for tomorrow. And Justin was basically obsessed with Bee, he didn't even try to hide it.

Yup, I was going to die third for sure. Or maybe he'd kill me first so he could steal James even faster…

"We're waiting, Penny," Justin said. He ducked his head into the limo. "It's fine," he whispered just so I could hear. "I won't let anything happen to you, I swear."

Which was exactly what a tricky serial killer would say before he killed you first or third. "I'm actually pretty tired. Do you mind if I just take a nap in here?"

"Penny, it's 1 in the morning. Bedtime isn't for another 2 hours."

I groaned. "There's a wedding tomorrow!"

"Yeah," he said and leaned in further. "And the wedding is going to be great. But I swear tonight is the main event. I did it partially for you. Come on."

Serial killer words. But Justin wasn't a serial killer. And now he'd really piqued my interest. How could whatever was behind that broken door be for me?

"Promise you won't kill me?" I asked.

He laughed. "Cross my heart." He put his hand out for me. "You're my favorite, you know that. I won't let anything happen to you."

Good. That meant Kristen was definitely getting offed first. And if Kristen died, I wouldn't stick around like bait. I'd run away before the murderers got me. Thank goodness I'd switched into a pair of flats. I grabbed Justin's hand and he pulled me out of the limo.

"Time to get our drink on!" Justin said.

Everyone cheered other than me.

Seriously…none of them were going to remember tonight *or* tomorrow at this rate. But a drink meant there was probably a bar inside. Which meant other people. I breathed a sigh of relief. I really hated this trend of top secret, password only bars in sketchy places like this. Why not just put it somewhere well lit?

A rat scurried past, and I swallowed a scream. And somewhere with less rodents?

Justin marched right up to the door. But he didn't do a weird knock or whisper a password. He just ducked under one of the broken boards. "This way!" he called back to me.

We took turns ducking into the building.

Justin turned on a flashlight to light the way. There was definitely no one else in here. And it definitely wasn't a bar. It was just a rundown building for sure. I heard something dripping and shivered. It hadn't rained recently. So what was leaking?

Bee screamed and grabbed my hand. "Was that a rat?"

"Probably," Justin said. "It's an abandoned warehouse. Now quiet, ladies," Justin said. "You don't want to scare them."

I gripped Bee's hand tighter. "Scare who?"

"Our murderers?" Bee asked.

I swallowed hard. Yeah, that sounded about right.

"Justin, I swear to God if you murder me before I get to walk down the aisle…"

"Daphne," Justin said in a calm voice. "I'm the best wedding planner in the city. How would I have a perfect 5-star rating if I murdered my brides?"

"Maybe because you murder all the ones that give you less than five stars," Daphne said.

He laughed. "Touché you sassy thing. Ah, here were are." He put his hand out to make us stop wandering around. And then he pulled out his phone. "Raphael, we've arrived."

"I thought he said Raphael went home," Bee whispered.

"We're definitely going to die here," Kristen said. "Or…we're about to get totally rammed by Raphael." She bit her lip.

"I don't want either of those things," Alina said.

Yeah, me either. But if I had to choose…

The lights went on, blinding us for a moment.

I blinked. Behind us was…sure enough…a warehouse from a horror movie. But in front of us? A fancy couch, velvet chairs, and tons of booze and snacks.

"Perfection," Justin said. "Time for a show." He closed the big doors behind us that I hadn't seen before and strutted toward the couch.

"What kind of show?" Daphne said and quickly followed him.

Bee and I both shrugged. Honestly, if there was a cheese plate then I was totally on board for any show. Although…since Raphael was involved, I was pretty sure it was strippers.

CHAPTER 25

Friday

We all sat down. Everyone started drinking, but I went right for the cheese and crackers. I was freaking starving.

Daphne was looking around like she was still scared.

I'll admit, the creepy warehouse on the other side of those big doors was terrifying. But this was like a five-star hotel lobby. And the food was divine. Although, I wasn't sure how they passed any kind of food-sanitary requirements since there were rats twenty feet back.

I looked down at the cracker in my hand and my stomach turned. I was not going to throw up any more during this bachelorette party. I quickly put the cracker back down on the table.

"Seriously, where are we?" Daphne asked.

"One of the many secret venues of Club Onyx," Justin said.

I looked over at Bee. "Did you know and were just playing along?"

She shook her head. "No. Ever since Tanner took over he's been expanding it like crazy. I had no idea."

I'd been really curious about Club Onyx over the years. But I'd never actually been in one of their locations before. *I think*. It was hard to know exactly because of the reason Bee just mentioned. They kept popping up with new hidden locations. For all I knew the Parrot Palace was actually a front for Club Onyx. I laughed to myself. That couldn't possibly be true. Because the Parrot Palace was the exact opposite of sexy.

Justin looked down at his watch and then pulled out his phone and shot off a text.

"Who are you texting?" Kristen asked. "Please tell me it's Raphael."

"Better," he said, holding back a smile.

"Better?" She raised an eyebrow. "Tell me more."

"Oh, baby girl, just wait for it."

As soon as he said it, a beat dropped from hidden speakers. And the wall in front of us began to shake.

"Earthquake!" Daphne yelled and tried to dive under the coffee table.

But Justin caught her around the waist. "No, it's the main event."

The wall parted and Rob slid into the room on his knees, like he'd just scored a goal in a soccer match. But that wasn't the alarming part. The alarming part was that he dressed just like a soccer player, but the shorts were way shorter. Like...waaaay shorter.

The beat dropped again, and he stood up at the same time he tore his jersey off and waved it over his head.

Oh my God.

He threw his jersey at Daphne.

She caught it with a laugh.

He did a little shimmy.

Oh my God, he's stripping. For...all of us? What the hell is happening?

Bee gave Rob a wolf whistle as he started thrusting.

He danced up to her and then turned around, shaking his butt in her face.

She laughed and smacked it.

He did similar moves in front of Alina and Kristen. He even let Justin give him an ass slap. And then he jumped up on the couch, his legs on either side of Daphne. And he tore off his shorts and thrust into her face.

He grabbed the bottom of her chin and tilted it up so that she could lock eyes with him. She'd stopped laughing. And there were stars in her eyes as she smiled up at him.

"I love you," she whispered.

"I love you back." He ran his thumb across her bottom lip.

All the shimmying and ass slapping was hot. But that moment had me squirming. How many times had James looked at me just like that before he pushed my back against a wall and kissed me like he was starving?

"Last but not least…" Rob said and practically fell over my lap, his ass in the air.

I laughed.

"You know you've always wanted to touch my butt," he said and gave me a wink.

"You're ridiculous."

"Don't make me spank you instead," he whispered so no one else could hear. "We both know you'd love that."

I swallowed hard. I should not have been aroused by this. It was James' brother for Christ's sake. But I think that was part of the reason why I shifted on the couch. Because they had the same dark eyes. And right now his were staring at me so intensely. And I'd just seen him look at Daphne like he was going to devour her.

And he was right. I fucking loved when James spanked me. And I was pretty sure that spanking Rob was somehow not as bad as him spanking me. So I did it.

He laughed and rolled off the couch, getting on all fours and crawling back over to Daphne.

Daphne was laughing so hard when he pulled her down into his practically naked lap and kissed her just like I'd thought he was going to. Like she was the air he needed to breathe.

It was so fucking hot.

Oh my God, what is wrong with me? I turned away from the heated kiss.

Rob always said inappropriate things to me. This wasn't any different than that. The only difference was tonight I was a little aroused. But I'm pretty sure it was just because I was missing James and my hormones were insane.

The music changed and Matt appeared where the walls had parted. He was wearing a football jersey, those tight little pants, and a helmet. Honestly, anyone else probably wouldn't have known it was Matt because of the helmet. But I knew these guys. And it was definitely him. Mostly because his eyes were staring directly at me.

Rob high-fived him on the way out and then Matt pushed himself off the wall and did a little spin.

I laughed, but it kind of died in my throat when he pulled off his helmet and shook his head so he wouldn't have helmet hair.

I swear it was straight out of one of those movies when the guy comes out of the ocean and is trying to get the water out of his hair. Or like he'd climbed off the back of a motorcycle. *Yeah, that one.* It was just like that.

He winked at me.

Shit. I should not be aroused by this too.

He dropped down onto the ground and started to do the worm. Of all the guys, I'd always thought Matt was the best dancer. I had no idea how he wormed his way up to us before standing up with a funny shimmy. Then he stood up, put his foot up on the table, and tore off his tight pants.

It was a bold move, removing his pants before his shirt. And somehow it worked for him, because Matthew Caldwell was packing. I was pretty sure Justin got his answer about the little Caldwell. And Matt was anything but little.

I immediately looked away.

Alina laughed and I turned back to see that Matt had just put his helmet on her head.

He pulled out a Sharpie from the waistband of his boxer briefs and put it in his mouth. And then he tore off his shirt.

Rob had the same build as James. Long lean muscles, with perfect 6-pack abs. Matt was just as in shape but…thicker. His shoulders were broader. Everything was just…bigger. Well, maybe not *everything*. It was hard to tell when his length was hidden behind his boxer briefs. But he definitely looked big. Like really big. *Why the hell am I staring at his boxer briefs?*

He made Kristen turn around and he smacked her ass with his jersey.

He did the same to Justin.

Justin laughed and thrust his ass out even harder.

Matt barely held back a laugh as he slapped him with his jersey again and then did a thrusting motion in front of Daphne.

I laughed at the shocked expression on her face. She'd been really into it when Rob did it. But not so much when Matt did.

Me? I loved watching both. Because my pregnancy was making me insane. James' friend should not be turning me on!

Matt tossed me his jersey and then pulled the sharpie out of his mouth. "Put it on," he mouthed.

I pulled it on immediately. In my defense, I was kind of used to being ordered around in the bedroom. Yup, I'd lost my mind.

He grabbed my hand and pulled me to my feet. He twirled me around and then pulled me in close.

He uncapped the Sharpie with his teeth. "Penny, you should not be looking at me that way. Because I've had too much to drink and I'm known to make terrible choices even when I'm not drunk."

"I'm not looking at you any way."

He smiled. "You are." He dipped me low and then pulled me back to his chest again. "James is one lucky guy. Now bend over."

What?

He spun me around, pulling my ass against his definitely erect penis.

Oh my God.

He kept one hand firmly on my waist as he signed his name on the back of the jersey with his other hand.

"All finished here." He spanked me and then stepped back.

I immediately stood up. I knew my face was flushed when I turned back to him.

He gave me another wink and walked through the opening in the wall.

Yeah, I was officially turned on. I really hoped James was next. But when the music changed, Brendan appeared.

He looked at me and the corner of his mouth ticked up.

Probably because of the huge jersey I was wearing. Brendan had liked me for all of 5 minutes. Surely he'd be giving most of his attention to Kristen, since she was the only one of us girls who was kind of available. Besides, I wasn't sure I could take getting any more turned on. This was all completely inappropriate. Justin knew that, right?

I pulled off the jersey and stared down at Matt's signature. As much fun as that was, his name didn't belong on me. I sat down.

Everyone started laughing.

I looked up to see Brendan doing this funny robot dance up to us. Which did not at all match the cowboy outfit he was wearing.

When he got in front of the couch he started doing this two-step thing in his cowboy boots. It looked like this was not his first time line dancing. I wasn't even sure if it was the first time he'd torn a plaid shirt off like that, the buttons going in every direction. Perfect chaos.

He grabbed Kristen's hand and pressed it against the front of his jeans.

It looked like she was going to faint.

Hopefully she'd be distracted by Brendan for the rest of the wedding weekend.

Besides Kristen, he didn't inappropriately thrust or spank anyone. But everyone was definitely distracted by his abs as he danced in front of the couch.

IVY SMOAK

Alina actually licked her lips as she stared at him.

Daphne's face had turned crimson as she shoved a cracker in her mouth.

I was surprised when Brendan tore his jeans off. All these costumes looked so real.

He tipped his hat at me and smiled.

"Hey, Brendan," I said.

"Hey? That's all I get?" He put his cowboy hat on my head, before pulling me off the couch.

I laughed, but my laughter died in my throat as he stared down at me. I'd been trying really hard not to look at him during his dance. Because he had a stupid perfect face and stupid perfect abs and I was already embarrassed enough about being aroused by Rob and Matt.

"Remember the last time I kissed you?" he whispered down at me.

My heart started beating faster. *Stop it, heart! Why are you betraying me?! I will not be turned on by you, Brendan.* I shook my head, even though I did remember.

He put his lips to my ear. "You really don't remember? It was a pretty great kiss, Penny." He pulled back and smiled at me. "And remember," he said in a surprisingly good Southern drawl. "Instead of riding a horse, next time ride a cowboy, darling."

I didn't know what he meant by that. Was he calling James a horse? Or was he just making the usual horse cowboy joke?

He placed a kiss on my cheek, like he wanted to remind me of what his lips felt like.

But I hadn't forgotten. And I didn't know if it was that, or the perfect Southern accent, or the cowboy costume itself but...he'd gotten me. I swallowed hard.

God, I needed James. Right this freaking second. But it wasn't James who appeared next.

It was Mason. And he was not in a costume at all. He was just wearing what I can only describe as a banana hammock. A gold banana hammock that shimmered slightly in the dim lighting.

Every one of his muscles and his firm ass perfectly exposed to the world.

What the hell are these guys trying to do to me?

"Now it's a banana party!" Kristen yelled.

I thought Matt was the best dancer, but Mason was the best dancer for this specifically. I wasn't surprised about that either. He'd surely seen enough strip shows. But it was weird that he'd already stripped.

Justin squealed in delight as Mason got down on his hands and knees and literally prowled toward us. He did something on the ground that wasn't quite the worm because it was way more sexual. His eyes trained on Bee as he basically humped the ground in front of her.

She fanned herself. "This is wonderful. But, Mason, what kind of costume is this?" Bee said with a laugh.

"I'm a stripper," he said.

She laughed. "Oh, I got that. But you jumped awfully fast to the last part."

"I didn't need some dumb costume to turn you on, baby." He stood up and did some kind of roll thing with his abs while leaning over her. It was freaking sinful.

I pressed my thighs together.

And immediately froze because he saw me do it.

The cockiest smile spread across his face. He did the same move, this time staring directly at me.

I immediately turned away. I never should have started this five months of seduction thing with James. It was like I needed sex 24/7 now. Like my body was trained for it.

But it was hard to look away when Mason stepped in front of me. He did the same move he'd just done to Bee, his gold banana hammock right in my face.

"It's okay Penny," he whispered, stopping when his pecs were right in my face. "We all thought about fucking you the first time we met you. It's okay that you've thought about how good it would feel to be underneath me. Or tied up in my bed, just the way I like it." He grabbed my hand and pressed it against his abs, pushing my fingers down to his happy trail.

Holy hell. Every inch of him was muscley goodness. I loved my husband. So fucking much. But it was like I couldn't look away.

"By the way, how's your new sex dungeon treating you?"

Oh God, he knows about that too? I'd blame Bee for blabbing, but I would have blabbed too if it had been me in her situation. "I…" But I had no excuse. If he knew he knew.

"Need me to show James a few things?"

I laughed.

"You would not be laughing if you belonged to me. I'd chain you up and have my way with you for hours."

"Jesus, Mason."

He laughed. "Not the first time someone's called me that in bed."

Yeah, I didn't doubt that.

"By the way." He held my hand a little tighter to his abs. "James is so fucking pissed at you right now." He dropped my hand and I was finally able to get it safely away from his abs. "You're welcome. Rumor has it you love a good spanking. I'm going to assume that'll happen to you tonight after you basically molested my abs while I was wearing virtually nothing. You dirty girl." He winked at me.

Oh no. It wasn't my fault. What was I supposed to do? Cross my arms and refuse to participate? James' friends were overly flirtatious. They always had been. This time they were just overly flirtatious and half naked. It didn't mean anything. At all.

James appeared in the entryway dressed like a professor. A scowl was etched across his perfect face. He was definitely pissed. And that just made me want him even more.

CHAPTER 26

Friday

Justin moved so he was sitting next to me on the couch. "You're welcome," he said and patted my leg.

Me? I didn't ask for this. And now my husband was furious with me. This seemed a lot more like a fantasy of Justin's...*oh*. It hit me. This was legit Justin's fantasy. No wonder Justin wanted to plan the bachelorette party. He wanted to watch all of our men do stripteases. And I guess this was what he'd planned for the bachelor party too. All the guys probably had stripper lessons tonight or something. Two birds, one stone.

And he'd kind of nailed it. The whole bridal party seemed to be having the time of their lives. Except for James.

And now me because I knew I was in so much trouble.

James' scowl intensified as the music changed and Mason left.

For a second, I didn't think he was going to dance at all. That he was just going to stand there looking like a furious professor.

But then he did a little spin as he pulled out his glasses from the pocket of his dress shirt. He put them on and then slowly rolled up the sleeves of his shirt as he stalked toward us, his hips moving to the beat. I loved when he rolled up his sleeves like that. Most men looked like they were more relaxed when they rolled up their sleeves. But if anything, it made him look more serious. More in charge. Like he was about to get down and dirty.

Yes, his hips were moving to the beat, but it was hardly a dance. It looked like he had a purpose out here…and it wasn't to do a fun striptease. It was to do a torturous one. Specifically designed to torture me.

Every single move he made was so erotic I could barely stand it. Especially with that scowl on his face. Each footstep landing perfectly to the beat.

Justin put his hand on my knee again and held his breath when James reached the coffee table.

The beat of the music changed and James ran his fingers through his hair as he gyrated his hips. In the exact same way he would if I was spread out naked beneath him.

But he wasn't looking at me as he did it. He was looking at Bee.

And when he loosened his tie, he stared at Alina.

And when he slowly unbuttoned his shirt to the beat of the music, he stared at Daphne.

Jealousy surged through me. I knew what he was doing. But it wasn't my fault that Rob made me spank him. Or that Matt gave me his jersey. Or that Brendan wanted me to ride him or something. Or that Mason made me molest his abs.

That had all been out of my hands.

But it was in James' hands as he jumped up on the table and tore his shirt off, looking everywhere but at me. He tossed his shirt at Kristen.

She cheered.

Yeah, I was really fucking jealous as my husband aroused every single one of these women with just his abs showing. He slowly unbuckled his belt, sliding it through the belt loops.

Justin put his hand to his forehead and fell backward.

I clenched my jaw. James wasn't really dancing like the other guys. Yes, his movements were to the beat, but they were methodical. Each one planned to arouse me. Sure, the other women too. But especially me. Yet he wasn't even giving me the time of day.

But he knew how much I loved when he rolled up the sleeves of his shirt like that. And the way he ran his fingers through his hair. And the way he unbuttoned his dress shirt.

He loosened his tie as he stared at Bee.

"Oh my God," Bee mouthed.

Yeah, I loved when he did that too. But I was used to his attention being trained on me. I'd been planning on asking Bee to help me somehow get James into our sex dungeon and at my mercy. But now I didn't want her anywhere near my sex dungeon. I didn't want any of these girls near it. Luckily they hadn't found it when they were in my apartment tonight.

James pulled out a ruler from his back pocket and slapped it against his palm.

I bit my lip.

"I heard one of you is getting married. But first you need one last crazy night. Who's the lucky bride?"

Daphne raised her hand.

"Stand up and turn around, you dirty girl."

Her jaw dropped. But she quickly obliged, turning around, arching her back slightly.

She was responding the same way I had to Rob. I got it. I did. But…I also hated it. James was mine.

James jumped off the table, his eyes locked on Daphne's ass.

Yes…Daphne's. Not mine. I was going to kill him.

He ran the ruler slowly down her back, tracing the path of her spine. And then he turned to me. He lowered his eyebrows as he stared into my eyes. And then he slapped her ass with the ruler.

I jumped slightly in my seat, almost feeling the sting of it.

He lowered his eyebrows even more and then turned away from me. He tossed the ruler at Alina and then tore off his pants in one swift movement. He tossed his pants at Justin, who leapt in the air to grab them.

He was giving pieces of clothing and props to everyone but me.

And he was standing there in just a tie and his boxer briefs. No one else should have been allowed to see him like this.

He loosened his tie again and then pulled it the rest of the way off. I thought he would spank someone with that too. But instead he grabbed Bee's hands and tied them together.

Her eyes grew round.

And I was pretty sure mine turned into slits. I didn't love watching him touch someone else like that. He tugged on the tie and she leaned forward slightly.

He whispered something in her ear and she smiled.

And I swear my stomach rolled. I knew this was how he had felt when his friends were out here doing stuff to me. But again…they were doing it *to* me. It truly had been out of my hands. And they'd only done it in good fun. He was purposely provoking me with things he knew I found sexy, and I was furious.

"You've all been very naughty girls," James said and winked at Alina. "I probably need to punish all of you."

I glared at him. Punish? Seriously? Of all lines, he had to use that one?

I swear, if he does anything with Kristen... My train of thought ended as he stepped in front of her.

No.

He raised his eyebrow at her and she practically melted into a puddle at his feet.

He was supposed to be raising his eyebrow at me, not her. That was our thing. He stared down at her through his glasses, and that somehow made him look a thousand times hotter.

Kristen stood up, pressing herself against him.

And James didn't step back. He put his hands on her waist, pulling her closer.

I clenched my hands into fists.

James glanced over at me as one of his hands lowered dangerously close to her ass.

I knew he could see the fury in my face. And yet...he didn't move. He just gave me the same hard stare back. *If you touch her ass I will murder you in your sleep.*

His hand moved a fraction of an inch lower as he glowered at me.

I got it. He was proving a point. But if he didn't remove his hands from Kristen's waist right this second I was going to cut a bitch.

Kristen pulled out the tie she'd stolen from his closet and draped it around his neck.

He smiled down at her.

No. He should have been freaking out that she'd stolen one of his ties! Not rewarding her with a sexy smirk.

She pulled on the ends of the tie, drawing his lips closer to hers.

If he kissed her I was going to lose my fucking mind.

He put his hand on the center of her chest, stopping her from pulling him any closer. And then he lightly pushed her back down on the couch.

I held my breath, expecting him to climb on top of her.

But he didn't. *Thank God.*

"I'll be taking this back," he said, pulling the tie off his bare shoulders. "Thank you very much, Miss Dwyer."

Him calling her Miss Dwyer made me just as jealous. I loved when he called me Miss Taylor.

"Do you want these clothes back too?" Justin asked.

James winked at him. "No, you're good."

Justin laughed.

But I wasn't laughing when James knelt down in front of Alina. He lifted up one of her high heeled feet and put it on top of his thigh.

Is he...he isn't... I was going to be sick. The imaginary image of him leaning down to kiss her inner thigh clouded what was actually happening in front of me.

I didn't realize my throat had made a weird squeaking noise until James looked over at me.

I watched as he lifted her other heel. He grabbed his belt off the table behind him and slowly tied her ankles together with the leather.

I hated the way his hands were on her skin. I hated that his belt was bound around her.

I could practically imagine the feeling of the leather biting into my own skin as I stared at him.

He lowered his eyebrows again as he stared back at me. But he kept his hands on Alina, not me.

My heart was beating so fast that I swore he could see my chest rising and falling. He had to know how pissed I was. So why was he still kneeling in front of a woman that wasn't me?

He slowly stood up. He was no longer even trying to move to the beat of the music. He stalked in front of me.

He looked so fucking pissed.

Well, tough luck. I was pissed too.

He leaned forward, putting his hands on the back of the couch. But not a single inch of him was touching me. He'd literally touched everyone else in the room but me.

"You've been a very naughty girl, Miss Taylor," he whispered in my ear. "I'll need to see you after class. Room 3B. You have exactly five minutes or this will be even worse for you."

He pushed himself back from me, being careful again not to touch me at all.

I had been so aroused earlier, but now I was just furious. Well, maybe still a little aroused. *Stupid professorly striptease!*

All James had left was his boxer briefs and the tie draped over his shoulders that he'd reclaimed from Kristen. He should have looked exposed. But the way he was staring at me was so domineering.

Yeah, I was definitely still aroused.

"That was so much fun!" Daphne said as James walked out of the room.

Everyone started cheering for encores and laughing.

But I didn't laugh. It felt like my heart was beating in my throat. Room 3B? It had to be somewhere in this building, because there was no way we were five minutes from any nice hotel. And it was probably somewhere through the opening in the wall. Because everything behind me was rat-infested.

It was like his words were echoing around in my head: *"You have exactly five minutes or this will be even worse for you."*

I had half a mind not to go, that bastard. I could just sit here and drown my sorrows in a cheese plate.

But I owed him a slap across the face. Or ten. I was going to kill him with his stupid necktie that smelled like Kristen instead of me. Before anyone could even ask me where I was going, I stormed off after him.

CHAPTER 27

Friday

I walked through the opening of the wall. Someone yelled my name from behind me, but I ignored them. I could only think about one thing…slapping my cocky husband.

There was a red curtain behind the wall, blocking off my path. I looked around, and then the ground started to shake. I looked behind me to see the wall behind me closing shut. *Shit.*

I had not thought this through. I had no idea where we were and no idea what was behind that curtain. And now I couldn't turn back to my friends.

But I could hear voices. I inched toward the curtain and the voices grew louder. I found a parting and pushed through it. And I stumbled into another curtained-off area. Five men in nothing but banana hammocks and big monkey masks all slowly turned toward me.

And for the second time tonight, I thought I was going to be murdered. I screamed at the top of my lungs and pushed through a different opening in the curtain.

Behind this one was a group of guys changing into stripper costumes. Probably about to do what my husband and friends had just done.

And even though a few of them were half naked, they were much less scary than the monkey men behind curtain #2.

"Where are we?" I asked and stepped toward the closest one who was already in full costume. He was dressed like a police officer.

He gave me a weird look. "The Society."

"The what?"

"It's invite only. Wait, did you not fill out all the forms?"

"Um…"

He took another step toward me. "Miss, how did you get in here?" He put his hands on his belt like he was about to pull out a taser or something.

Oh my God. I looked over at the other guys changing and they were all pulling on police uniforms. And now I wasn't sure they were about to be a stripper police office. Because the one in front of me was acting like a real police officer. I was about to be swarmed by cops.

"The Society, right. Of course I filled out all the forms." *What the fuck?!* "Gotta go!" I sprinted through another gap in the curtains and almost ran straight into Mason.

"Thank God," I said and breathed a sigh of relief.

Mason was fully clothed again in a freshly pressed suit. He stared down at me, a cloud of smoke around his head. He pulled the cigar out of the corner of his mouth.

"What are you doing back here?" he asked.

Tanner walked in through another curtain and waved his hand through the air. "So what do you think? It's a win, right?" He paused when he saw me and quickly lowered his arm. "Hey, Penny." He looked back and forth between Mason and me. "I didn't know you were a member."

"She's not," Mason said firmly. "It was a bachelorette party thing."

"Well, did you enjoy it?" Tanner asked.

Yeah, until my husband molested everyone but me. "Sure. I just…" I pointed over my shoulder. "I was trying to find James and I got lost in all those curtains. What is the Society?"

Mason cleared his throat. "The what?"

"The Society."

"The Society is a…" Tanner started but Mason elbowed him right in the ribs. He gave him a death stare. Tanner cleared his throat. "Never heard of it."

Seriously, what the hell was going on? "Look, I'm just looking for James. Do either of you know where room 3B is?"

Tanner smiled. "Room 3B, huh? Nice choice."

"Yeah…" But I didn't sound sure at all. Because Tanner looked so happy with himself and I was still really confused.

Tanner stepped to the side and opened another curtain. There was a fancy door with a strange ancient looking symbol etched onto it.

"Down the hall to the left," he said. "It's the room marked with the pencil symbol." He opened up the door for me, and I was happy to see that the hallway wasn't filled with strippers, monkey men, or police officers.

"Penny," Mason said before I walked through. "Don't go into any other rooms, okay?"

"Okay?"

"And have fun." He winked at me and turned back to Tanner before the door closed with a thud.

This had to be one of the strangest nights of my life. But I definitely felt safer in this hallway than I did running through all those red curtains.

I walked past a few doors with other symbols on them. Not strange ones like the one on the main door. I recognized these. A shamrock. An hourglass. A snowflake. A snake. There didn't seem to be any rhyme or reason to any of them. And they certainly didn't go together.

I stopped at the door with a pencil etched onto it. It also said 3B in very small font beneath it. For the people like me that had no idea what the symbols meant, I guess. I knocked on the door and waited a few seconds. But no one responded. I knocked again. Still no response.

James had said five minutes or else. I was pretty sure I was probably late. So where the heck was he? I wrapped my hand around the knob and was surprised to find it unlocked. I opened up the door. Everything inside was pitch black. But when I stepped in, the lights magically turned on.

I was standing in the middle of a classroom. Or...a replica of one. Because there was no way any parents would send their children to a place like this to learn. I walked past the rows of desks for students and up to the podium at the front of the room. There was an even bigger desk up here, I guess for the teacher. It wasn't like the college classrooms. It reminded me more of high school. I ran my hand along the top of the wooden desk and stared up at the chalkboard.

Thank God James and I had met in college rather than high school. Because if we'd met in a classroom like this and done the things we did...he would have ended up in jail rather than just losing his job.

I lifted up one of the notebooks on the desk. It was empty. Because...of course it was. I crossed my arms and stared at the chalkboard. It definitely wasn't a real classroom, because there wasn't even any chalk. Or even a single eraser smudge on the board. Or an eraser for that matter. Everything was too perfect. And the room smelled a little of fresh paint.

But I didn't have any more time to think about how weird it was that there was a classroom in the middle of all this insanity. Because I heard a click and the door to the classroom opened.

James walked in, fully dressed again. He started pacing back and forth. He clearly hadn't seen me. And for a few seconds, I just got to stare at him. That scowl was still stuck on his face. His eyebrows were lowered like he wanted to rip my head off.

And it was so incredibly sexy. I was still really pissed off at him. But seeing him seething like that? I couldn't help but want him to take his frustrations out on me. I couldn't wait for him to fuck me. Right after I gave him a piece of my mind.

"James," I said in my most authoritative tone. Although, I was pretty sure it wasn't authoritative at all.

He froze. His scowl turned to me in full force and I felt myself clench.

"What the hell was that?!" I said. "You put your hands all over everyone. And that Kristen girl? Wasn't she stalking you a few years ago? That was a really fucked up thing for you to do."

He lowered his eyebrows. "Are you done?"

"No." Actually, that was all I had to say. And I hadn't been expecting him to ask that. But I loved telling him no, so it had just slipped out. I cleared my throat. "The way you were looking at Bee? And Daphne? Completely inappropriate. And you practically went down on Alina."

"Now are you done?"

"No." *Yes.* What the hell else was I supposed to say? "I'm so royally pissed off at you. And where the hell are we?!"

He didn't say a word. He just walked over to me, past all the desks, the scowl on his face growing. Each step turned me on even more. And honestly, the whole classroom thing made it even sexier. How many times had I imagined James taking me right in the middle of class?

He stopped right in front of me. And I wasn't sure what came over me, but I slapped him across the face. The sound of the slap echoed around the empty room.

He grabbed my hand and pinned it against the chalkboard as he pressed his body into mine.

Holy shit.

"Did you think I enjoyed seeing your hands on Rob?"

I opened my mouth to respond, but he cut me off.

"Don't you fucking say a word."

I wasn't sure I'd ever seen him so pissed off before. Which was really saying something, because I pissed him off a lot.

"You think it made me happy seeing you in Matt's jersey? Or dancing with Brendan? Or fucking molesting Mason's abs?"

No. I was quite sure he felt the exact opposite of happy based on how he was glaring down at me.

"You drive me fucking crazy, Penny." He wrapped his fingers lightly around my neck.

I swallowed hard. "It was a strip show…"

"Did I say you could speak, Miss Taylor?"

Fuck, I loved when he called me that. "No, Professor Hunter."

He groaned and pressed his body more firmly against mine. I could feel how hard he was through his jeans.

He tilted his lips down to my ear. "I'm going to teach you a lesson. And I swear if you say another word you won't be able to sit down tomorrow. Are we clear?"

Oh God, I loved when he spanked me. I absolutely wanted that. I held back a smile. "Whatever you say."

His nostrils flared. "Put your hands on the podium. Now." He let go of my neck.

I took a deep breath. I was tempted to say something else, but I really had never seen him look so mad. This was going to be amazing. I stepped past him and put my hands on the podium, arching my back the way he loved.

He groaned from behind me. But he didn't instantly join me. I turned my head to look at him over my shoulder. He was leaning against the chalkboard, his arms crossed, just watching me.

"Face the class," he said.

I turned away from him. Each second that ticked by made me want him even more. And then finally I heard him come up to me.

His fingers traced up the back of one of my thighs. Pushing my skirt up over my ass.

"This is not the dress you left in," he said. "It's even more risqué. Were you trying to drive me crazy? Or purposely making my friends wish they were the ones fucking you instead of me?"

I gasped when he spanked me. But that was not his palm. I looked over my shoulder to see the ruler in his hand. *Fuck.*

"Face the class," he said again.

I immediately turned back around, my ass cheek singing with pain.

"It was the latter, right? You like the idea of my friends wanting to fuck you, you little slut."

He swatted my ass cheek with the ruler again.

Oh God.

"Were you dripping wet when you touched them?"

"No…"

The ruler hit my ass again. "Did I say you could speak?"

No, Professor Hunter.

His palm gently ran across my sore ass cheek before he swatted it again.

I was dripping wet now, desperate for his cock to fill me. For him to fuck away the pain.

"You love driving me crazy, don't you?" he asked.

I mean…a little. How could I not when this was how he reacted?

He spanked me again.

I inhaled sharply.

"Did it hurt to see my hands on your friends?"

I hated it. I hated every freaking second of it.

"I wanted it to be you, baby. I was dying to touch you. To show you who you belong to. But you needed to be taught a lesson." The ruler hit my skin again.

This time I yelped. It was too much. I just needed him.

And he knew it. He knew I couldn't take anymore. Yet he spanked me again, before tearing my thong off. The fabric made a terrible ripping noise before he tossed it on the ground. But I didn't have any time to react because he thrust himself inside of me. Hard.

My fingers gripped the podium.

It hurt. Not because he hadn't warmed me up properly. The spanking was plenty good for that. But the way his hips collided with my sore ass cheek. It only took a few seconds for him to have me moaning for more though. I'd always loved the mix of pleasure and pain. And I'd been so turned on all night, it was like I was desperate for him. Like I was fucking starving.

He grabbed my hips more firmly and slammed into me again. And again. And again. Each time his cock pounded me, the podium skidded forward a little. So that I was jutting my ass out even more in the air.

I'd actually had a fantasy just like this before. Only it was Tyler I'd been picturing instead of James. Each thrust of James inside of me made that other fantasy drift away. God, this was so much better than that dream.

He pulled back far enough to spank me again before slamming his cock even deeper inside of me.

So much fucking better.

"I swear to God, if you ever touch my friends like that again, I'll snap."

So this wasn't him snapping? I couldn't lie...now I was a little curious to see how far he would go.

He slammed into me again.

I moaned. I was barely holding on to the podium now. Before I completely lost purchase, he grabbed me around the waist, lifted me in the air while he was still deep inside of me, and pushed me down on top of the desk.

He grabbed a fistful of my hair, making me arch my back again, and then started fucking me even harder.

"Don't you even think about doing that ever again," he said, his voice tight. "You'll fucking kill me with jealousy."

I felt the same way about him. I'd go mad if he ever touched Kristen like that again. I'd almost lost it right then and there.

"Do you understand me?" He pulled my hair again.

I didn't dare speak. He was too far inside of me. His fingers were digging into my hips too hard. It was all too much. Too good. I felt myself start to clench around him.

"Fuck," he hissed and thrust deeper than before, his cum exploding into me as I screamed his name.

"James!" I couldn't help but speak. "God, James!"

He rode out my orgasm, each thrust making me scream his name again. Until we were both panting and silent.

My heart was hammering hard against my chest. "That was…intense," I said.

He slowly pulled out of me without responding.

I went to move my skirt back over my ass, but he pushed down on my hips, keeping me in place.

"I used to dream of this back when I was your professor." His hand gently massaged my ass where he'd spanked me. "Your ass in the air, begging for me to fill you. Right there in the middle of my classroom. I used to get hard just thinking about it. I'd jerk off in the shower to that very image. I'd imagine you touching yourself to that very same fantasy." His index finger slid inside of me.

God.

His fingers swirled around in my wetness. "I'd think about how tight your pussy was." He slid another finger in next to his first. "I'd imagine the way you'd clench around my cock as you came."

"James…"

"I couldn't get enough of you even before I ever had you."

"Me too." I'd thought about him incessantly. He'd been in all my dreams. I'd wanted him so badly that it hurt.

He moved his fingers faster and this thumb found my clit. He pressed down on it hard.

I came again, embarrassingly fast. His thumb continued to trace lazy circles around my clit. For a second I thought he was going to try to make me come for a third time. But then his fingers fell from my skin.

I heard the zip of his pants and then he came back into view. He sat down on the edge of the desk and stared down at me. He still looked pissed.

"I love you," I said.

The scowl on his face slowly eased away. He reached down and pushed some of my hair behind my ear. "I love you more," he said.

"Not possible."

He smiled, his fingers trailing down a lock of my hair. "Why is your hair all wet?"

I didn't need James to freak out about what Justin had done. Everything had turned out just fine. "It's a long story. I'll tell you some other time."

"And why was Justin wearing my clothes?"

I laughed. "I'm sorry about that." I looked up at him. "I'm sorry about all of it. I just…I'm horny all the time. I blame it on the pregnancy."

He laughed. "Come here." He tugged on my arm.

I wasn't exactly sure where he wanted me to go. So I just straddled him on the desk.

His hands settled on my hips and he dropped his forehead to mine.

"Where are we?" I asked. I was pretty sure we were in a sex classroom. And I was really glad the seats weren't filled with spectators.

I didn't have to look to know he was smiling at my question.

"I honestly have no idea," he said. "But let's go home."

"Home? We're supposed to go to the hotel. In separate rooms."

He shook his head. "We can sneak into the hotel rooms early in the morning. But I need you in our bed tonight, okay?" He breathed in my exhales.

"Okay." I doubted anyone would miss me tonight anyway. They were all shit-faced. Today had been crazy. And I just wanted to go home with my husband.

I'd tortured him tonight. He'd tortured me back. And I needed to make sure we were okay. "I love you most," I said.

His lips brushed against mine. "Impossible." One of his hands moved from my waist to my stomach.

He didn't say another word. But I knew what he was saying in the silence. That he loved our unborn baby too.

"Okay, let's go home. Besides, he needs his Harry Potter bedtime story." I put my hand on top of James'.

"Yes, *she* does."

I smiled to myself. I wasn't sure how I ever thought we'd be spending the night apart. But first we needed to find our way out of this warehouse maze.

CHAPTER 28

Saturday

"Baby."

I slowly opened my eyes to see James staring at me. I smiled at him. "Good morning, handsome."

He smiled. "I want to lie here with you all day...but we have to go."

I nodded but didn't move. And he didn't move either. We just stared at each other as the morning sun rays slowly filtered into the room.

I felt...off.

And I knew he could tell. It's why neither of us moved an inch.

My chest ached. It was almost like I was reliving the morning of our wedding. And that filled me with so much happiness, but also with fear. Our wedding day had been the best and the worst day of my life. I hadn't been to any weddings since ours. And I knew that Isabella wasn't out there anymore...but there was still this sense of doom in my chest. I wondered if weddings would always feel this way to me. Hope and fear, love and death, all colliding in my head.

I pressed my lips together.

"Today is gonna be okay," he said.

Was he thinking the same thing I was? Our wedding night was horrifying to me. But he didn't even remember it. He'd spent the night in a coma. I felt tears slide down the side of my face and onto my pillow. "I'm not sure I'll ever be able to go to another wedding without thinking about what happened at ours."

"Oh, baby." He pulled me into his arms and kissed the top of my head. "You have nothing to worry about today. Ian, Briggs, and Porter will all be there. And I hired extra security just in case. You don't have anything to fear."

I sniffled.

He kissed the top of my head. "We're safe now."

I knew that. I truly did. But I hugged him tighter anyway. I didn't want to spend the morning away from him. Hell, I hated spending even a second away from him. "Can't we just stay here a little while longer?"

"Of course." He held me tighter.

We just lay there in silence, wrapped up in each other. I pressed my cheek against his chest and listened to his steady heartbeat. And I let him run his fingers slowly up and down my back, calming me. His heart was still beating. He was safe. And healthy again. I closed my eyes tight and listened to his heartbeat for a few more minutes. There was nothing I loved more than hearing his heart beating, slow and steady.

"Okay," I said and tipped my head back so I could look up at him. "Let's do this thing."

He smiled down at me.

"Do you need to practice your best man speech or anything?"

He cupped my face in his hands. "No more procrastinating. If we're lucky none of them will catch us sneaking into the hotel."

"Easy. They were all so wasted last night."

He laughed. "They really were." He groaned as he sat up, stretching his neck.

"I'm sorry," I said.

He seemed to get a stiff neck whenever I insisted that we stay intertwined all night long.

He leaned down and kissed me again. "It was worth it. Now let's go before we get in trouble."

***

We stopped outside the hotel room door.

He pulled me in close and breathed me in. "We're safe," he said.

And I believed him. But I saw something else in his eyes this time when he said it. And as he held me a little tighter, like he didn't want to let me go.

I blinked fast so I wouldn't cry. For some reason all I could see was red. The blood sputtering out of his mouth and the fear in his eyes on our wedding night. I reached up and traced his lips with my index finger, just to make sure the vision was all in my head.

He kissed my fingertips. "I'll be waiting for you at the end of the aisle."

I smiled up at him. "Promise?"

He kissed my fingertips again and then pulled me in close. "I promise."

"Are you sure we can't just drive down together?"

"Rob insisted that he wanted a bros' morning." James shrugged. "But Ian's driving you guys down. It's going to be fine."

It was. It had to be. Because my heart couldn't take another night like our wedding night. It had almost broken me. "I'll see you tonight."

IVY SMOAK

"Until then." He leaned down. And kissed me. And kissed me. Until my head was dizzy. His fingers dug into my back as he pulled me even closer. And then he stepped back. The corner of his mouth ticked up. "See you later, wife."

"See you later, husband."

I watched him walk down the hall toward the hotel room where all the groomsmen were. I tried to shake away the feeling of doom in my tummy and turned toward my hotel room. It was game time. I did not want to get caught sneaking in.

I tiptoed into the hotel room. There were a few people asleep on the bed. And a few more on the fold out couch.

The floor creaked and a mess of blonde hair popped up from the bed.

"Did you just get in?" Bee asked with a yawn. She winced and pressed her hand to her head, which I'm sure ached.

"No, I was here all night," I said and pretended to yawn.

"Oh." She shrugged. "Last night is a little blurry. I need Advil." She pushed the covers away and climbed out of bed.

Daphne sat up with a yawn. "Where'd you sleep last night?" she asked.

"Here," I lied.

She frowned. "No you didn't. You ran off after the stripteases and never came back."

"I don't remember that."

"Lies," Daphne said with a laugh.

I laughed too. "Okay, you caught me. I really needed to see James. And I figured you were all too plastered to notice if I was gone."

"Oh, well…yeah. Every one of us was drunk. Except for you. Because you're the only pregnant one." Daphne quickly looked away from me. "I gotta hop in the shower! We gotta get on the road in less than an hour. Can you order brunch for us? There's a menu on the nightstand." She practically leapt out of bed and ran into the bathroom.

There was a whole lot about what she had said that was weird. But the thing that stuck out the most was that she was letting me order brunch. Without going over the menu a hundred times and being super anal about it. Which meant…she was definitely trying to get away from me. She'd started acting really weird when I said everyone else was drunk…

Oh my God… I sighed. She was pregnant, wasn't she? Bee had totally believed my lie about being here last night and she was nursing a hangover. But Daphne called me out right away and seemed perfectly chipper this morning. I thought back to last night. I hadn't ever actually seen her drinking anything. All I could picture was a glass of untouched champagne that Justin had forced into her hand. How had everyone seen it but me?

Damn it, I really didn't want to lose this bet. Hopefully I was just imagining it. Who knew…maybe Daphne was just a champ at holding her liquor. And I really didn't think this wedding was a shotgun thing. She and Rob were just head over heels in love. And pregnant. *Gah, no!*

But also…it was kind of perfect if they were. Their baby would be practically the same age as mine. They could grow up together and be best friends. I knew I was getting ahead of myself. I wasn't even sure Daphne was pregnant. But…it kind of seemed like she was. I couldn't believe I was going to lose another bet with James.

"What is with that Cheshire cat grin?" Bee asked and collapsed in the bed beside me.

"I'm pretty sure you're right about Daphne being pregnant. Did you see her drink at all last night?"

Bee scrunched her mouth to the side. "I honestly don't remember. I drank enough for all three of us."

I laughed.

She groaned. "Stop laughing so loud."

"She also said I could order brunch for everyone this morning. And didn't give me a detailed list of menu changes."

Bee propped herself up with a pillow. "That is weird. But she's probably just nervous about the wedding today, don't you think? She's probably freaking out. I mean…she's marrying Rob."

I laughed. "Rob is amazing."

"An amazing flirt."

"True. But he loves her. And now that he's settling down, I bet he'll be less flirtatious."

"I doubt it," Bee said. "He'll probably keep calling you sugar tits half the time."

I laughed. But she was so right. Rob would always be…Rob. And I loved that about him. "Okay, I need to order this food. Anything you know for sure that Daphne hates?"

Bee grabbed the menu from me. "Literally all of this."

I stuck my tongue out at her and called down to the front desk. I decided to hedge my bets by asking for everything on a separate plate. That way there was bound to be something Daphne could eat.

Kristen yawned and sat up on the couch bed. "You guys," she said and turned toward us. "I just had the best dream." She nudged Alina awake.

"What was your dream?" Alina mumbled and swatted her hand away.

"I dreamt that I slept with Professor Hunter."

"Okay," I said. "That's enough. Kristen, you cannot talk about my husband that way right in front of me. It's completely inappropriate and you're driving me crazy."

She laughed. "I'm so sorry. It's just so hard. You know how sexy he is."

"Like that! Stop saying that."

Bee laughed and I tossed a pillow at her face.

"Hey!" Bee rolled out of the way. "I wasn't hitting on James! You're the one who had your hands all over Mason."

"I didn't…"

"Yeah, you kind of did. But I don't blame you. Mason has abs of steel. It's hard not to touch them when they're right in front of you."

"He grabbed my hand."

"Mhm," she said with a laugh.

"He did! But none of that matters. We're even. You flirted with James too."

Bee shrugged. "I can't help it if I like being tied up."

Oh my God. I focused back on Kristen. "But you and I are not even. I mean, how would you feel if I kept saying stuff about your boyfriend…sorry…what's his name?"

"Tim," she said with a smile.

"How would you like it if I said Tim was my hall pass and I couldn't wait to screw him at the wedding tonight?"

"I'd say I'm so glad you said that, because I was hoping we could switch men tonight."

I groaned and fell backward on the bed. It was going to be a long day. But I had to say…I was very curious to meet the man that could apparently put up with Kristen. Because that girl was a lot.

"Just so you know," Kristen said, as if this conversation wasn't over. "Tim is an Olympic athlete. And that stamina in the bedroom? You'd definitely get your money's worth."

I stared at the ceiling. "So in this weird scenario I'm paying for your boyfriend to sleep with me?"

She laughed and jumped on the bed beside me. "It's just a saying. Tim would do it for free. He has a thing for redheads. And brunettes. And blondes."

I laughed. "It sounds like you need to keep him on a leash."

"I bet he'd love that."

Alina plopped down on the bed next to us. "Kristen, you are so weird sometimes. For the sake of everyone's relationships, can we just agree not to hit on each other's men for the remainder of the weekend?"

Kristen pouted. "But…"

"No buts." Alina put her hand into the middle of the bed.

"Fine by me," I said and put my hand on top of hers. I'd gotten jealous enough last night during James' striptease. I wasn't sure I could handle any more.

"I want to keep Mason's abs to myself," Bee said and put her hand on top of mine.

"He made me do it!" I protested.

She laughed. "I know. I'm just giving you a hard time."

"Kristen," Alina said. "Put your hand in."

She groaned.

"Kristen." Alina gave her a hard stare.

Kristen sighed. "Sober me agrees," she said and put her hand on top of Bee's. "But drunk me? I can't control that girl. She's wild."

Yeah…that was not agreement. But it was probably the closest we'd get from her.

"No hitting on each other's men on three," Alina said.

We all said the words. But not perfectly at the same time, so the words all jumbled together incoherently.

I laughed as we threw our hands into the air. I was pretty sure we'd just promised each other absolutely nothing. And tonight was about to get weird.

CHAPTER 29

Saturday

My hands were shaking as I put my earrings on. For some reason all I could see was myself staring back at me in that dingy hospital bathroom. As I'd tried to wash James' blood off my hands. As I'd tried to tear my blood-stained wedding dress off.

Bee's eyes met mine in the mirror. "Are you okay?"

I blinked again and saw myself in my bridesmaid dress. Safe. In the bridal suite of Hunter Creek Country Club. "Mhm." My voice sounded squeaky and strange. I finally slipped the last earring on. I needed to get myself under control. It would be easy to blame my crazy hormones. But…it was more than that. Each hour that passed brought us closer and closer to the wedding. Which brought us closer to tonight. And just the thought made my throat feel tight.

Bee leaned against the bathroom vanity and stared at me. "Does Rob have any crazy exes that you're aware of?"

"What?"

"Of all the girls that Rob dated, are any of them legit insane?"

"I'm honestly not even sure if Rob's had a real girl-friend before."

"Well…there you go. No psychos with guns at this wedding."

I sighed and leaned against the vanity too. "Every time I close my eyes I hear that gunshot. You know…I thought they were fireworks. Instead of looking at James I was looking up at the sky."

"Me too." She grabbed my hand. "But this is Rob's wedding. And Rob doesn't have an insane ex-wife."

I nodded.

"I know it's only been a few months since your wedding, but time heals everything. Maybe by the time my wedding rolls around you won't be thinking about that night anymore."

"Yeah. Maybe." I nodded, as if that would help make it happen.

"It's okay," she said. "You have time. I'm pretty sure Mason thinks that marriage is synonymous with babies because of you and James. And he is definitely not ready to be a father. Yet."

I laughed.

"There's my girl," Bee said. "Today is going to be so fun. And what could possibly go wrong here? Ian, Porter, and Briggs have got this place locked down."

I thought they did at our wedding too. "Isn't there another wedding here today?"

Bee waved her hand through the air. "Apparently it's this cute little old couple. They aren't a threat. And their guests are sectioned off. Now come on," she said and dragged me out of the bathroom. "The photographer should be here any minute and we need to get ready to strike a sexy pose."

I laughed. "I'm not sure I can pull that off right now."

Bee looked down at my stomach. "Nonsense. If you face the camera head-on you won't even be able to tell that you're pregnant."

Maybe. I did have to admit that the black color was pretty slimming. And I felt sexy with the way it criss-crossed in the back. I couldn't wait to see James drooling.

Justin strutted into the room looking like he wasn't hungover at all. Seriously...how did he do it?

"Ladies," Justin said and clapped his hands. "The photographer will be here in five minutes. We'll be doing pictures of the bridal parties separately so Rob and Daphne don't see each other before the big moment. The boys will be taking pictures outside first, so we'll be in here." He sat down on the couch and crossed his legs.

I loved that he was one of the girls with us. I sat down next to him, already happy to be off my feet.

"Last night was fun, huh?" he said.

"I think you probably had the best time."

He laughed. "What can I say? I like what I like." He started drumming his fingers on his thighs.

"Everything alright?" I asked.

"Yes, of course. I'm always just a little hyper on wedding days when there hasn't been a rehearsal. I tried to talk them into coming down last night and doing the rehearsal with a dinner and everything. But they insisted they wanted to spend the night in the city." He shook his head. "Now who knows what'll happen."

"I'm sure it'll be fine."

"I know. But the last huge wedding I planned was yours and it was perfect until that crazy witch ruined it. And now it's all anyone can remember." He pressed his lips together.

Apparently I wasn't the only one who was thinking about that. "Well, James and I did have a rehearsal and a rehearsal dinner. And it was a fiasco."

Justin shook his head. "No, everything was perfect. But I didn't expect the unexpected, that was the problem. Isabella ruined everything. I hate that woman. I hate her, I hate her, I hate her! I don't know how James could have married her after everything she did. I'll never forgive her for any of it." He huffed.

"Everything she did? Did you know her before they got married?" I knew for a fact that Justin hadn't planned James and Isabella's wedding. It was one of the reasons why I'd chosen him. Well, that and the fact that he was amazing.

"What?" he asked.

"You said how could James have married Isabella after everything she did. What did she do?"

"Oh." He shook his head. "No. I just meant...I hate her." He pressed his lips together and stared straight ahead, lost in thought.

First Daphne had been acting secretive.

And now Justin was too.

I looked over at Bee. She was sipping on a mimosa, watching us. She seemed equally perplexed by Justin's comment about Isabella.

I cleared my throat. "Well, at least she's dead." I'd never wished harm on anyone before Isabella. But I meant what I said. Isabella was a menace to society, and I was glad she was six feet under.

"If it had happened sooner, everyone would have been a lot better off," Justin said.

I nodded. Wow, he really did hate her. I thought I hated Isabella more than anyone else, but Justin was winning that competition. I stared at him. It seemed…personal. What had Isabella done to him?

Justin cleared his throat. "You look lovely," he said to me. The change in subject was not at all subtle.

"Thank you. But…you have me so curious now. Did you know Isabella before what happened at my wedding?"

Justin shrugged and looked down at his watch. "No, not personally. An old friend of mine…" He swallowed hard. "Isabella hurt a good friend of mine."

"I'm sorry. Well, I'm sure your friend is happy Isabella is dead too."

"No," he said. "She passed away a long time ago. Way before Isabella got what she deserved."

"Justin, I'm so sorry."

He shook his head. "I just get emotional at weddings. She was the first person who believed I could do all this, you know?" He gestured around the bridal suite. "And every now and then it just hits me. I owe everything to that girl. And she never got to see it."

I grabbed his hand. "I'm sure she'd be so proud of you."

He shook his head and opened his mouth like he was about to respond. But he snapped his mouth shut when the photographer came into the room. He leapt to his feet, literally running away from our conversation.

If Justin had lost his friend years ago, before Isabella died, she must have been so young. I felt tears welling in my eyes. There was nothing worse than a life cut so short. I put my hand on my stomach.

"That was very strange," Bee said and sat down next to me.

"Yeah." I stared at Justin who was talking animatedly to the photographer. "You don't think he was implying that Isabella killed his friend?"

"I don't know."

"Isabella really had a way of wrecking peoples' lives."

"She didn't succeed in ruining yours. You got the fairytale ending."

With a dose of everlasting fear. That I hoped each day would go away. I just nodded.

Daphne emerged from the changing room. Alina was walking behind her, adjusting her veil. But it didn't really need any adjusting. Daphne looked perfect.

I exhaled slowly. My new sister was getting married. This was not a time to be thinking about Isabella and doom and death. This wedding was a fresh start for all of us. I put my hand on my stomach. *Right, little man?*

Bee smiled at me and then grabbed my arm to pull me over to where the photographer was already snapping photos.

I didn't bother trying to stand straight to hide my baby bump. I didn't want to hide it. This baby was the blessing that had kept me going after what happened to James. He'd given me strength. I owed this baby everything. I wasn't sure I'd still be breathing without him.

I put my hand on my stomach and smiled at the camera. And when Daphne pulled me to the side for a picture with just her, I knew everything had a way of working out. My whole family was here. I was safe. We were all safe. And I started to feel those butterflies in my stomach. The same ones I'd felt before I walked down the aisle on my wedding day.

I pressed my cheek to hers as we cheesed at the camera.

This felt like a do-over. And this time James and I would get it right.

***

The golf cart attendant drove slowly, doing their best not to mess up our hair in the wind. The leaves hadn't started to change yet like Justin hoped. But the golf course was stunning in the setting sun.

We pulled up close to the willow tree. The arch they'd set up was covered in white flowers with sprigs of green. It was absolutely gorgeous. It looked like it belonged there. The aisle was dotted with white rose petals and all the guests were seated. There was an electric buzz of anticipation in the air.

Rob and all the groomsmen were standing several feet behind where all the wedding guests were seated. I smiled as I watched James straighten Rob's tie.

But when Rob saw the bridesmaids, he hurried over to us.

"Is everything all set?" he asked me and grabbed my hand, helping me out of the golf cart. "Daphne hasn't run away yet?" He flashed me a smile to let me know he was pretty sure that wasn't what was about to happen.

I laughed. "Of course she hasn't."

"Good."

"Nervous?" I asked.

"No." He shook his head. "Excited."

I smiled. "Daphne is amazing. You did good, Rob."

"You too, sugar tits."

I groaned.

"What, you thought I'd stop with the fun nicknames once I got hitched? Not a chance."

I was actually kind of happy about that. Rob was the brother I'd never had. The very inappropriate brother. I gave him a hug. I wanted to thank him for everything he'd done for me after my wedding. How he'd been my rock. But I didn't want to remind him of that. So I just said, "I love you."

"Hitting on me on the day of my wedding, huh? It's too late for us now."

I punched his arm.

"Everyone line up, right this second!" Justin screamed. "We're late, we're late!"

I swore he'd come out of nowhere.

"And don't look that way," Justin said and grabbed Rob's arm, forcing him to look down the aisle at the empty altar. "Daphne is already en route." He pulled Rob toward the chairs and pushed him to make him start walking up the aisle.

I turned my gaze to James. He was staring at me, his hands shoved into the pockets of his tuxedo jacket. He glanced over at the willow tree and then back at me. And then he raised his eyebrow.

Was that him propositioning me? We had a wedding to attend in one minute. So I just stuck my tongue out at him.

He put his hands over his heart like I'd wounded him and I laughed.

"Alina, you're with James," Justin said. "Maid of honor and best man, hold hands this instant!"

Alina slid her hand into my husband's.

After last night, I did not love that. Honestly, I'd never love that.

"Penny, you're with what's-his-name." Justin gestured over to Matt.

"His name is Matt," I said.

"Yeah…Mike. Whatever. Hold hands, please and thank you."

"I think Justin hates you," I said and grabbed Matt's hand.

I expected Matt to laugh. But he didn't respond at all. He was just staring straight ahead at the altar.

"Matt?" I squeezed his hand.

"Hm?" He looked down at me.

"Are you okay?"

"I'm…working on it."

I pressed my lips together. What did he mean by that? "Don't tell me you're having flashbacks to my wedding night too?"

He frowned. "Don't picture that, Penny. Living in the past can do ugly things to you."

"Yeah." He was definitely right about that.

"You're shaking," he said.

"I'm sorry." I didn't realize I had been.

He dropped my hand and put his arm around my shoulders, spreading some of his warmth to me.

"You know…" his voice trailed off as he hugged me into his side. "I always thought I'd be the first of my friends to get married. I used to want a big family. All of that. A long time ago."

Used to? I looked up at him. "I can't picture you getting married first. I thought you loved playing the field. Or whatever you guys call it."

James and Alina started walking down the aisle.

"I can barely picture it anymore either." Matt took a deep breath, his chest rising and stretching the fabric of his tuxedo. And then he slowly exhaled. "Right now I'm looking forward to being an uncle." He smiled down at me.

"Me too," Mason said.

I looked over my shoulder at Mason and Bee holding hands. They were lucky that they got paired up. Behind them were Kristen and Brendan.

"A nephew is fun," I said to Mason. "But a good uncle would give him a cousin to play with."

Mason laughed. "Maybe. But we're not getting married any time soon."

Bee was right. He definitely thought those two things were the same.

Bee rolled her eyes at me.

"You two look awfully cozy," Mason said. "Get ready for James to lose it."

I laughed and turned around. After last night, James had to know I belonged to him and only him. "Tonight is going to be fun," I said to Matt, ignoring his brother.

"Mason is right. James is probably already pissed at me for having my arm around you right now," Matt said. "Might as well make him really mad. Save me a dance?" He smiled down at me.

"Always," I said with a laugh. James wasn't upset about my friendship with Matt. We were all friends. Matt was the other brother I'd never had. And Mason the other older brother I'd never had. James had nothing to worry about.

"You two are up," Justin said and snapped his fingers in my face. "Mattias, you're doing it all wrong. Hold her hand!"

Why did Justin keep messing up Matt's name? At least Mattias had Matt in it.

Matt laughed and dropped his arm from around my shoulders. He squeezed my hand. "No thinking about the past today, okay? We've got this."

I nodded and he escorted me down the aisle.

It was hard not to feel safe when I was beside Matt. He'd been lost in thought, but when he'd seen that I was scared, he put his whole attention on that. He really would make a great husband to some girl one day.

Speaking of great husbands…I locked eyes with James who was standing to the side of the altar.

His eyes were trained intently on me, like he was taking me in. He looked amazing in his tuxedo. Seriously, no one deserved to look that good in clothes. And the way the sun was setting behind him made him almost look ethereal. Like I'd dreamed up the perfect man.

He glanced over to the willow tree again and raised his eyebrow at me.

Was he trying to make me blush?

I waved at James' sister, Jen, and James' father who were sitting in the front row. I wasn't surprised that James' mom wasn't here. I hadn't talked to Rob and Daphne about it…but I kind of assumed his mom wasn't invited. And I was relieved not to see her. She gave off some serious Isabella vibes.

Matt gave my hand one last squeeze as we split in front of the altar.

I felt James' eyes on me and looked over at him instead of down the aisle.

It was easy for me to read him today. There was a heat in his gaze. An electricity in the air. And I knew without a shadow of a doubt that before the end of the night James was going to have me right against that willow tree.

CHAPTER 30
Saturday

I broke my gaze with James' as the music changed.

Daphne stepped into view and everyone stood.

I held my breath as she started walking down the aisle. And I felt a tear slide down my cheek. This was going to be the best day of her life. And there wouldn't be anything at the end to ruin it. Tonight would just be…perfect.

James was right. Bee was right. Matt was right. We were safe here. This wasn't an outdoor venue in the middle of Central Park. We weren't exposed to any strangers. We were in a cute little corner of Delaware, tucked away from the rest of the world. There weren't even any paparazzi trying to get in. The whole wedding had been very hush hush. And thousands of women would be crushed when the headlines hit Monday morning that one of the most eligible bachelors in New York had been taken off the market.

But there was no one more deserving of Rob's love than Daphne. I was still getting to know her. But I could tell that they couldn't get enough of each other. And they made each other laugh every day. And they had so much in common. But all that mattered was that they were both smiling as they stood right here in front of all their family and friends. And Rob was right…they weren't nervous. They were excited to spend the rest of their lives together.

Rob pulled Daphne in for a kiss before the pastor even started speaking.

There were a few whistles in the crowd.

The pastor cleared his throat. "Jumping the gun a little, aren't we?"

Rob laughed as he finally broke the kiss. "Can you blame me?" The smile on his face was contagious.

And I knew I looked crazy. Smiling so hard it hurt, as tears rolled down my cheeks. I barely heard the pastor speaking as my eyes locked with James'.

His eyes were watery too. "It hurts me to see you cry," he mouthed silently at me.

Which just made me cry more. Because he'd said those exact same words to me on our wedding day.

"I'm crying because I'm so happy," I silently mouthed back to him.

"The happy couple decided to write their own vows. Take it away Rob."

I tried to blink away my tears as I turned my attention back to Rob and Daphne.

"Daphne," Rob said as he held her hands in his. "You know I could go on for hours about all the reasons why I love you. But I love a good party, so I'm gonna cut to the chase."

That got a few laughs from the audience.

Rob smiled. "Because it all comes back to one simple thing. You're terrible at making choices, and I barely think anything through. So we balance each other out."

Daphne laughed. "I hope you thought this marriage through."

He put his hand on the side of her face. "I didn't have to think about it. In all seriousness, Daphne, you're the first person in my life I've ever been able to talk about everything with. I've felt your pain. And I would never let you face that alone. I'll never let you face anything alone ever again."

There were tears in Daphne's eyes again.

He grabbed both her hands again. "I promised you that if you gave me your hand...I'd never let it go. And I'm here promising it again. Take this crazy leap with me. Let's explore the world together. Let's make a family. Let's do life together. The two of us. All of us." He laughed and looked over at his groomsmen. "My boys and I are kind of a package deal."

Daphne nodded and removed one of her hands from his grip to wipe her eyes. "A family," she said and kept wiping under her eyes. "I've so badly needed family. That's what you are to me, you know. As soon as we met...I tried really hard to fight my feelings for you."

"I know," Rob said with a laugh.

"But you feel like home to me. I had a whole speech planned, but I just need you to know that one thing, Rob. You'll always be home to me. Promise you'll never let me go?"

Rob dropped his forehead to hers. "Not in a million years, baby."

"You taught me what it was like to live again," she continued. "That the best things are crazy and fast. You're the best thing in my life. I owe you everything. I love you. Every piece of you. I waited my whole life for you, Robert Hunter."

"Robert Hunter? We're barely married, am I in trouble already?"

"That depends." She blinked away the tears in his eyes. "Kiss me." She tilted her head up to kiss him. His hands slid to her ass as he kissed her back.

The pastor cleared his throat.

I smiled when Rob and Daphne didn't even care.

The pastor cleared his throat a little more. "Daphne, do you take Rob to be your lawfully wedded husband? To have and to hold until death do you part?"

Daphne pulled back. "I do. The easiest decision I've ever made."

Rob reached out his hand and James handed him the rings. He slid one onto Daphne's ring finger.

She smiled up at him.

"And Rob, do you take Daphne to be your lawfully wedded wife? To have and to hold until death do you part?"

"Damn right I do," he said. He tossed Daphne the other ring and she almost dropped it.

She laughed as she slid it onto his finger.

"Then by the power vested in me by the state of Delaware, I now pronounce you husband and wife. Go ahead and kiss again already," he said with a smile.

Rob smiled down at Daphne. "It's the start of our love story," he said. "Let's make it memorable." He grabbed Daphne's hips and lifted her up. She wrapped her arms behind his back and her legs around his waist as their kiss turned sinful.

I cheered at the top of my lungs.

Rob threw his fist in the air as he continued making out with his new bride.

And everyone stood up from their chairs and started cheering too.

The gunshot rang out, and I stumbled backward. And ran straight into James' hard body.

"It's okay," he whispered. "It's just fireworks." He pointed into the sky. The sun was just setting behind the trees. And another loud bang went off and the sky was ignited.

I hated the noise. I hated everything about it. I flinched when another went off.

James wrapped his arms tighter around me. "We're okay." He kissed the side of my neck. "I tried to talk Rob out of them, but he swore they were necessary."

Rob would think they were necessary. As if their amazing vows weren't enough to wow the guests.

I winced again.

"I'm right here," James said. "I'll always be right here."

I turned to face him. I didn't care about seeing the fireworks. I'd always take a view of him instead. "When we promised that to each other under the altar, I almost lost you."

"But I'm still here. And if you think I'll ever leave you, you're dead wrong. I can't get enough of you, baby." He pulled me closer.

I wasn't worried about that. Yes, I was quick to get jealous. Last night was evidence of that. But I knew James wouldn't leave me in that way. I was more worried about him being forced to leave me. With a gunshot. "Can't get enough of me, huh?"

"Never."

The fireworks faded away in the distance when I was wrapped up in him.

"I'm sorry about today," I said. "I…I'm going to be okay. I was just feeling…"

"It's okay. I was too." He slid his fingers into my hair and pulled lightly. "Let's face it together, head-on, okay?"

I would have nodded if he wasn't holding my head in place.

"Us against the world, Penny. The three of us." His free hand slid to my stomach.

I linked my arms behind his neck and pulled him back into a kiss. We were supposed to be walking down the aisle toward the reception. But I didn't even care. When he kissed me I was reminded of our wedding day. But this time, it was the good parts.

When I cried at the altar and got so nervous I forgot my words.

When his hand steadied me.

When he promised me a lifetime of him.

It felt like my world was caving in around me today. But tonight in his arms? His love was enough. His love would always lift me up out of the darkness.

"You're all I've ever wanted," he whispered in my ear.

I loved that he remembered what he said to me on our wedding day. I pressed the side of my face against his chest and listened to his heartbeat. "You're all I've ever wanted," I said back and held him tight.

"What in the ever-living Hades are you two doing?" Justin said and stomped his foot. "It's time for pictures and you're holding everyone up. Didn't you notice all the guests head out to the cocktail hour?"

"No. I did not," James said, his eyes glued to me.

"Uh. To be young and in love. Snap out of it!" He snapped in front of my face for the second time today.

I really didn't love when he did that. "Justin, it's fine," I said, reluctantly turning toward him. Rob and Daphne were still making out and the rest of the bridal party was just hanging around chatting. "We're not even the only ones being bad."

"But I have my eyes on you right now, honey."

I laughed. "Okay. Where do you need us to be for pictures?"

"We already got plenty up here during the ceremony." He pointed over to the willow tree. "So get over there. Now."

"Yes, sir," I said.

I grabbed James' hand and pulled him toward the willow tree.

"I knew I'd get you over here tonight," James said.

I laughed. "Everyone else is about to join us for pictures. We don't exactly have time for tomfoolery."

"Tomfoolery?" He laughed. "I wouldn't call what I have planned for you tonight tomfoolery."

"What exactly do you have planned?"

He dropped his lips to my ear. "You'll have to wait and see."

A chill ran down my spine and then Bee gave me a huge bear hug from behind and squealed. "Party time!"

I laughed and turned toward her. I hadn't even seen her sneak off to the bar.

"It's such a bummer that you can't drink," Bee said. "It would have been so much fun to go nuts tonight."

I'm pretty sure she was going to go plenty nuts without me. "I'm still fun," I said.

"Gah." Bee kicked off her high heels.

"Bee!" I leaned down and picked them up. "We're about to take more pictures."

"More? We already took a billion."

I laughed. "But now the bride and groom can be to-gether in them."

"Gah," she said again.

Mason wrapped his arm around his fiancée and started laughing.

"You're both wasted," I said.

"Me?" Mason pointed to Bee. "Or her?" He pointed to me.

I laughed. They were so drunk. I looked up at James. If they had gotten this drunk at our wedding, I didn't re-member it. He started laughing too.

"Where are Matt and Brendan?" Rob asked as he and Daphne joined us.

I looked around his shoulder. Matt and Brendan were standing there talking to...*oh no*. They were talking to Tan-ner. Who Rob didn't know was coming. *Shoot*. Maybe Rob was as drunk as Bee and Mason and wouldn't even be mad...

Rob followed my gaze. "Party crasher," he said. It looked like he was about to storm over to them, but I grabbed his arm.

"Tanner didn't crash your wedding. Matt invited him as his plus one."

"His plus one? To my wedding? Matt knows I fucking hate that guy. Why would he do this to me today of all days?"

"Rob...Tanner is so nice. Can't you just ignore him?"

"At my wedding?!"

"Yeah. Just focus on Daphne. Pretend Tanner isn't even there."

Rob scowled at me. "It's a little hard when we're supposed to be taking pictures and Matt and Brendan are chatting Tanner up like he's a smoking hot drunk chick."

I laughed. "You're ridiculous."

"You're ridiculous." And then he laughed and pulled me into a hug. "I got married!" He lifted me up and twirled me around.

I wasn't sure if he'd had more to drink than I realized or if he was just drunk on happiness.

"Whoa, whoa," James said and put his arms around me to stop Rob from twirling me around. "Be careful."

"Right," Rob said and released me from his embrace. "Gotta be careful with the pregnant ones. I don't want your baby to pop out and steal the show."

"Of course," I said with a smile.

Rob reached over and grabbed Justin's arm. "Go get the rest of my groomsmen and that stupid idiot they're talking to."

Why does he want Tanner to come over? Is he gonna murder him?

Justin looked over at Matt, Brendan, and Tanner. "You mean the one in that fabulously fitted tux?" Justin asked. "The tall one with the fantastic haircut? The one with the piercing eyes? The one that's making all of your hot friends laugh so hard?"

"No, the hideous unfunny one," Rob said.

Justin looked confused.

"Yes," I said. "His name is Tanner. He's the one in the fabulously fitted suit with the fantastic haircut and piercing eyes and amazing sense of humor."

"I'll be right back then," Justin said. He hurried off as he straightened his tie.

Rob glared at me.

"Jealousy doesn't suit you, Rob," I said and patted his chest.

"It doesn't suit you either," Rob said.

"What?"

He nodded over at James.

Kristen was practically all over him, a cocktail glass in her hand. *Son of a bitch.*

"We're even," Rob said.

"We are not even. I'm mad that some girl is throwing herself at my husband. You're upset because your best friend has another friend."

"Same difference," Rob said.

I shook my head.

"Smile," Rob said and wrapped his arm around my shoulders. The cameraman started taking pictures.

"One with my new sister-in-law!" Daphne said and joined me on the other side. She squeezed me tight and we smiled at the camera.

But out of the corner of my eye I saw Kristen laughing at something James just said.

Mother fucker. So maybe I was quick to judge Rob. Because I was really jealous right now too.

I heard her laughing again and I tried to focus on the pictures we were taking.

But it was really hard when I was seconds away from punching Kristen right in her perfect stupid face. God, when had I turned into Rob?

CHAPTER 31

Saturday

"Smile!" The cameraman said as he took another picture of Rob and James together, back-to-back with their arms crossed.

It was adorable. And somehow sexy at the same time. I couldn't wait to get copies.

I heard Kristen sigh.

I'd been trying really hard to ignore her. But I was seconds away from cracking. Luckily Justin chose that moment to pull Matt, Brendan, and Tanner over.

Rob scowled and broke his pose. "Tanner."

"Robert," Tanner said.

Rob lowered his eyebrows at him. "So we meet again."

Tanner laughed. "Thanks for inviting me," he said and put out his hand for Rob to shake.

Rob didn't shake it.

For the love of God. Just shake the man's hand! I didn't care if I was being a hypocrite. Because if Kristen put her hand out for me right now I'd grab it and make her slap herself.

"I brought a gift," Tanner said and pulled an envelope out of his front pocket. "I've had my private island reserved for you and Daphne for your honeymoon. All expenses paid, including travel. Five-star resort living without any other patrons." He handed Rob the envelope.

"We already have our honeymoon planned. How utterly thoughtless of you."

Tanner shrugged. "I promise this'll be better."

"Than the honeymoon I planned myself for the woman I know better than anyone else in the world? I doubt that."

"I was just trying to…"

"Well it didn't work," Rob said. "You and I will always be enemies."

Wow this was going so much worse than I expected. "Should we start taking more pictures?" I whispered to James.

James shook his head. "This is too good not to watch."

"Enemies?" Tanner laughed. "I have enough of those. Come on, man. I'm trying to clear the air here."

"Well, all I need for you to do is admit that you wear goblin shoes and a man bun every Tuesday night."

Tanner frowned. "Yeah…but I don't. So…"

"Lies! At least admit that I'm Matt's best friend, not you."

"Come on, Rob," Matt said and put his arm around Rob's shoulder. "Today's all about you. Let's get these pictures taken so we can start this epic reception."

Rob sighed. "Fine. Away with him though."

"I've got it," Justin said. Justin looped his arm through Tanner's. And Tanner laughed but casually sidestepped away from Justin. I looked over at Rob and gave him what I hoped was an "I told you Tanner isn't gay" look.

Rob just glared at me. "Trash gift," he said and shoved the envelope against James' chest. "Let's get these pictures taken." He pulled Daphne into a hug.

She whispered something to him and Rob's anger melted away. He leaned down and kissed her.

Hopefully she'd told him to be nice. The gift Tanner had just given them was lovely. They were crazy not to take him up on that offer. I couldn't imagine what kind of crazy stuff was on an island owned by Tanner Rhodes.

I heard giggling and turned to see Kristen all over James again. *For the love of God!* She was supposed to be posing in pictures. Not acting like a homewrecker.

I walked over to them and grabbed James' hand. "Picture time, lover." *Lover?* Why had I just said that?

James suppressed a smile. "Of course, lover," he said back. "Lead the way."

He managed to not laugh until we were a few feet away from Kristen.

"Lover?" he asked.

"I wanted to make sure Kristen knows I'm pleasing you on a regular basis."

"I could be pleased right now…" he reached down and squeezed my butt.

I swatted his hand away. "I swear, if they captured a picture of that…"

He silenced me with a searing kiss. "Silence, lover."

I started laughing, but it died away when he kissed me again. His hands slid to my ass again as he pulled me closer. And I didn't even care that there was most certainly a picture of this now. I wasn't sure if this kiss was more for me or more to get Kristen to finally leave him alone. Probably both.

"Think she got the hint?" I asked as I smiled up at James.

"I don't know. We might have to get caught under the willow tree with your skirt bunched around your hips and me deep inside of you."

I swallowed hard.

"Pictures first though," he said, and pulled me toward where Justin was corralling everyone again.

Justin split us up like we were at the altar again. Boys to the right and girls to the left.

"How much do you want to bet that tonight ends with two fist fights?" Bee whispered to me as she struck a sexy pose. "Rob and Tanner. And you and Kristen?"

"I'm not going to punch Kristen." *Even though she definitely deserves it.*

I yelped as a bunch of doves were released from behind us. I put my hand to my chest. Was the goal tonight to give me a heart attack? If Justin thought that was going to make for a good picture, he was dead wrong. Because I wasn't the only one who screamed. I got that they wanted this wedding to be extravagant. But some of these surprises were terrifying.

Matt dodged one of the birds pooping just in time for it to not hit his tux.

I shook my head. I wasn't sure I even wanted to see what they had planned for the reception.

"Well...what about Rob and Tanner?" Bee asked. "I could see Rob taking a swing."

"Who do you think would win that fight?"

"I don't know..." Bee's voice trailed off as she looked over at the cocktail reception. "Tanner's taller. But he didn't strip for us last night, so I don't know how ripped he is."

"He fills that suit out nicely."

Bee laughed. "You naughty girl." Her eyes dropped lower as she stared at Tanner.

"I didn't mean his package. I meant it looks like he has muscles."

"Oh." Bee laughed again. "I think he has big both. You should see him do a business deal. I really have a thing for guys who own every conference room they walk into."

"Like Mason."

"Mason and Tanner are the only guys I've ever seen do it. I bet James can do it too. Or else he couldn't have sold his first company for so much. They're all packing, for sure."

I laughed.

"I wish we had one more single friend to set up with Tanner. Hey, what about Melissa?"

"I think she's gonna give it another go with Josh."

"Really? Ah, that's so exciting!"

"Yeah. They're amazing together."

"I'd set my friend Kendra up with him, but as adventurous as she is, she has a no-sex-club-owner rule." She shrugged.

"About that… Where were we last night?"

"I don't know. Something new that Tanner's working on."

"Someone said it was called The Society?"

Bee shrugged. "I'm honestly not as in the loop with the Club Onyx business as I used to be. Bee Inspired Media Group is growing so fast…it's hard to keep up with everything else. But Tanner has been amazing. He's already doubled our profits at the club."

"That is amazing."

"He's a magician with making companies boom. Pretty sure he's the most successful venture capitalist in the whole country."

"Impressive." It kind of felt like she was pitching him to me. "Maybe we should tell Kristen about him."

Bee laughed. "Tanner is well dressed, but not as well dressed as Tim." She pointed to someone drinking a martini in a bright blue tuxedo with perfectly coiffed hair.

"That's Tim? Wow, I was not expecting all *that*."

"Mhm."

"I kind of thought he'd look like James. Or at least less…um…"

"Gay? Yeah. Weird, right? But he's not gay, surprisingly enough. Because he's dating…"

"Kristen. I got that. Huh. I really have terrible gaydar."

"Don't beat yourself up about it," Bee said. "I thought the same thing when I first talked to him at the bar. He's just very metrosexual. It's good when a guy cares about himself though." She shrugged.

Yeah. But James cared about how he looked too. That was why he was always going for runs and lifting weights. Not styling his hair and waving his hands around like that. And Tim seemed *very* cozy with Justin. Tanner had slid out of that conversation and was surrounded by a few blonde girls I didn't recognize.

"I'm just glad we're not single," Bee said. "Dating is getting weird."

I laughed. "I'm very happy to be hitched."

"Okay, enough chitchat," she said. "Time to pose."

I laughed again. She was the one that had started talking. I shook my head and smiled at the camera.

I swear we stood there for over an hour, moving around in different groups. I looked longingly over to the cocktail hour. My stomach growled. I wanted all those amazing hors d'oeuvres. But they were funneling the people under the big white tents they'd constructed for the reception.

I sighed. Maybe I could sneak off into the kitchen later and eat a bunch of mini crab cakes once the dancing started.

After taking another few pictures, the cameraman finally called it quits and let us go.

"Time for your grand entrances, people," Justin said. "Get with your partners from earlier. And if you haven't thought of a dance, I will literally kill you."

Whoa. Justin! This was the first time I was even hearing of an entrance dance.

I looked over at Matt.

"I got us covered," Matt said and downed the glass of scotch he was drinking.

"I hope so." I looped my arm through his as he escorted me to the tent. "Because here I was thinking that no one was going to try to kill anyone tonight."

Matt laughed.

"So what's the plan?" I asked.

"Don't you trust me?"

"Yeah...but..."

"I said I've got us covered, Penny."

That wasn't exactly a plan. And I was supposed to be dancing too. This didn't seem like a well thought out plan at all.

But the DJ was already announcing the best man and maid of honor. James and Alina did this hilarious shimmy thing and then pretended to strike poses at the end, like there were paparazzi taking pictures of them.

I laughed.

"Ready?" Matt asked.

No...

He ducked down behind me and put his head under my skirt. Holy shit, what the hell was he doing? Bee's bet about there being two fights at this wedding was suddenly looking much more likely. James was going to kill Matt before the end of the night.

Matt grabbed my thighs and stood up.

I screamed as he lifted me in the air. I was sitting up on his shoulders and my head almost hit the top of the tent. I looked down and Matt's head was still hidden beneath my skirt. *Jesus.* I grabbed the fabric and lifted it over his head, hoping I wasn't showing all the guests my underwear.

"Hold on," Matt said, his fingers tightening on my thighs.

What?

He started dancing past the tables, moving his shoulders way too much. I grabbed onto his neck with one hand and buried my fingers in his hair with the other.

He twirled in a circle and I had to dodge one of the many chandeliers hanging from the top of the tent.

I didn't mean to pull on his hair, but he was trying to kill me, and I didn't know what else to hold on to.

He looked up. "I like when you're rough with me, Penny." He winked at me before spinning us in a circle again.

I leaned forward, wrapping my arms under his neck so I wouldn't tumble off his back. "Put me down!" I said with a laugh.

"Okay, I'll be honest, I have no idea how to get you down now."

"Matt!"

"And I really like the way the lace of your thong scratches the back of my neck."

I swatted the back of his head.

He laughed and knelt down in the middle of the dance floor. "You can dismount me now, you kinky girl."

He was ridiculous. I leaned forward and kind of hopped off his shoulders. I looked behind me and his head was still under my skirt. I pulled my dress back in place.

"What are you doing?" I asked.

He was grinning up at me, still on his knees. "I'm a dead man, aren't I?" he said.

"Yeah. You are." But I put my hand out for him anyway to help him to his feet.

Before Matt grabbed it, James came over and grabbed my hand instead. And then he grabbed Matt by the lapels of his tuxedo jacket and pulled him to his feet.

"If I ever see you with your head up my wife's skirt ever again, you're dead." He shoved Matt backward.

Whoa. It was all in good fun. I stepped in front of James. "Matt was just messing around. Let's go sit down." I was not going to cause a scene at Rob's wedding.

I pulled James off the center of the dance floor and tried to get him to sit down at Table 1. At least…I thought Table 1 was our table. I was rather distracted by the ice sculpture in the middle of it. Was that Rob and Daphne naked? In ice? I had so many questions. First and foremost…had they posed for that?

But James grabbed my hand, led me right past our table, and ducked out of the tent.

"James…we're part of the wedding party, we can't just…"

He pushed my back against one of the bars constructing the tent. There was a hunger in his eyes. And I was pretty sure it had nothing to do with the crab cakes we'd missed out on.

"James, we can't miss Rob and Daphne coming in…"

He pushed my skirt up, moved my thong to the side, and slid two fingers inside of me. *Jesus.*

"Your pussy is mine," he said.

I gripped the back of his neck.

He moved his fingers slowly in and out of me before picking up the pace.

I tried not to moan. I could hear the DJ announcing the next people in the wedding party. I could hear the guests cheering. And if I could hear them, they'd be able to hear me too. Hell, anyone could just walk out here and…

Just that second I saw Porter turn the corner. He saw us and immediately turned his back to us. But he didn't walk away. He stood there with his arms crossed, making sure no one else would see us.

"James, Porter is…"

"You think this is the first time Porter has caught me with my hand up your skirt?"

I knew for a fact that it wasn't.

"You're soaking wet, baby. You love when people watch us."

I moaned and clapped my hand over my mouth.

"Half of me wants to go down on you right in the middle of the dance floor. To show everyone that you're mine." He pumped his hand faster.

God. I let my hand fall from my mouth.

"Every inch of you is mine." He reached up with his fingers, hitting a spot that had me so close to the edge.

"Yes!"

"Say it, Penny."

"Every inch of me is yours."

"Good girl." He removed his hand right before I came.

My throat made a weird squeaking noise. "James…"

He slid his fingers into his mouth as he stared down at me, the hunger still in his eyes.

God.

He licked off every drop, the intensity in his eyes only growing.

"I was so close," I said. I lifted my skirt slightly, trying to tempt him to come back to me.

He leaned forward and grabbed the hem of my skirt.

Thank God.

"You tortured me," he whispered, his breath hot in my ear. "Now I get to torture you." He dropped my skirt back into place.

I was so frustrated that I could scream. "I didn't ask for Matt to do that."

"You also didn't slap him and tell him to stop."

I just stared at him. "But…James…"

"You can beg me to let you come later when you're on your knees choking on my cock."

Holy shit.

"But right now they're about to announce Rob and Daphne coming in. And like you said…we can't miss it."

He walked backward and ducked under the flap of the tent, leaving me panting out here all alone.

Screw that. I wouldn't be the one begging him later. He'd be the one begging me.

CHAPTER 32

Saturday

I ate another forkful of the plate of mini crab cakes that had magically arrived in place of the first course.

I knew James had arranged it. Which was incredibly sweet. But he hadn't been sweet ten minutes ago when he finger fucked me until I was two seconds away from coming and then stopped. I licked the side of my fork. It was really fun to do. Because I was pretty sure the fork was made of pure gold. All the silverware was. And so was the little tray underneath the inappropriate ice sculpture.

James lowered his eyebrows as he stared at me.

"Girl, I get it," Kristen said. Who for some reason was seated next to me. "You suck Professor Hunter's cock on the regular. Stop rubbing it in."

I was so shocked by what she'd said that I dropped my fork onto my plate. I opened my mouth to say something salty back to her, but I stopped when I saw Tim's arm around her shoulders. He'd had zero reaction to what Kristen had just said. How was he not fuming?

"You must be Tim," I said and reached across her plate to shake his hand. "It's so nice to finally meet you."

"The pleasure is all mine," Tim said. But instead of shaking my hand, he pulled it to his lips and gently kissed the back of it.

"I have to say, the two of you make a perfect couple," I said as I quickly pulled my hand away from his lips. I wasn't sure if they actually made a perfect couple or not. But I sure wanted Tim to start being more possessive of Kristen. Kind of like the way James was possessive of me. Driving me slowly insane.

Tim touched his chest. "Why thank you, you gorgeous specimen."

"You're very welcome. Seriously, you two look perfect together."

Kristen raised her eyebrow at me.

"We really do, huh?" Tim said, pulling Kristen closer to his side.

My work here was done. Hopefully he'd hold her closer for the rest of the night. "Mhm. Absolutely." I took another big bite of crab cakes.

James put his hand on my thigh. "Aren't you going to thank me?" he asked.

"For what?" I looked up at him. "For sexually torturing me?" I whispered and took another slow bite, licking the side of my lips.

He lowered his eyebrows.

I'd recognize the heat in his gaze anywhere. He wanted me. Well, good. I wanted him too. I bit my bottom lip as my gaze dropped to his mouth.

"I have to make a speech any minute," he said. "So eat your crab cakes and stop giving me sex eyes."

"Are you sure you're not just aroused by the ice sculpture?"

James laughed. "I'm sure."

I took another very seductive bite.

James groaned and adjusted his tuxedo pants.

I smiled to myself when I saw that there was a tent in his pants. I hoped he did have a huge erection when he stood up to give his best man toast. *Wait…no.* I didn't want that. Because Kristen would be staring at him.

"Dead kittens," I said, because it was the first unsexy thing that popped into my head.

James frowned. "What?"

"Just tons of them. Dozens of dead kittens." I frowned. *Gross.*

"Why are we talking about dead kittens?"

I leaned closer to him. "I don't want Kristen to see what you're packing. I'll stop torturing you now, I swear. Just undo…that." I gestured toward his pants.

"By thinking of dead kittens?" he asked.

I nodded.

He took a deep breath and sighed. He looked up at the ceiling of the tent. And for some reason staring at the tent thankfully made the tent in his pants start to disappear.

"It worked," I said.

"Mhm." He took a sip of his drink.

"Was it the kittens thing?"

"No." He leaned closer to me so no one could hear. "I was thinking about Kristen staring at my junk."

I smiled at him. "Thank you," I mouthed to him.

He put his arm behind my back, pulling me closer to him. "You have nothing to worry about with her. You act like you don't know how pretty you are. When I tell you on a daily basis. I want you and only you."

"Then have me."

He leaned back, letting his arm fall from my shoulders. "Dead kittens," he mumbled and stared up at the lights that were strung around the top of the tent.

I smiled to myself. I loved James' domineering side. But I loved his sweet side just as much.

Justin popped up out of nowhere behind James. "James," he whispered.

James jumped in his seat. Apparently he hadn't seen Justin approach either.

"It's time for your speech." Justin rubbed his shoulders. "Are you ready? Do you need anything at all?" He kept rubbing his shoulders.

Dude, I just got Kristen out of the way, and now I had to get Justin to stop hitting on James too. And I kinda wanted him to give me James' pants back while we were on the topic of inappropriate things.

"Yeah, no, I'm good," James said and gave him a weird look.

Justin sighed and removed his hands. "Okay then. I'll let you get to it. And remember the grand speech finale."

The grand speech finale? What was Justin talking about?

The light music faded completely as James stood up and tapped his knife to the side of a champagne glass.

The room hushed as all the guests turned to him. It reminded me of what Bee had said earlier. How sexy it was when a man could control a room like that. She was damn right. I crossed my legs under the table.

James looked over at the sweetheart table where just Rob and Daphne were sitting. "Rob took his sweet time asking me to be his best man," James said with a laugh.

I smiled up at him.

"And honestly? I would have been a little offended if he'd asked anyone else. Rob has been by my side through so much. The good. And the bad. And I'm sorry that there's been so much bad." He nodded to Rob.

Rob smiled. "I forgive you."

James smiled back. "I think usually little brothers say this to their big brothers. But Rob, I don't know what I would have done without you by my side growing up. You always had my back. 100%, without any question. Even in fights with our friends." He nodded toward Matt and Mason. "And God knows I was usually in the wrong."

I knew that James had lost touch with Mason and Matt after college. I wondered if that was what he was referring to. I was so glad they all found their way back to each other.

"And you always make me laugh, especially when I need it. I gotta say...I'm used to having your undivided attention. And I'm a little jealous that I have to share you now."

Daphne laughed.

"But seriously...you and Daphne? I see the way you look at her. And the way she looks at you. I've always wanted the best for you. And I'm glad you took your damn time to settle down. Because Daphne is the best. She understands you. And she'll pick up the slack when I'm not always a good brother."

Daphne smiled again, but there were tears in her eyes now.

"Welcome to the family, Daphne." He looked back at Rob. "I love you, man," James said. "And I love that you found love. Because if I've learned anything over the past couple years...nothing is more important than that."

"I love you too, big bro," Rob said and lifted his glass in the air.

"Now what eloquent thing did you say when you were the best man at my wedding?" James pretended to think.

"Oh, right. I can't wait to be an uncle to all the kids you're certainly going to have because you never wear a condom." James winked at Rob.

Rob laughed.

And so did I. I was so shocked when Rob had said that at our wedding. It was completely inappropriate. Payback was supposed to be a bitch, but Rob just kept laughing.

"Ow ow!" Bee yelled.

Mason and Matt both whistled at the same time and then started laughing.

And Daphne looked very, very pale.

I exhaled slowly as I looked from her pale face to her untouched glass of champagne. *Damn it.* I had for sure lost the bet. She was already pregnant. The Hunter brothers really should wear condoms more often if they didn't want millions of kids running around.

James sat down to the applause of the guests.

I leaned over and kissed his cheek. "Very eloquent speech."

He laughed. "Right?"

There was a loud popping noise and I almost screamed again. But then I saw it was just all the waiters popping more champagne. Well…not popping. They'd just cut off the tops of the bottles with freaking swords.

What the actual hell?

"What is all this weird stuff?" James said with a laugh. "I'm pretty sure Justin gave Rob a list of all the craziest things they could do at their wedding, and Rob said yes to all of it."

"Sounds about right. I guess this was the grand speech finale?"

James shrugged.

I plopped another mini crab cake in my mouth and rested my head on his shoulder.

"Barehanding the food now?" he asked with a smile.

"I'm a barbarian."

He kissed the top of my head and barehanded another crab cake to feed me. As I ate the last bite, I swirled my tongue around his thumb.

"Fuck," he groaned.

I tuned out the next few speeches as I just stared up at James.

He'd promised to get me alone under the willow tree. Was now a good time? I almost asked him to sneak away but the main course had just come out and there was bacon wrapped something involved, so I wasn't moving an inch.

You're welcome, little dude, I said to myself and put my hand on my stomach.

I looked over at James. He was smiling at me.

"What?"

"Are you talking to her again?"

"*Him.* I'm right about this one."

"This one?" He raised his eyebrow.

I sighed and put my fork down. It was time to admit defeat. "I think that Daphne is…"

"Ladies and gentlemen, may I please have your attention!" Rob said, cutting me off from having to concede. "We have so much to celebrate tonight." He grabbed Daphne's hand and pulled her to her feet. "My beautiful new wife." He kissed her cheek.

A little color went back to her face.

"And a beautiful family." He lifted his glass in the air.

Well…I mean…he could have just been referring to all of us sitting at Table 1. *Maybe. Possibly. Probably not.*

Bee leaned around the ice sculpture so she could see me. "Shotgun wedding," she mouthed silently at me from across the table.

Yeah, I know. Gah! I really hated losing bets.

Rob wrapped his arm around Daphne, the biggest smile on his face. "A family of three," he said and put his hand on Daphne's stomach.

"We're pregnant!" Daphne shouted.

Son of a bitch. I pressed my lips together at the thought. I didn't mean that. Daphne was lovely. And I was super happy for them.

"Huzzah!" Rob yelled and threw his glass on the ground.

Everyone around him started throwing their glasses and yelling "huzzah" at the top of their lungs.

Daphne threw one of the plates like a frisbee across the tent. It shattered into a million pieces and then more people started throwing glasses and plates down on the ground.

Bee took one more bite off her plate and then lifted it in the air. "Huzzah!" she slammed it on the ground and then everyone at our table started doing it too.

A glass shattered dangerously close to my foot. And I was pretty sure Kristen had done it intentionally. I leaned into James so I wouldn't get cut.

And then a bunch of confetti started raining down from the top of the tent.

I coughed and waved my hand in front of my face.

James smiled down at me.

"Don't even say it," I said and pushed confetti off my shoulder. "Maybe that was the grand speech finale? The glass seems like a hazard for dancing if you ask me." But there were already a bunch of waiters rushing out with brooms.

"You're changing the subject when what we should really be discussing is…I win."

I laughed. "I said not to say it."

"She's going to have a best friend for life now," James said and put his hand on my stomach.

I'd tell him that he was wrong, and that I was most definitely going to have a boy. But I'd just lost a bet. And I didn't feel quite as confident about the sex of our baby anymore. I was terrible at bets. "That's all that really matters," I said. "We should go congratulate them."

"Well, the bet still matters," he said as he helped me to my feet.

"What are you going to make me do?"

"You'll see," he said and winked at me.

I swatted his butt as all of us ran over to Rob and Daphne.

Mason was already hugging Rob. And even though Bee had guessed it, there were tears in her eyes as she hugged Daphne.

"I knew it," Matt said.

"Me too," said Mason.

Apparently I was the only one who really believed it wasn't a shotgun wedding. I was a sucker for love.

I gave Rob a big hug. "Congratulations."

He kissed my cheek. "JJ and RJ are going to be best friends, I just know it."

I laughed. "There is no way that James is going to name our son James Junior."

"You never know," Rob said. "Why are you crying?" He cupped the side of my face.

"I seem to do that a lot recently. I'm just…so happy."

Rob pulled me back into his embrace.

"I'm so happy for you," I said.

He squeezed me tight. "I'm terrified. But so excited. Is that normal?"

"100 percent." I'm pretty sure I bounce back and forth between those two emotions on a daily basis. "But you're going to be a great dad. You took care of James when he needed you."

"Hopefully my son won't have as strong of a left hook. No. Scratch that. I hope he does."

I laughed, even though I'd never heard the story of James punching Rob. I'd have to hear that another day though, because James pulled Rob into a hug.

I kept blinking away my tears.

Daphne grabbed my hand. "I'm sorry. I wanted to tell you as soon as we found out. But Rob wanted it to be a surprise. I thought we were going to tell you at that parrot restaurant, but Rob surprised me with a proposal."

I'd known something weird was up that night. *God, why hadn't I followed my instincts?* I should have won this bet. Instead I'd totally lost. But I couldn't be mad at myself. It wasn't bad to be a believer in true love. And despite the fact that Rob and Daphne were expecting a child, I truly believed they were meant to be together regardless. They were like two puzzle pieces that just…fit.

"That's okay," I said with a smile. "You told us now."

"That was part of the reason I was acting weird too," added Daphne. "Too many secrets! I hate keeping secrets from you."

I gave her a big hug. "They're going to be best friends, you know. Just like James, Rob, Mason, and Matt were."

"I hope so. I have the cutest picture of them when they were little. Rob showed it to me."

I smiled. "They used to be so cute, huh?" I turned to look at James and Rob all grown up. They were standing with Mason and Matt laughing. Everyone looked so happy. I wanted this moment to last forever. "I guess they're still cute."

Daphne laughed. "They really are. Maybe we'll each have two boys and they'll be just like the four of them."

"Well, hopefully not exactly like them. We'll be better moms than Mrs. Hunter."

"Oh, so much better," Daphne said.

"I can't believe you guys didn't invite her because of us."

"Are you kidding? We love you and James. And as far as I'm concerned, that woman is not part of our family."

I gave her another hug, trying hard to blink away my tears. This was what I wanted. For us to be friends. And I'd been too foolish to realize that we already were.

Bee put her arms around us and I laughed.

"Group hug!" she said.

I laughed. "You're so drunk."

"Not yet." She downed a shot that I hadn't seen in her hand a second ago. "But I'm about to be! Best night ever!"

"Best night ever!" Daphne yelled.

Yeah. They had a good point. "Best night ever!" I yelled.

CHAPTER 33

Saturday

I smiled as I watched Rob dip Daphne low.

Despite what everyone said, this wasn't a shotgun wedding. They were perfect together.

"You're crying again," James said.

"What?" I reached up and touched beneath my eyes. Sure enough, I felt the tears.

"You're so cute." He pulled me into his side.

"I'm not cute. I'm very sexy."

He kissed the top of my head.

"Speaking of sexy," Kristen said and leaned in way too close. "Threesomes are very sexy."

"Okay." I put my hand out to prevent her from leaning in any further. "Kristen, we talked about this. No hitting on my husband." I emphasized the word husband. Although I wasn't sure she understood the concept.

Kristen shrugged. "It's just an offer. One you can't refuse, I hope." She stood up. "Want to dance, Professor Hunter?"

The music had just changed and guests were flooding onto the dance floor.

James didn't even look up at her. "I think I owe my wife a dance," he said and put his hand out for me.

At least he was being well behaved. Well…kind of. Because he was giving me all kinds of sex eyes. Not the threesome kind, just the normal kind.

He led me to the dance floor and pulled me in close. A smoke machine must have been turned on somewhere, because it was like we were dancing on a cloud. This was one thing I could get behind. *Nice work, Justin.* James twirled me around and the smoke swirled in the air away from my skirt. It truly was like we were dancing in the air.

James pulled me back in close. I was pretty sure this was just what love felt like. Security. I smiled up at him. "No threesome tonight, huh?"

"I've had enough of those for one lifetime."

I couldn't help it. I kicked him right in the shin.

"Ow."

I glared at him.

"Please don't tell me this is when you're finally going to demand my actual number."

I shook my head. I knew it was a lot. And I didn't care. Because he'd chosen me. Besides, I didn't want the knowledge of his sexual history to get in the way of the stars in my eyes as I looked up at him.

The slow song switched to a fast paced one and Bee gave me a bear hug, almost knocking me to the floor.

"Time to dance!" she screamed.

That was fine. I was happy to dance with her. As long as I stayed close to James all night. I didn't want to leave him alone. Kristen would see it as a peace offering or something. And I didn't want peace with her. I wanted her to stay away from my man.

***

I felt drunk even though I wasn't. I just felt fucking alive. The sweat dripped down the back of my neck, and James' hands were on my hips, pulling me closer.

I wasn't sure how long we'd been dancing. But based on how overheated I was and how hard I was smiling? Probably a while. And I'd only had to practically shove Kristen away four times. Which seemed on the low side to me since James was looking fine as hell tonight.

I heard laughter and looked over at Justin on the dance floor. Tim was bent over in front of him and Justin was spanking his ass. I had so many questions. But it looked like they were all having the time of their lives. Including Kristen. Who was now spanking Justin's ass. Maybe that was the threesome that was about to happen.

"Everyone is so drunk," I said.

"Not me." James' hand swept over my stomach, pulling me closer. He nuzzled his nose into the side of my neck. "And I need you," he whispered into my ear.

I tilted my head back so that I could see him. "Then take me."

He bit down lightly on my earlobe.

I tried my best not to moan right on the dance floor. I expected him to pull me out of the tent. Especially since the song had just ended.

Instead, he spun me around so that I was facing him. I exhaled slowly as I stared up at him. Earlier today, I'd been terrified of this wedding. Like the whole world had been caving in on top of me. Like I couldn't breathe. I exhaled slowly. But I felt so safe in James' arms. James was the best thing I'd ever have. He was the best part of my life.

"Baby." He ran his thumb beneath my eye. "You know it hurts me when you cry."

"I love you," I said.

"I love you more."

I pressed my lips together. "Impossible."

He ran his fingers through my hair. "Trust me, it's possible. Whatever you're feeling...I don't know how it could be as consuming as what I'm feeling for you."

"Our baby is going to have a best friend."

James dropped his forehead to mine.

"This isn't a slow song," I whispered.

"It feels like one."

Every song felt like a slow song with him. Like time stopped when our bodies were pressed against each other.

"Do you want to get out of here?" I said and looked up at him.

"You're not scared we're gonna miss something? They haven't even cut the cake."

"I've seen a cake cut before. It's hardly momentous."

James smiled. "In that case." He stepped away from me and put out his hand. "Are you ready for the time of your life?"

I had no idea what he meant by that. But I'd always take his hand when he offered it.

Before he could pull me out of the tent though, Justin stepped in front of us. "Where do you think you two are going?" he asked.

"A walk," James said.

"It's almost time to cut the cake." He looked down at his watch. "You have 20 minutes, tops. And if I have to come find you, I'm going to be very upset. I might just have to punish the two of you."

I laughed. I loved the idea of James punishing me. But I didn't think I'd love Justin's punishment. He'd probably force me to help plan another rushed wedding. Or get me covered in glitter again. Or make me do unspeakable things with Tim and Kristen. I shuddered at the thought.

"We'll be back in 20 minutes then," James promised.

"Okay. You don't want to miss this. It's going to be epic. They're going to cut the cake with a sword. Damn it! Why'd I just ruin the surprise? I'm a mess tonight." He fanned his face. "Sometimes I get a little loopy when I've had too much to drink. Oh well! Time to get back to grinding on the dance floor, bitches!" He blew us each a kiss and ran back onto the dance floor.

Yup, he was definitely drunk.

I laughed as James pulled me out of the tent. "Now that we know the cake is being cut with a sword, we probably don't need to hurry back. Besides, there's no way he's going to come find us. He's having the time of his life."

"My thoughts exactly."

We walked hand in hand over to the little waterfall. For a second we just stood there and stared. The very first time we'd been here there were still lightning bugs. But they'd disappeared early this year as the chilly fall air swept in.

James pulled my back to his chest. And his hand slid down my thigh, hiking up the skirt of my dress.

I shivered, but not from the cold. James lightly traced my thigh with his fingertips. His other hand slipped down the front of my dress and grabbed my breast.

Before I could protest, he moved my thong to the side and slid his finger inside of me.

God. I let my head fall back on his shoulder.

His thumb brushed against my clit.

And it was like the shock of electricity woke me up. "James," I hissed. "Anyone can walk out here and…"

He thrust another finger inside of me.

Jesus. I grabbed his forearm to stop him, but instead I found myself guiding his movements.

"Baby, you've always loved the thrill of almost getting caught."

I pushed my ass back, rubbing it against his growing erection. His slow exhale made me shiver. I needed him inside of me. Because he was right. I loved the idea of getting caught. He'd always known it. He'd just had to show me that it was true.

"I can feel how much you love it," he groaned.

I did. So fucking much.

"You're soaking wet."

I moaned.

"I'd dare you to take this off like last time," he whispered against my neck. "But I love bunching up your skirt and fucking you hard."

Just putting that image in my head made me moan again. But before I could respond, he grabbed my waist and lifted me over his shoulder.

My laughter drowned out the music from the reception.

He pushed my skirt up and lightly nipped my exposed ass cheek.

It was déjà vu. From our first night here. Even more so as I felt the soft leaves of the willow tree against my skin as he dipped us beneath the branches.

It was quieter underneath the tree. Like we were tucked away and hidden from the world. And when James set me down on my feet it was almost like I was transported back in time.

I wanted to call him Professor Hunter. And I wanted him to fuck me against this tree. Desperately.

"Hmm…" I twirled around beneath the branches. "Should I lie down? Or will the fertilizer give me a terrible rash?" I'd never asked him how he knew about such things. And I never would. Because his past didn't matter. This moment did. We did.

"Put your hands on the tree trunk," he said, ignoring me.

But he was right there with me. Back in time. Before we were really an us. When we'd both just started falling. God, who was I kidding? I'd fallen for him the moment I fell into his arms in that coffee shop.

I followed his instructions and put my hands against the tree trunk. "Time to teach me a lesson, Professor Hunter?"

He groaned.

"Because I've been a very naughty girl." I hiked up my skirt and arched my back.

I heard the zip of his pants and I clenched. I needed him inside of me. He was right. I was fucking soaked. And I needed him. I always needed him.

He grabbed my hips and thrust himself inside of me.

I gasped, my palms digging into the bark. God, I loved that. The pain and the…

He thrust again.

Pleasure. Yes! Just like that.

He fucked me harder. Faster. A couple weeks ago, he'd been gentle with me. Worried about his baby growing inside of me.

But it was like he'd lost control the past few days. He fucked me like it was just the two of us. Like we were in love and nothing else mattered.

His fingers dug into my hips. Painfully so. And I loved every fucking second of it. I'd always liked it rough. And he knew it.

I pushed against the trunk of the tree, matching his thrusts. I was so fucking close to coming. And I didn't even care if I screamed loudly enough for the whole reception to hear. It felt too good. Too consuming. Too much.

But he pulled out of me far too soon.

I turned around to see him, my skirt still bunched up in my hands. I watched his chest rise and fall as he caught his breath, his cock standing at attention through the zipper of his tuxedo pants.

Last time we'd done this, he'd fucked me against the tree so hard that my back was sore for days from the little cuts from the bark. I'd been fully expecting that again.

Instead, I watched him pull off his jacket and toss it on the ground.

"Lie down," he said.

There was a difference between being a dirty little secret and the love of someone's life. And as much as I loved getting fucked against a tree... I sat down on top of his jacket in the grass and slowly spread my legs.

For a second he just stood there and watched me.

I ran my hand up the inside of my thigh as I stared up at him. His Adam's apple rose and fell. And before I reached my wetness, he took a step toward me.

He got down on his knees and leaned over me, thrusting himself inside of me again.

Yes! I gripped the muscles in his back. Yes, I liked being his dirty little secret. But I loved being cherished by him too.

He grabbed my ass, pulling me even closer. The shift of angle made me cry out.

"Baby, you're just trying to get caught."

I moaned again.

"You really are a dirty girl. And I fucking love it."

I pulled his lips down to mine. I didn't care if we got caught. I just wanted him inside me. Faster. Harder. *God, yes!*

He bit down on my lip as he thrust faster.

"James..."

"Come with me, baby." He pulled my hair so I'd meet his gaze. And that was it. The little bit of pain mixed with the excruciating pleasure.

"Fuck," he groaned as I tightened around his cock.

He kissed me as I came. His kisses growing more ragged as he released himself inside of me.

I blinked up at him. "That was...not the same as last time." It had started off very similar. But it ended up being a lot more gentle. Loving. Perfect. I ran my fingers through his hair.

"I didn't want to hurt you." He ran the tip of his nose down the length of mine before pulling out of me.

"And you wanted to back then?"

For a second he looked confused.

I felt so empty without him inside of me. "You wanted to hurt me back then?" I asked again.

"No. Not at all. But I think a part of me still wanted to fuck you out of my system." He smiled down at me. "And somewhere along the way I fucked you into my system instead of out of it."

I laughed and looped my arms behind his neck, pulling him back to me. "What an eloquent way to put it."

"I'm only kidding. I was infatuated with you. It was like I couldn't breathe without you."

I stared into his eyes. "I felt exactly the same way. You completely captivated me. I dreamed about you every night we weren't together."

He ran his fingers through my hair. "I dreamed about you too. Sinful dreams."

I smiled up at him. "Me too." I'd had so much fun tonight. And I knew the party was still going on, because I could hear the music blaring. But...I just wanted to go home with my husband. As fun as it was to be part of the bridal party...I needed some time just the two of us. "I know it's still early. But do you want to head home?"

James smiled down at me. "I actually have a better idea." He pulled out an envelope from his pocket. "Want to go to Tanner's private island for the week?"

"Seriously?"

"We got robbed of our honeymoon. Let's take it now."

I didn't actually want to go home. I just wanted to be alone with him. It didn't matter where we were. And a surprise honeymoon at Tanner's private island sounded amazing. It was a great gift. Rob was ridiculous. "A thousand times yes."

James' lips met mine.

I couldn't wait to kiss him senseless on a private island. "The rest of this year is going to be amazing. The island, the Caldwell Halloween party, Christmas!" And I still needed to get him tied up in our sex dungeon and have my way with him. I had so many wicked plans for what I was going to do to his naked body.

James smiled down at me. "And a baby in the New Year," he said.

"Mhm." I was really excited about that too.

He dropped his forehead to mine. "And don't forget five months of seduction."

"How could I possibly forget that?" If he thought the last few weeks were sexy...he was going to be very surprised about everything I had planned for him. The five months of seduction had only just begun. I bit my lip as I looked up at him. "What time does the plane leave?"

"Not until the morning."

I grabbed his tie and pulled him closer. That gave us plenty of time for round two.

STEAMY BONUS SCENE

Professor Hunter and Penny are so hot together! And I can't stop writing about them. Which is why this super steamy bonus scene exists.

James' office isn't the only place where James and Penny are heating up campus…

To get your free copy of James and Penny's steamy bonus scene, go to:

www.ivysmoak.com/seduction-pb

WHAT'S NEXT?

James and Penny face their biggest hurdle yet when her pregnancy has life-threatening complications. And for the first time ever, see their story unfold through James' point of view.

James and Penny's story continues in *The Light to My Darkness*…available now!

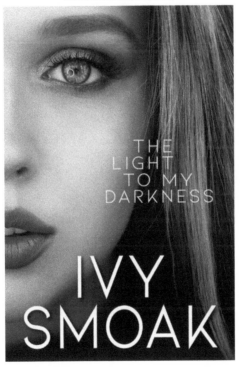

A NOTE FROM IVY

When I first started writing this book, I wanted it to be a short story about the annual Caldwell Halloween party coming back. A fun Hunted/Empire High series mashup.

That didn't exactly happen. Because when I started writing, I couldn't stop. My soul needed this book. I can't even explain how much I missed writing about James and Penny. And Rob! Don't even get me started on Rob. I can't believe it took me this long to write about his wedding.

And now that I've started writing about James and Penny again? I don't know when I'll be able to stop!

I mean…there's still 4 and a half more months of seduction, right? And I didn't even write about the Caldwell Halloween party yet!

Okay, it's officially happening. I can't even help myself!

But while you wait for the next Seduction book, keep reading James and Penny's story in The Light to My Darkness. There's still so much you haven't learned about this couple yet. And writing/reading about them will always feel like coming home to me.

Ivy Smoak

Ivy Smoak
Wilmington, DE
www.ivysmoak.com

ABOUT THE AUTHOR

Ivy Smoak is the Wall Street Journal, USA Today, and Amazon #1 bestselling author of *The Hunted Series*. Her books have sold over 3 million copies worldwide.

When she's not writing, you can find Ivy binge watching too many TV shows, taking long walks, playing outside, and generally refusing to act like an adult. She lives with her husband in Delaware.

Facebook: IvySmoakAuthor
Instagram: @IvySmoakAuthor
Goodreads: IvySmoak

Recommend *Seduction* for your next book club!

Book club questions available at:
www.ivysmoak.com/bookclub

Lightning Source UK Ltd.
Milton Keynes UK
UKHW010855310123
416239UK00005B/343